NEXT DOOR TO MURDER

NEXT DOOR TO MURDER

Anthea Fraser

This first world edition publi
SEVERN HOUSE PUBLISI
9–15 High Street, Sutton, Su
This first world edition publi
SEVERN HOUSE PUBLISH
595 Madison Avenue, New Y

British Library Cataloguing in Publication Data

Fraser, Anthea
  Next door to murder
  1. Parish, Rona (Fictitious character) - Fiction 2. Women
  authors - England - Fiction 3. Murder - Investigation -
  Fiction 4. Detective and mystery stories
  I. Title
  823.9'14[F]

  ISBN-13: 978-0-7278-6614-1   (cased)
  ISBN-13: 978-1-84751-051-8   (trade paper)

All Severn House titles are printed on acid-free paper.

Typeset by Palimpsest Book Production Ltd.,
Grangemouth, Stirlingshire, Scotland.
Printed and bound in Great Britain by
MPG Books Ltd., Bodmin, Cornwall.

One

M ax Allerdyce came clattering down the basement stairs to the kitchen, kissed his wife, patted the dog, and announced, 'It looks as if someone's moving in next door.'

Rona nodded. 'So I noticed. Wonder who we'll get this time.'

The house next door, a four-storey Georgian like their own, had been empty for several months. Its owners lived abroad, and over the years there'd been a succession of tenants, most of whom had taken it for the minimum period of six months. Some of them Rona had barely seen during their tenure, some she'd known only to say 'Good morning' to, and, very rarely, some they'd had in for drinks. Usually, the tenants were couples with school-age children whose jobs had moved them to the locality, and, intent on finding a place of their own, they'd had neither the time nor the inclination to strike up an acquaintance with temporary neighbours.

'Seen anything of them?' Max enquired, taking out a couple of glasses.

'An elderly man went up the path at one point. If he's the one moving in, it'll be a change from the usual age group. Not that it'll make much difference; I doubt if we'll see much of them.' She took the drink he handed her. 'Thanks. How did the classes go?'

Once a week, Max held art classes in the afternoon for those who couldn't attend in the evenings – mainly housewives and the retired.

'OK, but it was unpleasantly hot in the studio. The fans are pretty useless; all they do is move the air around. If this weather continues, I'll have to think seriously about air con.'

'One problem we don't have here, with these thick walls,' Rona commented. 'It stays cool in the highest temperatures.'

'And the lowest!' Max said with a laugh. 'Thank God for central heating.' He glanced outside. 'The sun's off the garden now; let's take our drinks out before I make a start on dinner. I thought we'd have a barbecue while the weather holds.'

Max was the chef of the family. Rona loathed cooking, and on the evenings he had classes she existed on take-aways, salads and visits to the conveniently close Italian restaurant.

He slid back the patio door, and she went ahead of him into the small paved garden. After the cool of the kitchen, the air was warm on her bare arms, and she inhaled with pleasure the mixture of scents drifting on it. She loved this small, private area, with its urns and baskets overflowing with flowers, and its small, half-hidden statues reminiscent of Italian court-yards. It was surrounded on three sides by a high wall of mellow, rose-coloured brick that now, in the evening sunlight, gave back its warmth.

Gus, the golden retriever, flopped down on the sun-baked flagstones, his tongue lolling. He seemed resigned to his evening walks becoming later and later, postponed till the heat of the day had abated.

Max and Rona strolled in contented silence to the end of the garden, from where they could see that the upstairs windows of the house next door were wide open.

'It's been empty quite a while, hasn't it?' Rona commented. 'I hope the agents gave it a good clean and airing before anyone moved in.'

'If it's an elderly couple, at least we should be spared screaming children in the garden!'

He leant against the wall and lifted his face to the sun, eyes closed. 'Why did we spend a fortune on that holiday, when the weather's just as good here?'

They'd returned only days earlier from four weeks in Greece – longer than they usually took, but Rona's last assignment for *Chiltern Life* had been a trying one. She'd been subdued for weeks afterwards – hardly surprising, in view of what had happened – and Max had felt she needed a complete break.

'Because here,' she answered lazily, her own head tilted back, 'there's no warm sea, or golden sand, or ouzo, or tavernas, or—'

He laughed. 'OK, you have a point.' He pushed himself away from the wall. 'I'd better start sorting out the food. I'll give you a shout when I need your input.'

She walked back towards the house with him, and sank into one of the loungers by the open door.

He took her empty glass. 'Like a top-up?'

'No thanks, I'll wait for wine with the meal.'

He disappeared inside and she could hear him moving about, the fridge door opening and shutting, cupboard doors sliding. Gus ambled over and lay at her feet, yawning prodigiously, and she reached down to scratch his ears.

She admitted to herself that she'd needed that holiday. So much had changed over the past months; at the time it had carried her along with it, but the stresses and strains of that last project and the emotions aroused had proved the final straw. It was good of Max to have recognized that, and taken measures to rectify it.

Eighteen months ago, she reflected, life had seemed set in its smoothly running pattern. She'd been about to start on her fourth biography – of the recently deceased thriller writer, Theo Harvey. Her twin sister Lindsey, a solicitor, was bouncing back from her divorce from Hugh, and their parents, if not particularly happy, appeared to be rubbing along together as they had for years.

Now, all that had changed. Rona's own career seemed to have switched – at least temporarily – to that of freelance journalist at the glossy magazine *Chiltern Life* – a move that, while seeming innocuous enough, had flung her repeatedly into violent and distressing situations, a trend that her present series, on the history of long-established family businesses, was continuing to uphold.

Lindsey meanwhile had lurched from one unsuitable lover to another – including Hugh himself, who was now back on the scene – and her latest was, in Rona's view, an arrogant and opinionated millionaire, whose cavalier attitude left Lindsey miserable and unsure of herself.

Most dramatic of all, her parents had separated and Pops was now living in a flat in town, waiting for two years to elapse before divorcing to marry Catherine, an ex-headmistress. While Mum had miraculously metamorphosed from a drab, discontented shrew into a smartly turned-out woman with a part-time job and a paying guest.

How had it all come about? What 'tide in the affairs of men' had been responsible for dropping her family into a kaleidoscope and giving them all a good shake? A mixed metaphor if ever there was one, Rona thought with a self-deprecating smile.

Only Max hadn't changed. In addition to his commissioned paintings and teaching at the art school, he continued to hold classes at Farthings, a cottage ten minutes' walk away, and spend three nights a week there following the evening sessions. Yet, though he was unaware of it, even their relationship had come under threat during that last assignment. Furthermore, though she longed to put the whole episode behind her, including the death of a young woman she'd considered her friend, she was prevented from doing so. For Curzon, local manufacturers of fine china whose history she'd been researching, would celebrate their hundred and fiftieth anniversary in two months' time, and, although all the work had been done on them, the articles were being held over to coincide with that. It was as though a small black cloud hovered over her, and however hard she tried, she couldn't escape it.

Max's call came as a welcome diversion. 'OK, time to prepare the salad.'

She swung her feet to the ground, narrowly missing the dog. 'Coming!' she said.

Lindsey phoned the next morning.

'I'm fed up. Are you free for lunch?'

'I'm free for anything at the moment,' Rona answered wryly.

'Still not back in gear? That's what four weeks away does for you.'

'I needed it, Linz.'

'I need it too, but I'm not likely to get it.'

'One of the advantages of self-employment. Max organizes his own classes, and the students had no objection to the four-week break. Which just left the art school, and as he only teaches there one day a week and was able to arrange a stand-in, it wasn't a problem. And to answer your question, yes, I'm free for lunch. Where shall we go?'

'The Gallery at one? Then I can shop my way down.'

'I'll be there.'

The next call was from Barnie Trent, features editor at *Chiltern Life*.

'How's my favourite journalist?'

'Guilt-ridden,' Rona replied.

'Well, far be it from me to heap coals, but I *was* wondering—'

'When, if ever, you were going to hear from me? It is an *occasional* series, Barnie. I always stressed that. I might abandon you at any time to do another bio.'

'If that's on the cards, fair enough; but until you take that decision . . . Look, I know there were hiccups over the last venture, but it's behind you now.'

'Not till it's in print, it isn't.'

'Well, the hiccups must be, surely. The series is very popular, you know; I keep getting hints from local businesses that they wouldn't be averse to some publicity. In fact, quite a queue is forming.'

'I'm flattered but surprised, considering each one so far has turned up something untoward. Or do they subscribe to there being no such thing as bad publicity?'

'Whatever. How about it, Rona? Are you prepared to get down to a new one?'

She sighed. 'I suppose I must. The trouble is, I can't get up any enthusiasm.'

'Work at it,' he said briskly. 'Call in next time you're passing, and I'll give you a list of those who've approached me. One of them might provide the necessary spark.'

'Will do,' she said.

The Gallery Café was approached by a wrought-iron staircase leading to a walkway above the shops on Guild Street, the main shopping area. Enclosed by ornate black railings, the parade also included a couple of boutiques and galleries, but the café held pride of place since, like Willows' Fine Furniture beneath it, it rounded the corner into Fullers Walk, thus offering its patrons a choice of views over the busy thoroughfare. It was a popular eating place, and Rona, arriving just before one o'clock, was not surprised to find all the tables occupied.

She hesitated, wondering whether, since Lindsey's lunch hour was limited, to wait for her outside and try somewhere else, and was on the point of doing so when her name was called, and she turned to see her friends Georgia Kingston and Hilary Grant waving at her.

'We've finished, Rona – you can have our table.'

Rona walked thankfully over to them, Gus at her heels, and as she pulled out a vacant chair, he went to his accustomed place under the table. 'Thanks; I'm meeting Lindsey, and was about to give up.'

'We're just waiting for the bill,' Hilary said. 'Haven't seen you lately; where did you get that fabulous tan?'

'In Greece; we had four weeks there, and it was sheer heaven.'

'Lucky you! We can't get away till September, thanks to Simon's deadline.' Simon Grant was an artist friend of Max's.

'How's your series on family businesses going?' Georgia enquired. 'I haven't seen any for a while.'

'We're holding the Curzon one, to tie in with their anniversary.'

'So who's your next prospect?'

Rona grimaced. 'You're as bad as my editor!'

'You said some time ago that the Willows were on your list, and asked me not to mention it till you'd approached them.'

'So I did,' Rona remembered. 'And you told me that in your youth, you went out with Julian.'

'Only for a month or two!' Georgia protested. 'But look – if you want an intro or anything, why don't I ask him and his wife to dinner with you and Max? Would that break the ice?'

Rona hesitated. Was she ready to plunge back into work? But wasn't that just what Lindsey and Barnie, not to mention Max, had been urging her to do?

'Tell you what,' Georgia said, gathering up her shopping as the waitress at last brought their bill, 'I'll fix it anyway, and leave it to you whether or not to approach him.'

'That's good of you, Georgie. Thanks.'

'I'll ring you and suggest a few dates. Enjoy your lunch.'

Lindsey arrived minutes later. 'Sorry, there was a phone call just as I was leaving. Well done, getting a window table.'

'I was in luck – Georgia and Hilary were about to leave. I've ordered wine – house white; we usually enjoy it, and it's light for lunchtime.'

'Fine, though a double G and T wouldn't go amiss.'

'You'd fall asleep at your desk! So – what's the matter?'

'Dominic, what else? Ro, I haven't heard from him for a *month*!'

'Then write him off,' Rona said briskly. 'You still have Jonathan and Hugh.' Jonathan Hurst, a fellow partner at Chase Mortimer, was another of Lindsey's admirers.

'Neither of them can hold a candle to Dominic.'

'Not having a private plane or chauffeur-driven Daimler?'

'Don't be vile; you know quite well what I mean.'

Rona passed her the menu. 'We'd better decide what to eat. If we don't order it when the wine comes, it could be a long wait.'

They settled on quiche and a side salad, and when the order had been given and the wine poured, Rona asked, 'Seriously, are you still stringing those two along?'

'I wouldn't be, if Dominic was more reliable.'

'Perhaps he's out of the country.'

'More than likely, but he could have *told* me.'

'Linz, he's been like this from the start. Either it doesn't occur to him to inform you of his plans, or he considers them none of your business. You have to take it or leave it. And – admit it – that's part of his attraction.'

Lindsey sighed and sipped her wine. 'I bet bloody Carla knows his every move.'

Carla Deighton was Frayne's personal assistant. Cool and glamorous, she was bitterly resented by Lindsey.

'It's her business to. Now, snap out of it, there's a love. Any day now you'll get a phone call, and life will be rosy again – provided you don't let him know you've been fretting. If you do, you can kiss him goodbye.'

'Auntie Rona's Advice Column,' Lindsey said sourly. She straightened. 'Sorry. How about you, anyway? You still haven't settled back to work?'

'No, but as it happens Georgia reminded me just now that I'd been considering the Willows.' She tilted her head downwards, in the direction of the furniture emporium beneath them. 'She offered to invite us to dinner with Julian and his wife, so I'd have the chance to sound him out.'

'Good. That'll get you back on track. So what else is new? We've not really caught up since you came back from holiday.'

'Nothing much; it's been a question of ploughing through

all the mail, phone calls and emails. The only bit of news, for what it's worth, is that the house next door has been let again. I think it's an elderly couple this time.'

Lindsey nodded absently. 'Have you spoken to Mum or Pops since you got back?'

'Yes, both of them. Pops was telling me about Catherine's little granddaughter.'

The baby's birth had disrupted a family lunch at Easter.

'He's quite besotted with her,' Lindsey confirmed.

They leaned back in their chairs as the quiches and salads were placed in front of them.

'He suggested we might like to go to Catherine's one weekend, when Daniel and Jenny are over,' Rona added.

'I hope I'm not included in the invitation. Babies do nothing for me.' Lindsey unfolded her napkin, then looked up as a thought struck her. 'They won't be at our lunch, will they?'

It was the twins' birthday the following Saturday, and there was to be a celebration meal at the Clarendon Hotel.

'No, it's immediate family only,' Rona said. 'Catherine's going over to Cricklehurst – largely out of tact, I suspect, since Mum wouldn't have come otherwise.' Although their parents were now on reasonable terms, meetings between Avril and her replacement were strained.

Lindsey reached for the salad dressing. 'What are you doing the rest of Saturday?'

'Max is taking me to the theatre. We'll have supper after, and spend the night at the Argyll.'

'Very nice too. What are you seeing?'

'*The Sound of Music*. It'll be interesting to see the new production, after all the publicity. Remember Mum taking us to the film, when we were little?' She topped up their glasses. 'How about you? What have you planned?'

'Hugh's taking me out. Dinner somewhere, I think, though I told him I wouldn't be hungry, after a large lunch.'

'Very gracious of you.'

'Well, it's true.' She paused. 'It'll be like old times, spending my birthday with him.'

'You realize you're on dangerous ground?'

'He knows the position.'

'Does he know about Dominic?'

'There's not much to know,' Lindsey said bitterly. 'Anyway, enough of that; tell me about Greece. Where did you stay?'

Forty minutes later, as they emerged on to Guild Street, Rona said suddenly, 'Let's have a look round Willows'.'

'Thinking of splurging on a three-piece suite?'

'No chance, and if we were, I doubt we could afford their prices. I just want a look round, to get a feel for the place.'

'You're seriously considering them, then?'

'Linz, this has all come up in the last hour. I'm weighing possibilities, that's all.'

'Won't it look odd if you come across Julian, then meet him again at the Kingstons'?'

'He won't be there. None of the family work on the shop floor.'

'Too grand, I suppose,' Lindsey said with a sniff.

'Georgia says there's a title in their ancestry, which is why they give themselves airs.'

Lindsey snorted. 'And further back, a barrow-boy, so the story goes. Bet they don't dwell on that.'

'Actually, I think they're quite proud of it.'

'Inverse as well as actual snobbery? You'll be walking on eggshells.'

'Nonsense, it'll be fine. I barely know Julian and have never met his wife, but they can't be that bad if they're friends of Patrick and Georgia. Let's suss it out. Gus won't be welcome, though; we'd better leave him here.'

She tied his lead to some railings, gave him a pat, and, pushing open the swing door, they went inside, to be immediately engulfed in opulence. A thick carpet covered the floor, low music played in the background, and the coolness of circulating air was balm after the heat outside. On all sides, stretching back into the interior, were room settings of exquisite furniture, gleaming richly in the soft lights. Dining tables in modern or reproduction styles were set with delicate china – some of it Curzon, Rona noted; beds were made up with exotic spreads or duvets and piled high with plump, colour-coordinated cushions, while in living-room settings, leather sofas and low, lamp-lit tables suggested the ultimate in comfortable relaxation.

'Would you like any help, ladies?' enquired a smooth voice, and they turned to find a young man smiling at them.

'We're just looking, thank you,' Rona said.

'Fine; but should you need any information on prices or availability, please don't hesitate to ask.'

He moved away, leaving them to their browsing.

'It makes me want to throw everything out, and start again,' Lindsey said.

'That's a bit extreme, isn't it?'

'Seriously, Ro, I'm realizing that my tastes have changed. The furniture in the flat is what Hugh and I chose together, and split between us when we divorced. I can still picture him sitting in the chairs, which can be disconcerting when I'm with Jonathan. The idea of updating hadn't occurred to me, but it's very tempting.'

'Well, go slowly, for goodness' sake – a chair or table at a time.'

'But that could end up looking bitty. Better, surely, to take advice from an interior decorator or someone?'

'It would double your expenses, for a start.'

Lindsey sighed. 'No doubt you're right.' She glanced at her watch. 'I must be getting back; my lunch hour's nearly up.'

'Your lunch hour-and-a-half, you mean.'

'Very funny.'

With a noncommittal smile at the hovering assistant, they made their way outside, where the hot air met them like a suffocating blanket.

'Max is thinking of air con for the studio,' Rona remarked, as she untied Gus from his railing.

'I don't blame him; we couldn't survive in the office without it.' They exchanged a quick kiss. 'See you on Saturday,' Lindsey said, and, crossing Fullers Walk, she continued along Guild Street in the direction of Chase Mortimer.

Rona rounded the corner into the side street, glancing in Willows' windows as she went. Fullers Walk remained commercial for about a third of its length, accommodating, beyond Willows', a florist's, a bakery, a delicatessen and several smaller outlets, before the shops tailed off to give way to residential houses. Two roads led off it: halfway down on the left, Dean's Crescent curved back towards the eastern end of Guild Street, and, having crossed it, became Dean's Crescent

North, where Max had his cottage; while a hundred yards farther on, the Walk was bisected by Lightbourne Avenue, the road in which they lived.

As she walked home, Rona's mind was on the possibilities that had opened up, and she'd taken out her key before she realized there was someone in the garden of the house next door.

She paused and, glancing over the low wall, saw an elderly couple standing at the foot of the steps, the door of the house open behind them. They were examining a rather tired-looking plant in a pot, but, sensing Rona's presence, they looked up enquiringly.

'Good afternoon,' she said. 'I'm Rona Parish, and I live next door.'

'Oh – how do you do?' They moved uncertainly forward, and the man added, 'Barbara and Keith Franks.'

He had, Rona noted, a slight transatlantic accent.

'Are you settling in all right?'

His wife gave a nervous smile. 'There's a lot of sorting out to do.'

'You've come from abroad?'

'Yes, Canada. We're actually English, but we've lived over there for some time.'

There was a brief, almost embarrassed, pause. Then Rona said, 'Well, if there's anything we can help you with, please let us know.'

They nodded their thanks, and she continued the few yards to her own gateway and, still aware of their proximity, went self-consciously up the steps and into the house, Gus at her heels. And that, she thought resignedly, might well be the last words they'd exchange. Certainly they hadn't been forthcoming, but it must be unsettling for them at their age – which she estimated to be mid-seventies – moving not only house but country. She wondered idly why they'd gone to Canada, and, more particularly, why they'd come back. No doubt she'd never know.

'I've established contact with our new neighbours,' she told Max, when he phoned later, 'but I doubt if it will progress any further. They seemed pretty reserved. Their name's Franks, and they're from Canada.' She paused, her thoughts moving on. 'Have you ever met Julian Willow?'

'That's an abrupt switch! No, I know him by sight, that's all. Why?'

'I saw Georgia at lunchtime, and she offered to invite him and his wife to dinner with us.'

'Nice of her, but again, why?'

'Because I'm considering Willows' for my next assignment.'

'Ah! Well, I'd say it's a good choice. They're a well-known Marsborough family, after all.'

'I've not reached a firm decision, but Linz and I had a sniff round the shop. It's very plush.'

'And pricey, I should think. Look, love, the class will be arriving any minute. I'll have to go, but I'll give you the usual call later, to say goodnight.'

Rona looked out at the garden. The sun was off it now, which made it a good time to do some watering. She went outside, filled the can at the outdoor tap, and began the time-consuming routine. There were at least a dozen urns and containers to attend to, and several hanging baskets.

It was as she was reaching up to a basket on the dividing wall that a movement caught her eye, and she glanced up at the house next door in time to see a curtain at an upstairs window twitch back into place.

Rona paused, feeling vaguely uncomfortable. Someone up there had been watching her, she thought. Why? Then she shook herself. She was being neurotic; no doubt whoever it was – probably Mrs Franks – had simply been straightening the curtain.

She risked another, furtive, glance up at the house, but nothing else moved, and she continued her watering. That was the second time she'd felt slightly uneasy about her new neighbours, and both times, she told herself roundly, totally without cause.

Resolving to put them out of her mind, she finished her watering and went back into the house, closing and locking the door behind her.

Two

Mid-morning was a quiet time at Belmont Library, and they were enjoying a cup of coffee in the minute staff room.

'How are you getting on with your lodger?' Mary Price enquired.

Avril Parish put down a book she'd been flicking through. 'Fine, thanks, though I'm still on a learning curve.'

Mary smiled. 'You said she has a will of her own.'

'Oh, she has. A very determined young lady.'

'That's schoolteachers for you, even young ones! Perhaps they're born, not made.'

It was through Mary's good offices that Sarah had come to her – Mary having a friend at the school, who'd heard she was looking for accommodation – and Avril didn't want to seem ungrateful. 'In fact, it's working very well,' she added. 'If she's not out, she spends the evenings in her room, so we don't impinge on each other, and so far, she's been going home to Stokely at weekends.'

'So far?'

'Well, I'm not sure how long that'll continue. She's acquired a boyfriend.'

'Ah! Have you met him?'

'Briefly, when he called for her one evening.' She paused. 'Actually, Mary, I might be anticipating difficulties where none exist, but—'

'No gentlemen callers above stairs?'

Avril gave a relieved laugh. 'Exactly. Does that make me sound like a dinosaur?'

'Not at all. It's your house, and if you don't want any shenanigans, you're at liberty to say so. Is there anywhere else they could go?'

'There's the dining room. It already has one easy chair; I could find another.'

'Then pre-empt them by suggesting that. You know: "Why don't you ask So-and-So in for coffee? You could have the dining room to yourselves." They mightn't want to stay in, but if they did, you'd be covered.'

'You're brilliant, Mary. Thanks.'

'Any time,' said Mary Price. She passed Avril the packet of biscuits. 'It's your weekend off, isn't it?'

'Yes, fortunately. It's the girls' birthday tomorrow, and we're having a family lunch.'

'Including Tom?'

'Including Tom.'

'And his lady friend?'

'No, thank God. She's visiting her new grandchild.'

'It should be good, then; you and Tom are OK now, aren't you?'

'Oh, very civilized,' said Avril drily.

'You're doing fine, Avril,' Mary assured her. 'I really admire how you've pulled yourself together and made a new life for yourself, instead of sitting at home moping.'

Avril was surprised and gratified. 'That's nice of you; thanks.'

She *did* manage to keep busy, she acknowledged to herself, as she went to relieve Liz and Rita; what with working here four mornings a week and alternate Saturdays, spending Wednesday afternoons at the charity shop, and playing bridge on Thursdays. Not to mention becoming a landlady. Then there were bridge parties at friends' houses and – though these had decreased since Tom's departure – the odd invitation to dinner. All in all, as Mary had said, she was doing pretty well. The only thing she was lacking was male company, and there was not much she could do about that.

Georgia phoned at lunchtime.

'I've been speaking to Felicity Willow,' she began. 'Not surprisingly, they've a lot on at the moment – when haven't they? – and then, of course, there's the added difficulty of Max being unavailable three evenings a week. Still, they are free next Friday – a week today. Is that any good?'

'I'm sure it is,' Rona said. Max's evening classes frequently interfered with their social life. 'Thanks, Georgia, that would be great.'

'I didn't mention an ulterior motive,' Georgia went on, 'so no big deal if you decide not to go ahead with them.'

'It's good of you to go to all this trouble.'

'No trouble. We owe you dinner anyway, and it's always pleasant to introduce one set of friends to another. I'm asking Hilary and Simon, too, to make up the numbers. Eight for eight thirty?'

'We'll look forward to it.'

'See you then.'

She rang off, and Rona entered the engagement on the kitchen diary, relieved to see that a scrawl of Max's hadn't forestalled her.

The more she thought about it, the more she felt she'd like to research the Willow family. They went back a satisfyingly long way, and the founding of their business, from what she'd heard, largely coincided with the development of Marsborough itself. The firm and the town had grown up together, and fashions in furniture were known to reflect social trends – wide chairs to accommodate crinolines, and so on. There were all kinds of angles she could cover, she thought with mounting enthusiasm. She'd check out the development of furniture styles on the Internet, so she wouldn't appear a complete ignoramus when she met the Willows.

Feeling more positive than she had for months, she opened a tin of sardines for her lunch.

'Lindsey? Dominic Frayne. I was wondering if by any chance you're free on Sunday? I'm flying over to France again, and it would be good to have company.'

Lindsey sat down abruptly, willing her voice to remain calm. 'Dominic. That sounds exciting.' *And where the hell have you been for the last four weeks?*

'We'd arrive in time for lunch, and return after dinner. The forecast's good, so it should be a pleasant outing. Would you care to come?'

'I should, very much.'

'Excellent. I'll collect you at ten thirty. Better bring your passport, just in case.' And he rang off.

Lindsey sat for several minutes, the phone still in her hand. Though they had met three months ago, this would be only the third time she'd been out with him. The first occasion was dinner at the Savoy, the second a visit to Cheltenham races. Each time, they had been conducted there and back in his chauffeur-driven car, and on each occasion he had been charming, courteous and attentive. But he hadn't as much as touched her hand. And she'd been told – though admittedly by Jonathan – that he was a serial womaniser. It was certainly hard to believe, she thought ruefully.

'Moving into second gear?' Carla Deighton enquired, without turning.

She was standing at the window of Dominic's flat, from where she had an eagle's eye view over Furze Hill Park to the cluster of roofs and steeples that was the town of Marsborough. There was a breeze this evening, and in the park several brightly coloured kites were flying.

'How do you mean?'

She turned and looked across at him, leaning comfortably back in his chair. 'Only a selected few are taken to France.'

'I enjoy her company, certainly.'

'She's very decorative,' Carla remarked judiciously, 'and you like to be seen with beautiful women.'

'Which is one reason why I enjoy her company. I'm not sure what you mean by second gear, but I'm not putting my foot on any accelerator.'

'Very wise. You might have more need of brakes – for an emergency stop, even.'

'You're being very enigmatic this morning, Carla,' he remarked, with a touch of irritation.

'Just sounding a word of warning. This one might not be the sort of woman who's content to be ignored for weeks on end, and then phoned on a whim.'

'You know damn well that wasn't—'

'I imagine she has some pride, and from what I hear, she's not short of admirers.'

He raised an eyebrow. 'I wasn't aware you listened to gossip, my dear.'

'I always take an interest in your *objets d'amour*.'

He gave a snort of laughter, and reached for his spectacles.

'Talking of which,' she continued, 'what about your little heiress in Kensington?'

He sobered, and she saw she'd touched a nerve. 'No longer in the frame,' he said briefly.

'Really? What went wrong.'

'It was getting altogether too heavy; I ended it some weeks ago. Now, enough of my affairs. Did Ballingers ever come back to us?'

And Carla, sliding effortlessly from confidante to business persona, lifted a file from the table and handed it to him.

Catherine came into the room as Tom put down the phone.

'That was Rona,' he said. 'It'll be good to see her tomorrow – and Lindsey, of course.'

'You missed her, didn't you, while she was in Greece?'

'Yes – silly, isn't it? It's not as though we're in each other's pockets, but we speak on the phone once or twice a week, and I missed that.'

'And you've also been worried about her,' Catherine said gently.

He sighed. 'That Curzon business hit her hard – the girl's death and everything. Max was right to whisk her away. I hope the rest has restored her balance.'

'I'm sure so; she's very resilient. Give her my love, won't you?' And she added, as he had, 'And Lindsey, of course.'

Tom smiled at her. 'I will. I'm sorry you won't be there.'

'This is Avril's call, not mine, but hopefully I'll see the girls before long.'

Or at least Rona, she added privately. Lindsey was still inclined to be prickly, having sided firmly with her mother over the separation, but Catherine was genuinely fond of Rona.

'If you're determined to go home, I'll walk you back,' Tom said, as she retrieved her handbag from the chair.

'I'd better, my love. I want to make an early start tomorrow; you know what the traffic can be like at weekends.'

They walked together down the stairs and out into the warm summer night. Tom's flat was only a stone's throw from Catherine's home – one reason why he had chosen it. He'd been adamant that, although they enjoyed most of the benefits of marriage, they wouldn't move in together till they were free to marry. He didn't want Catherine to be the subject of gossip, and this way they maintained their independence, each having a home their children could visit without the constant presence of another partner.

'You're staying in Cricklehurst overnight?'

'Yes, I'll be back Sunday evening.'

'And in the meantime you'll be worshipping at young Alice's cradle.'

She laughed. 'At every opportunity.'

They had reached Catherine's gateway, and he kissed her gently. 'Drive carefully, and give me a ring when you're home again.'

'I will.'

'Love to the family.'

He watched her walk up the path and let herself into the bungalow. Then, returning her wave from the open door, he walked slowly home.

Max and Rona had had their supper outside, grateful for the breeze that had come with evening, gently ruffling Gus's fur as he slept on the warm flags. Light from the kitchen behind them threw a pool of brightness over the table, but the far end of the garden lay in shadow, urns and containers blurring into the gloaming.

As always on Friday evenings, they had filled each other in on what they'd been doing since Max was last home on Wednesday. Though the nightly phone calls covered major incidents, there were always small things to report and amusing incidents to share. Now, though, they were silent, content to sit in the dusk and relax at another week's ending.

Finally, Max stirred and began to stack their plates. 'Well, this time tomorrow, you'll be a year older!' he said.

'Don't remind me!'

'And we'll be eating in rather more exotic surroundings.'

'But without the scent of stocks, no doubt.'

'True.'

Rona helped him carry their supper things indoors. Gus, who'd had his walk earlier, had already retired to his basket.

'I'll go on up,' she said, as Max slid their plates into the dishwasher.

'I'll not be far behind you.'

The old house creaked comfortably about her as she walked up the stairs. She must remember to get the camera from the desk drawer, she thought; birthday lunches were always recorded. In fact, she'd get it now, before she forgot.

The study was lit by reflection from the patio below, but as she retrieved the camera, the room was plunged into darkness as Max switched off the kitchen light. Rona glanced out of the window, and as she did so, something in the next-door garden caught her eye and she paused, moving back slightly. There it was again – a red glow, presumably a cigarette. By straining her eyes she could just distinguish the pale outline of a woman's dress against the denser darkness of the shrubs; and was aware of faint surprise. She wouldn't have put Mrs Franks down as a smoker.

'What are you doing in the dark?' came Max's voice from behind her.

'There's someone in next door's garden.'

'Taking the night air, no doubt, as we were.'

'Polluting it, actually. She's smoking.' Rona drew her brows together. 'It's a woman, but she looks taller than Mrs Franks.'

'A visitor, perhaps. Come on, love; we don't want to spy on them.'

She followed him silently out of the room. When they'd been sitting out there, had the Franks been just the other side of the wall? she wondered. And if so, could they have overheard their conversation? Though they'd said nothing private, it was a disturbing thought.

Sarah had, after all, left as usual for the weekend. It would seem strange, Avril reflected, when school broke up in two weeks' time, and she'd be alone again. Though her relationship with Sarah was a business one, the knowledge that there was someone else to cook breakfast for, to expect home in the evenings, and to be in the house overnight, was a source of great comfort. Conversely, she'd not wanted the girl under her feet, and Sarah had appreciated that. She was, in fact, the perfect PG; Avril only wished she could warm to her more.

Since she volunteered nothing personal, the existence of the boyfriend had come as a surprise. Answering the doorbell one evening, Avril had reached the door just ahead of Sarah, who'd had no option but to introduce him. Clive Gregory, his name was, and she'd added that he was a sports master at the school. He'd seemed a pleasant young man, tall and tanned and with a ready smile. It had reminded Avril, on a wave of nostalgia, of when similar young men had come calling for her own daughters.

She wasn't sure of standard practice covering long absences, but she'd hinted to Sarah that should she want to spend the odd night in Marsborough over the holidays, her room would be available, and the girl had seemed grateful. Perhaps, Avril thought now, on her way out to the car, she'd take the opportunity to go away herself, though as most of her friends were married, it might be difficult to find a companion. She'd heard there were holidays catering for single people, but didn't feel brave enough to consider one.

The Clarendon Hotel was almost as familiar to Avril as her own home. It had run like a thread through her life; childhood parties had been held there, both in her own infancy and later for her daughters. It had been the venue for postpantomime teas, exam celebrations and New Year balls, and had also hosted all three of their family wedding receptions, although, she reflected soberly as she went through the swing doors, only Rona and Max's marriage had survived.

'Mrs Parish!' Dorothy Fairfax came towards her, smiling her welcome. 'How good to see you.' Tall and straight and in her eighties, Dorothy was the doyenne of the establishment and still, it was rumoured, had the final say in any major undertakings. She, too, had had family problems, and of a more serious nature than Avril's, but from her calm exterior and gracious bearing, it seemed she had weathered them.

'You too, Mrs Fairfax,' Avril replied, taking her hand. 'I was just thinking that coming here is almost like coming home.'

'What a charming thought. Thank you. I believe it's your daughters' birthday? They're all awaiting you in the bar.'

Avril smiled acknowledgment, and moved away as Dorothy turned to greet other guests. She'd avoided the word 'husband', Avril registered; no doubt it was now common knowledge that she and Tom had parted.

He and Max stood to greet her as she went into the bar. Kisses and presents were exchanged, and champagne cocktails, another family tradition on such occasions, were ordered. It was almost possible, in a suspension of disbelief, to imagine that all was as it had been, that they were still a united family meeting here, as they had so often, to celebrate another birthday.

'You're looking very glam, Mum,' Lindsey said approvingly. 'Love that dress.'

'Thank you, dear.'

It was true, Tom thought, Avril did look good. It still came as a slight shock to see her so svelte and well-groomed, after years of self-neglect. And still, too, came the niggle of guilt that this transformation, which she'd made such an effort to achieve, should have coincided with his decision to leave her.

A waiter came to tell them their table was ready, and they were led through to the restaurant. Menus were produced, snowy napkins unfolded and placed, with a flourish, on their laps. The wine waiter approached, and while Tom discussed the list with him, the others settled down to studying the menu.

Avril was deciding on her first course when a voice above her said, 'Mrs Parish? It is, isn't it?' And she looked up to see Guy Lacey smiling down at her.

'Mr Lacey! Hello. Is Sarah with you?'

'No, I begged leave of absence, so she's meeting friends for lunch. I'm attending a retirement party.'

Avril, aware of the family's intense interest, remembered her manners. 'Mr Lacey is the father of my lodger,' she told them. And, to him, 'May I introduce my daughters, Lindsey and Rona, my son-in-law Max, and –' she hesitated briefly – 'my almost-ex-husband, Tom.'

'Guy Lacey,' he said, his smile encompassing them all. 'Delighted to meet you.' His eyes returned to Avril. 'I hope my daughter's behaving herself with you?'

'Oh, she's a model guest.'

'That's good to hear. Well, I mustn't intrude. No doubt we'll catch up with each other before long.'

And he moved away to join the rest of his party at a table across the room.

'Nice man,' commented Lindsey, observing her mother's faintly flushed cheeks. 'When did you meet him?'

'He came with Sarah when she first moved in,' Avril explained, adding quickly, 'That's the only time we've met.'

Tom, noting her slight embarrassment and intrigued by it,

came to her rescue. 'Has everyone made their choice?' he asked. And wondered, privately, if there was a Mrs Lacey.

'So – have you enjoyed your birthday?'

Lindsey looked across the candle-flame at her ex-husband. 'I'm still enjoying it.'

'I'm glad to hear it. How was the salmon?'

She looked ruefully at the half-fillet still on her plate. 'Delicious. I'm sorry, Hugh, I simply have no more room.'

'That's all right. You did warn me.'

But at these prices, Lindsey thought guiltily, there must be a good eight pounds' worth going to waste. A meal at Serendipity, the in-place to eat in Marsborough, did not come cheap, and he'd also bought her a very pretty bracelet.

The candles, the wine and the soft music playing in the background were working their magic, and she was acutely aware of Hugh's proximity. It was this strong physical attraction that had brought them together in the first place, and held them in thrall through five turbulent years. Even when love had gone – at least on her part – it remained a powerful force.

She looked up, saw his eyes on her face, and for a heart-stopping moment wondered if he'd been reading her thoughts. He reached across the table and gently took her wrist, idly turning it as though examining the bracelet.

'Would you like to see the dessert menu?' he asked.

Lindsey forced a laugh. 'Little girls who don't finish their main course don't get any pudding.'

'This little girl may, if she'd like some.'

'No, really, thank you. Just coffee, perhaps.'

'Tell you what, then,' he said quietly, still not looking at her, 'you've never seen my flat, have you? How about our going back there for coffee, rather than having it here?'

Lindsey's heart started thumping in slow, agonizing beats. It was a long time since she and Hugh had made love, and it was becoming increasingly difficult to withstand him. She had, to her shame, put him on hold pending a positive move from Dominic. But although he'd finally contacted her, the trip to France tomorrow would surely be as formal and platonic as their previous two outings. If she waited for his advances, she reflected, she'd be waiting a long time.

She looked up, meeting Hugh's intent, anxious gaze.
'That would be lovely,' she said.

Avril, curled up on the sofa with a glass of spritzer, was thinking back to the lunch party. The girls seemed pleased with their presents, which was gratifying, and Tom – well, Tom had been his usual charming self. She still regretted the way things had turned out – largely, she knew, due to her own behaviour. Had things been right between them, he wouldn't have spared a second glance for Catherine Bishop.

Too late to think of that, though. And before she could stop it, her mind turned to Guy Lacey and their brief exchange in the restaurant. *No doubt we'll catch up with each other before long.* What had he meant by that? That he'd be coming to help Sarah pack up for the holiday? But there was no need, surely; she had her own car to transport her belongings.

Avril swung her feet impatiently to the floor, telling herself she'd imagined the admiration in his eyes. He was attractive, though; from the first, she'd liked his easy manner and the way he'd made her laugh. There hadn't been much laughter in the last year or two – again, largely her own fault. Well, given another chance, she'd make far better use of it; a sentiment she preferred not to analyse too closely.

It had been an enjoyable evening. The theatre was packed and the show excellent. They'd emerged into a heat scarcely diminished since midday, and made their way through the crowds to one of their favourite restaurants, where Max had booked a table.

'The tunes are still going round in my head,' Rona commented. 'It was lovely to hear them all again. Thanks for taking me, darling. I know it wasn't really your scene.'

'A bit sentimental for my taste,' he acknowledged, 'but it was your birthday, so your choice.'

'It's been a good day altogether,' Rona said contentedly. 'I enjoyed lunch, and the parents seemed in good form.'

'Odd, your mother seeing that chap she knew.'

'Oh, I don't know. Everybody meets everybody at the Clarendon; it's like the Champs Elysées.'

'That's not quite what I meant. She blushed very prettily.'

'Come on now, Max!' Rona protested. 'You're imagining things.'

'I think not. I shouldn't be surprised if we hear more of Mr Guy Lacey in the future.'

Rona stared at him. 'You're serious?'

'Not entirely. All I would say is, watch this space.'

'Good Lord!' Rona considered for a moment. 'It would be great if she *could* find someone, now Pops has Catherine.'

Max topped up their glasses. 'Did I gather Lindsey's seeing Hugh this evening?'

'Yes. I'm not altogether sure that's wise.'

'Very *un*wise, I should say. She's surely not considering getting back with him?'

Rona sighed. 'Who knows, with Linz? She needs a man in her life, that's always been her problem. Trouble is, she usually chooses the wrong one.'

'Like that Hurst man she works with.'

'Among others.'

'Ah yes, the multi-millionaire.'

'Not sure about the multi!' Rona said.

'How are things on that front?'

'Slow-moving, I think. He sounds an awkward devil.'

'How so?'

'Oh, hardly ever contacting her, and when he does, being formal in the extreme.'

'That wouldn't suit Lindsey,' Max said shrewdly.

Rona flushed. 'If she could only meet the right one, she'd be fine.'

A change of subject seemed to be called for. Unfortunately, the one he had to broach wouldn't be any more acceptable than criticizing his sister-in-law. His best bet seemed to be to come straight out with it.

'I've a piece of news for you,' he said abruptly. 'Adele Yarborough's back home.'

Rona drew in her breath. Adele was a student of Max's who had formed an attachment to him and caused an unconscionable amount of trouble. She'd spent the last few months at a psychiatric unit up in Norfolk.

'How long have you known?'

'Since yesterday. Philip phoned me, as a matter of courtesy, and I've been waiting for a suitable time to tell you.

Obviously, she won't be coming back to class, but he thought Lindsey might see her, with them living in the same road, and that it was as well to be forewarned.'

'Is she – better?'

Adele had been suffering from a form of Munchhausen's syndrome.

'Philip says so. I've no intention of checking.'

After a moment Rona said, 'It'll be good for the children to have her home.'

'Yes.' Max allowed himself a breath of relief. Thank God that was over.

He sat back in his chair, his eyes moving casually over their fellow diners. Then his gaze narrowed.

'Isn't that your pal Julian Willow over there?'

'Where?' Rona looked about her.

'At the table in the corner.'

Following the direction of his nod, she studied the couple indicated, recognizing the lean, rather bony face and pale hair. 'Yes, so it is. Small world. His wife looks attractive; I look forward to meeting her.'

'They seem very engrossed in each other.'

Rona smiled. 'Perhaps that's what people have been thinking about us.'

He smiled back, his hand closing over hers. 'And they'd be quite right. Happy birthday, my darling, and many more.'

'Amen to that,' she said.

Three

Lindsey had forgotten how much she loved France. They hadn't, as she'd expected, flown to Paris, but landed in a field outside a small village in Normandy. She'd not associated Dominic with rustic pursuits, and, seeing her surprise, he offered an explanation.

'We're here because a few miles down the road is one of the best restaurants in France. I thought we could amuse ourselves bucolically during the day, and dine regally before returning home. If that appeals?'

'Very much,' she said.

He was, she thought, a man of surprises. She'd never before seen him dressed other than formally, and in his cords and open-necked shirt he looked at once younger and less formidable. For the first time, she felt able to relax with him.

A hire car had been awaiting them, and, having agreed a time to rendezvous with the pilot, he drove her the mile or so into the village and parked in the main square. They then spent a couple of hours wandering the cobbled streets, buying the ingredients for an al fresco lunch, and exploring the tiny stone-built church. It shouldn't have surprised her that Dominic spoke easy and fluent French. She didn't comment, but later, when they were seated at one of the pavement cafés, she placed her own order equally fluently, and had the satisfaction of a raised eyebrow.

'Quite a dark horse, aren't you?' he commented.

'I spent a year in Angers while I was at university.'

'You told me you'd always lived in Marsborough?'

'It's been my permanent home, yes; but that doesn't make me a provincial mouse.'

'Obviously not. So – which university, and what did you read?'

'Durham, Modern Languages.'

'Impressive. Then, presumably law school?'

'That's right; I didn't decide on law till I was halfway through my degree course. The parents weren't impressed.'

'Understandably.' He studied her inscrutably from behind his sunglasses. 'It strikes me I know very little about you.'

'You've never asked.'

To his surprise, he realized that was true. 'Then please enlighten me.' He settled back, crossing his long legs. 'Starting with your family.'

She waited till the waiter had set down their coffees and *pains au chocolat*.

'Only if you'll reciprocate.'

'If you insist.'

She stirred her coffee reflectively. 'As to family, my parents separated at Christmas, but seem to be coping well. And I have a twin sister, Rona, who writes biographies, though at the moment she's concentrating on journalism.'

Dominic leant forward. 'Hold on a minute. Rona Parish? *Pitt the Elder*?'

'It seems her fame has gone before.'

'It was a damn good biography. She's your twin, you say? God, I never made the connection.' He paused, seemingly reflecting on what he saw as a coincidence. Then he gestured apologetically. 'But I interrupted you. Please go on.'

'There's little else to tell. I passed my law exams, joined Chase Mortimer, married, and then divorced. End of story. Now it's your turn.'

'Not so fast. Tell me about your ex-husband. What possessed him to let you go?'

Lindsey looked up quickly, but again the sunglasses hid any expression in his eyes.

'We were pretty explosive together,' she answered after a minute.

'And that wasn't good?'

'It made for a stormy existence.'

'Storms and explosions,' Dominic said consideringly. 'At least life wouldn't have been dull. So what does he do, and do you still see him?'

Memories of the previous night, exceedingly unwelcome in the circumstances, flooded Lindsey's mind, and she prayed her colour wouldn't rise.

'He's a chartered accountant, and since he lives in

Marsborough, yes, I see him from time to time. How about your ex-wives?' she added quickly, to pre-empt further questions. 'Why did *your* marriages fail?'

He held her eyes for a long moment, and she wondered if he resented the question. But, she defended herself, it was no more personal than those he'd asked her.

'Not for such dramatic reasons as yours,' he said eventually. 'I dare say incompatibility pretty well covers it.'

Lindsey would have liked to probe further, but this was their first intimate conversation and she was chary of going too far. Instead, she asked, 'Are you still in touch with them?'

'Occasionally; we're on reasonable terms.'

'Both of them?'

'It requires a balancing act, but yes. It's only fair on the offspring.'

'Tell me about your children.'

'Hardly children; Crispin is twenty-three and at medical school, Dougal at twenty-one is training to be a surveyor, and Olivia's nineteen and recently become engaged. My second ex and I are trying, so far unsuccessfully, to persuade her not to opt out of university, so you'll appreciate we need a united front.'

Though Lindsey was curious to know more – about his business and his relationship with the glamorous Carla – she sensed he'd said as much as he intended, at least for the present, and accordingly held her peace.

As Dominic called for the bill, it struck her that she'd instinctively shown him a different side of herself from that presented to either Hugh or Jonathan – or, for that matter, to her family. How multi-faceted we are, she thought; far from being a freak of nature, multiple personalities are the norm.

As they left the café to resume their stroll, he took her hand and threaded it through his arm. It was, amazingly, the first time he'd touched her, and she felt a surge of excitement. This man intrigued as well as attracted her; she must take care not to let him slip through her fingers.

Tom Parish did not like Sundays. In the past, when the girls came home to lunch, it had been a highlight of the week, and during Avril's most difficult phase, their visits were a welcome respite. Now, they were all scattered and the day had no cohesion. Furthermore, since the arrival of her grand-child, Catherine frequently visited her family at weekends, leaving him even more adrift.

God knows what Avril was doing, he thought, staring dis-consolately out of the window. Perhaps that fellow they'd seen at lunch had been in touch. Tom had the impression that if so, he would not be unwelcome. Rona and Max, of course, would be involved with their own affairs, but it was just possible Lindsey was at a loose end.

On the off chance, he rang both her home and mobile numbers, but reached only the answermachine and voicemail. And what could he have said to her, if he'd got through? Damn it, they'd been together only yesterday; she'd not want to see him again so soon.

It was a lovely day; pity he hadn't a garden to potter in. The flat had a communal one, but it was tended by contract gardeners, and though Catherine willingly let him help in hers, he couldn't avail himself of it in her absence.

Perhaps he should get a dog; it would at least be company, and he could take it for walks to fill in the time. Though he no longer had the patience to puppy-train, a rescue dog was a possibility. On second thoughts, though, animals were a tie, and this interregnum was of limited duration. Once he and Catherine were married, Sundays would resume their former character. In the meantime, he decided on a flash of inspiration, he'd drive down to the golf club, and see if he could get a game.

Feeling instantly more cheerful, he went in search of his clubs.

They had driven into the countryside for their lunch, and Lindsey watched with amazement as Dominic extracted a folding table and two chairs from the boot.

'I ordered them when I booked the car,' he told her.

'Any candelabra?'

'Regrettably, we'll have to manage without.'

She helped him set out the food, together with the plastic knives and glasses and the large paper napkins they'd had the foresight to buy. The brie was running in the heat, and the skin of the apricots warm to the touch. She and Hugh had often enjoyed similar meals on French holidays, though they'd never risen to table and chairs. She could imagine Hugh's derision if she'd suggested them, but somehow, with Dominic, it seemed quite natural.

Everything was perfect, Lindsey thought: the dappled shade, the line of distant poplars, the murmuring of the stream a few feet from them. The wine, she noted, was *ordinaire,* and her initial surprise gave way to the acknowledgment that it, too, was just right, its slight roughness complimenting the crusty baguettes and soft, pungent cheese. Life didn't get much better than this, she thought contentedly.

They ate slowly and for the most part silently, savouring their surroundings and, in Lindsey's case, the new-found ease between them. She didn't want it to end, wanted to remain indefinitely in the warm sunshine of this French idyll.

But then the meal was over and Dominic, having tossed the last crust to a hovering bird, was picking up the almost-empty wine bottle. When he rose and came over to her, she expected him to pour the last of it into her glass. Instead, to her confusion, he tilted back her head, and, as she looked questioningly up at him, bent to give her a brief but forceful kiss. Then, without a word, he did indeed tip the last of the wine into her glass before returning to his chair.

Above the clattering of her heart, Lindsey was relieved that instinct had prevented her from attempting to prolong that remarkably thorough kiss.

'Have you been to Mont St Michel?' he enquired, as though the incident had never happened, and Lindsey, hastily collecting herself, shook her head. 'It's a couple of hours' drive from here, but if you'd like to see it, we've plenty of time; we shan't be dining until nine.'

'That would be lovely,' she said.

Until the previous year, Marsborough's weekly market had traditionally been held on the pavements of Market Street, which, though adding colour to normally sober surroundings, had caused a certain amount of congestion. Recently, therefore, the town council had opened up a large area further down the road to provide a designated site, and this July Sunday, the new Market Square was playing host to a French market.

'There was no need for Lindsey to go to France,' Rona remarked, surveying the Tricolore flying from improvised poles, and the blue, white and red bunting decking the stalls; 'France has come to us!'

The air was filled with French voices calling out their wares, while the stalls themselves presented a tempting array: char- cuteries offering succulent slices of ham, pies and pasties; bread of all shapes and sizes; pâtisseries displaying glazed apple and pear flans; herbs from Provence, and stalls piled high with fresh fruit and vegetables.

It was as they paused in front of the cheese booth that a jovial voice behind them said, '*Bonjour, mes amis! Comment ça va?*' and they turned to see their friends Gavin and Magda Ridgeway smiling at them.

'Isn't this great?' Magda said enthusiastically. 'If I bought everything I covet, I wouldn't have the strength to carry it home!' She glanced into Rona's almost-empty basket. 'How are you doing?'

'We've only just arrived. We spent last night in London, but I was determined to get back in time for this.'

'Have a good birthday?'

'Wonderful; and thanks so much for the earrings.' She pushed back her hair. 'As you can see, I'm wearing them.'

'I thought you'd like them. You spent the day in London, then?'

'No, we had the standard family lunch at the Clarendon, then went in to see *The Sound of Music,* followed by a theatre supper and a night at the Argyll. It was all perfect. So – what goodies have you found?'

'Oh, the usual, really: bread and croissants and preserves and some luscious-looking ham; we were stocking up on cheese when you arrived. By the way, there's a fabric stall over on the far side, that has lots of Provençal goods – place mats, napkins, bread containers and so on.' She unearthed a package from the bottom of her own basket and pulled it open to show Rona the contents. 'They'll be ideal to take as gifts when we go to dinner parties.'

'That's an excellent idea,' Rona agreed. 'We're invited to the Kingstons' next Friday, and I was wondering what to take apart from the usual bottle.'

'I don't know about you,' Gavin cut in, 'but my feet are giving out. There's a place over there dispensing food and drink, and I spy a free table. How about it?'

They followed him to where an enterprising stallholder had cordoned off a small area in which he'd set up three tables under striped umbrellas.

'Lindsey's gone to France for the day,' Rona said, as they sat down. 'I was saying to Max that she needn't have bothered!'

'Oh, I don't know,' Magda said. 'I'd always go for the real thing, given the chance.'

'What do you mean, given the chance?' demanded Gavin. 'You hop over there at the drop of a hat, to all the fashion shows.'

Magda owned a string of boutiques. 'But that's business,' she protested, 'and I really only see Paris. It's rural France that I love – hanging villages and fields of lavender and squares where old men play *boules* under spreading plane trees.'

'Well, close your eyes and pretend you're there! The accordion should help!'

They ordered a bottle of wine and, since it was lunchtime, some savoury crêpes, and sat back, watching the colourful crowds swirl past their enclosure.

'Is Lindsey over there for anything specific?' Magda enquired.

'Just a day out, I think. Her latest admirer has a private plane.'

'Very civilized! And who is this desirable escort?'

Rona hesitated, but Lindsey had not requested secrecy, and thankfully, unlike Jonathan Hurst, this one wasn't married. 'Dominic Frayne,' she replied.

'Dominic Frayne?' repeated Gavin, with raised eyebrows. 'Better tell her to watch her step.'

'What do you mean?' Rona asked sharply.

'Oh – nothing concrete. I've heard he's pretty hard-headed in the business world, but that wouldn't impact on Lindsey.'

'Yet you said she should watch her step,' Rona persisted. 'Is there anything I should warn her about?'

Gavin looked embarrassed. 'I was probably speaking out of turn. It's just that his name's been linked with several society women, and I wouldn't like her to get hurt. Tell her not to get in too deep, that's all.'

Nothing more was said on the subject, but his warning weighed heavily on Rona's mind for the rest of the day.

* * *

Lindsey didn't reach home till the early hours, but although tired, she was unable to sleep. Her mind was continually whirling through the events of the day; the flight out in the morning, their leisurely stroll through cobbled streets, and particularly Dominic's sudden and unexpected kiss. Then the afternoon drive through lush countryside to the impressive mound of Mont St Michel, and the long climb up to its abbey.

Dinner at the chateau, now converted into a five-star hotel and restaurant, was as sumptuous as he had promised, each course meticulously cooked and presented. They'd eaten on the veranda by candlelight, watching winking lights in the darkness of the valley below them.

Yet now she was filled with a bleak sense of anticlimax. After that tantalizingly brief kiss at lunchtime, she'd felt sure they'd drawn closer, that at last they would come together. But throughout those long hours, other than a cautionary hand on her arm at the Mont, he'd made no further attempt to touch her. And on the final stage of their journey home, despite the screen between them and the chauffeur, they'd sat as decorously apart as if a searchlight were shining on them. No good-night kiss, simply a brushing aside of her thanks, thanking her in turn for her company.

Her dreams during brief intervals of sleep continued the theme, replaying in distorted form various incidents of the day, woven in with vivid but imaginary events, so that, when she tossed herself awake, she couldn't be sure which of them had actually happened.

Minutes, it seemed, after she'd fallen into her first deep sleep, the alarm clock dragged her up from dizzying depths to the awareness of a raging thirst and an agonizing headache. Too much wine, she diagnosed; she'd been too distracted on her return to drink the requisite glasses of water to fend off dehydration.

Should she phone to thank him? she wondered, holding up her face to the stream of water jetting from the shower. He'd left his number when he'd called that first time. Or would it seem too eager? Perhaps a brief note – but she didn't know his address. In fact, she thought in frustration, despite the more relaxed atmosphere between them, she still knew virtually nothing about him. The names and professions of his children: what earthly use was that?

God, she'd be like a limp rag at work today, and she'd a
new client coming in this afternoon. Black coffee and para-
cetamol were the order of the day, and it was to be hoped one
wouldn't cancel out the other.

Rona's uneasiness concerning Dominic Frayne overlapped
into the next morning, and she agonized over what, if anything,
to say to her sister. Lindsey would no doubt ring later with
an account of her day in France, and she'd have to temper
her response, or Linz would take the huff and clam up. On a
flash of irritation, Rona reflected that she spent more than
enough time worrying about her twin's complicated love life.
    Through the open study window came the sound of Gus
barking in the garden below, and she went to see what was
exciting him. The answer was apparent in the shape of a ginger
cat, now sitting safely on the wall and glaring defiantly down
at him. From the cat, Rona's amused glance slid to the garden
beyond the wall. There was a bench under the apple tree, and
sitting on it, apparently engrossed in a book, was a woman
who was definitely not Mrs Franks. Could she be the owner
of the cigarette that had glowed in the dark? If so, she must
be a regular visitor, and seemingly very much at home, since
then, as now, she'd been alone.
    Rona studied her a little guiltily. Dark glasses hid her eyes,
but her heavy black hair hung in a long straight bob, with a
fringe that reached the top of her glasses. She was wearing a
printed cotton dress, and her bare arms and legs were pale,
as though they'd not been exposed to the sun.
    Rona turned away. Whoever she was, it was no business of
hers.

'Your little heiress is proving persistent,' Carla remarked.
'Following last week's calls, she's phoned three times in the
last two days. I thought you'd signed her off?'
    Dominic looked up from a report, reluctant to be reminded
of what he'd hoped had been cleanly and fairly dealt with. 'I
did, over dinner at the Savoy.'
    'It seems she's not accepted it. Would you care to make it
more plain?'
    He ran a hand distractedly through his hair. 'I'd prefer not
to have to speak to her.'

'So I keep on saying you're unavailable, or out of the country, or in a meeting?'

'If you would. Eventually, perhaps, she'll realize I'm being cruel to be kind.'

'I shouldn't count on it,' Carla said darkly.

Jonathan, who'd overridden Lindsey's refusal to have lunch with him, leaned back in his chair and studied her across the table.

'You look pretty wiped, I must say.'

'Thanks; that makes me feel a lot better.'

'No need to snap, sweetie. So what's wrong? Were you out with your ex again yesterday?'

Lindsey looked up sharply, and winced as the movement sent a pain through her head. 'What do you mean, again?'

'I mean after having dinner with him on Saturday. You're not going to deny it, are you? My spies are everywhere!'

'Why should I deny it? You have dinner with your wife *every* night.'

'Honey, I'm not making an issue of it. Have dinner with whomever you choose.'

'Thank you.' Lindsey took a long draught of mineral water.

'I'm just trying to find out what's put you in such a foul mood. It can't only be the hangover, surely?'

'For the last time, I have *not* got a hangover. I simply had a bad night.'

Jonathan shrugged. 'Have it your way.' He put a tentative hand over hers. She moved impatiently but did not withdraw it, and, encouraged, he leaned forward and said quietly, 'I could manage an hour or so this evening, if that would help?'

Lindsey felt an absurd desire to cry. How had she come to make such a wholesale mess of her love life?

'No, it would not,' she said.

On the afternoons that Avril played bridge, she arrived home roughly an hour after Sarah. It had become the custom that whoever was last back called to the other to announce their arrival, and this Avril proceeded to do. To her surprise, the response, unusually muted, came from the kitchen, and she pushed open the door to see Sarah standing at the sink with her back to her.

'I was getting a glass of water,' she said.

'Fine. Will you be out this evening?'

The girl still hadn't turned. 'No,' she said baldly.

Avril paused, a little nonplussed. 'Right,' she said.

As she hesitated, Sarah, unable any longer to avoid turning, passed her in the doorway with lowered eyes, and went up the stairs. It was obvious she'd been crying.

Slowly Avril followed her and went to change out of her best suit, feeling somewhat at a loss. Had it been one of her daughters, she could have attempted to find out the cause of her distress, perhaps offer some comfort, but she and Sarah hadn't that kind of relationship, and personal exchanges were kept to a minimum. Yet the girl was clearly unhappy, and away from home.

As she came out on to the landing, she heard muffled sobbing from behind the closed door, and, making up her mind, went to tap on it. The sobs stopped abruptly and there was silence.

'I don't want to interfere,' Avril began, 'and I'll go away if you ask me to, but might it help to talk things over?'

A long silence, and Avril, defeated, was turning away, when a choked voice said, 'I don't think so.'

Encouraged to have elicited some response, Avril ventured to ask, 'May I come in?'

Another pause, then, 'If you like.'

Sarah was sitting at the dressing table, a wad of Kleenex in her hand. Avril sat down on the edge of the bed and waited. When Sarah didn't speak, she said hesitantly, 'Is there any way I could help?'

Sarah swivelled round to face her, her eyes red and puffy. 'I don't mean to be rude, but I think this is something I have to weather by myself.'

'Is it – to do with your young man?'

Fresh tears filled her eyes. 'We had a row, and it was my fault; but that's only part of it. It's not working out at school.'

'In what way?'

'The staff don't like me.'

'Oh, I'm sure—'

'I overheard them, when I was in the loo. They think I'm bossy and have a high opinion of myself. And tonight, they're all going to Polly's engagement party, but I'm not invited.'

'That's rather hard,' Avril agreed, 'but there's not a lot you can do about it. However, if the row with – Clive, is it? – was your fault, you could always try phoning to apologize. That might at least clear up half the problem.'

'Suppose he doesn't want to know?'

'That's a chance you'll have to take. If you think he's worth it.'

'Yes,' Sarah said in a low voice. 'He is.'

Avril stood up. 'Then you do that. As for the staff, go out of your way to be friendly, and they'll soon come round. It's almost the end of term, so take in a cake or something, for you all to share.'

She was rewarded by a watery smile. It was hard to reconcile this dejected young woman with the confident and – yes – slightly bossy person Avril was used to. There was indeed a prickliness about her that prevented overtures; perhaps this unhappy experience would persuade her to lower her defences.

Ten minutes later, there was a tap on the sitting room door and Sarah came in, looking decidedly brighter. 'I took your advice,' she said, 'and smoothed things over with Clive. We're meeting at eight thirty, and going for a drink.'

'Well done,' Avril said heartily.

Sarah hesitated a moment, then walked quickly over, bent down, and kissed Avril's cheek.

'Thank you!' she said, and hurried from the room.

Avril sat for a moment staring at the closed door. Then, with a little smile of satisfaction, she returned to her newspaper.

'By the way,' Max said on the phone that evening, 'I met our neighbour as I was leaving the house this morning. Seemed a pleasant enough chap. He was asking about the various estate agents; they haven't exactly been inundated with details.'

'What are they looking for?'

'Detached house, not too large, in a pleasant area; with a bit of a garden. Shouldn't be too hard to find, one would think.'

'Might price be the problem? Property's pretty expensive round here.'

'Not a question I could ask.'

Rona, losing interest, remarked, 'I'm going to have one of those French quiches for supper. It looks and smells delicious.'

'Well, don't scoff the lot before Wednesday! I'm looking forward to sampling the cheeses.'

'Don't worry, there's plenty left. I hope these markets become a regular event.'

'Did you tell Lindsey about it?'

Rona frowned. 'Actually, I've not spoken to her. I thought she'd be on the phone first thing with a blow-by-blow account, but there's been a deathly silence. In view of what Gavin said, I'm a bit concerned.'

'Why didn't you ring her?'

'She doesn't like discussing personal things at work.'

'Well, I shouldn't worry,' Max said briskly. 'She's old enough to take care of herself.'

'She should be home by now, though. I think I'll give her a ring.'

'Let's face it, if lover-boy has ditched her, it mightn't be such a bad thing.'

But Rona, aware of her sister's vulnerability, wasn't so sure.

'Yes, thanks. It was – very pleasant.'

Pleasant? Lindsey had spent a day in France with the man of her dreams, and that was all she could say? Driven by an equal measure of curiosity and concern into making the call, this wasn't what Rona had expected.

'You don't sound exactly carried away,' she probed.

'Oh, Ro, for God's sake! I enjoyed it, right? But I've had a diabolical headache all day, and because of that I mishandled an important interview, and risk losing a prospective client. I'm not exactly on top of the world.'

'I was expecting you to phone, that's all, but if you don't want to talk about it, fine.' Rona, feeling snubbed, was about to let it go; but, remembering Gavin's warning, she added incautiously, 'He *was* OK with you, wasn't he? Dominic?'

'Look,' Lindsey said, in a voice laden with patience, 'we had a picnic lunch – "a loaf of bread, a flask of wine"-type thing – after which we explored Mont St Michel, had dinner in a fabulous chateau, and travelled home by private plane. I'd say that was pretty much OK, wouldn't you?'

'That's all I wanted to know,' Rona said mildly. She didn't dare ask how the evening with Hugh had gone.

Four

Tuesday morning, and Rona was feeling unsettled. It was always the same when she was between jobs, this sense that she should be doing something, but there was nothing to do. In the field of writing, that is. She could give the house an extra clean, take Gus for a long walk, write some letters she'd been putting off, but none of these tasks appealed. The sooner she met Julian Willow and was able to start work, the better.

She glanced dispiritedly at the papers on her desk, brightening as her gaze alighted on a book token, a birthday present from a friend. She decided to go into town and choose a book, then spend a lazy afternoon in the garden reading it.

Gus, asleep on the doormat, looked up expectantly as she came downstairs.

'Yes, we're going out,' she told him, 'but only into town. We'll have a proper walk later, when it's cooled down a bit.'

Registering only the word 'walk', he wagged his tail and waited for his lead to be clipped on. Rona slipped the token into her bag and let them out of the house, mentally running through the reviews in last Sunday's papers, and already anticipating the pleasure of browsing.

They'd gone only a few yards when a voice behind them called, 'Hello!' and Rona turned to see a young woman hurrying after them. Her first thought was that she must have dropped something; then, as recognition came, wasn't this . . .?

'We haven't met,' said the newcomer, holding out her hand, 'though I've seen you coming and going. I'm Louise Franks.'

Rona, slightly bewildered, took her hand. 'Rona Parish. So – you're Mr and Mrs Franks' daughter?'

'That's right.' Seeing Rona's puzzlement, she added, 'Is that a problem?'

Rona collected herself. 'I'm sorry. No, of course not; it's

only that when I met your parents last week, they didn't mention you, and I'd assumed there were just the two of them.'

It was illogical to be surprised, Rona told herself; after all, what more natural explanation for her being in the garden? What *was* surprising was that it hadn't occurred to her; perhaps because Mr and Mrs Franks had seemed so – self-contained, presenting a united and somehow exclusive front.

'Are you going into the town?' Louise Franks was continuing.

'Yes, that's right.'

'Would you mind very much if I came with you? I haven't been out yet, and don't know my way around. Or would I be in the way?'

Though aware this would disrupt her browsing, Rona had little option but to agree. 'I'm only going to the book shop, but you're welcome to join me.'

'Thank you.' Louise bent to pat Gus, who was patiently waiting for his walk to resume. 'I'd love to have a dog,' she said a little wistfully.

'Perhaps when you get settled?' Rona suggested, as they began walking again.

'Settled?'

'In your new home. You're only temporarily next door, aren't you?'

'Oh, I see. Yes.'

There was a rather taut silence, and to break it, Rona asked, 'Haven't you been well?'

Again, it seemed she'd said the wrong thing, because Louise spun to face her, her thick hair swinging across her face. 'Why do you say that?' she demanded.

'You – said you'd not been out.'

'Oh, I see,' Louise repeated, but she didn't answer the question.

The flare of tension subsided, and Rona drew a cautious breath. Conversation with her new neighbour was proving unexpectedly difficult. In the hope of avoiding further awkwardness, she decided to act as guide.

'As you see, we've now turned into Fullers Walk. It leads to the main shopping area, Guild Street, which runs across the top of the road, where you can see the traffic. You'll find most things there, but there are also out-of-town supermarkets within easy driving distance.'

She'd no idea if the Franks had a car; none of the houses in Lightbourne Avenue boasted a garage, but she knew that a rented one in Charlton Road went with the house.

Louise made no comment, though as they passed Dean's Crescent on the other side of the road, she roused herself to ask, 'Where does that lead?'

'It curves round and comes out at the east end of Guild Street. There's a good Italian restaurant along there, and some antique shops, if you're interested in that kind of thing?'

The inflection in her voice indicated a question, but Louise didn't reply. This, Rona decided, was like wading through treacle. The only facts her companion had vouchsafed were that she'd not been out before – though she'd avoided giving a reason – and that she'd like to have a dog. If all her opening gambits fell on stony ground, how would she survive the next half-hour?

Guild Street was, as always, crowded, and Louise kept close by her side as they started along it. Once inside Waterstone's, however, she seemed to relax, and to Rona's relief, moved away, leaving her free to browse and not, in fact, rejoining her until, having made her choice, she was queuing at the checkout.

'Not found anything yourself?' she asked.

Smilingly Louise shook her head.

'This is the latest by one of my favourite authors. Have you read him?'

A hesitation. Then, 'I'm – not sure.'

Rona flipped the book open to display the backlist. 'Any of these titles ring a bell?'

But Louise had turned away. Resignedly, Rona handed over her token and, back on the pavement, freed Gus from the post to which he'd been tied.

They'd started back towards Fullers Walk and her ordeal seemed nearly over, when Louise said suddenly, 'Let me buy you a coffee. To thank you for letting me tag along. I know I'm not the easiest person to be with.'

'Oh, nonsense!' Rona lied gallantly. 'It's been good to meet you, but I really—'

'Please! I don't know when I'll have the chance again. My parents don't like my going out alone.'

Rona stared at her. After a moment, she said lamely, 'You're here now.'

'Only because I disobeyed them.'

It seemed an odd word for an adult to use.

'Father had a dental appointment,' Louise continued, 'a root filling – and as he couldn't drive home after the anaesthetic, Mother had to go with him. They wanted to take me, but I refused; so I was given strict instructions not to leave the house.'

Rona frowned. 'I don't understand.'

'It doesn't matter. *Will* you come for coffee?'

As luck would have it, they'd reached the iron staircase leading to the Gallery, and since Gus, following his familiar routine, had already started up it, Rona felt further protest would be useless.

'Then thank you. There's a café up these stairs.'

Luckily, there was a table free. Gus settled himself beneath it, they gave their order, and, seated opposite her, Rona was, for the first time, able to take a proper look at her companion. At a guess, she was in her early thirties, give or take a few years either way. The dark, bobbed hair with its heavy fringe she'd seen from the study window, but now Louise had removed her sunglasses, her eyes were revealed as a vivid blue, a striking contrast to the blackness of brows and lashes. Today, she was wearing an open-necked cheesecloth shirt and designer jeans. There were no rings on her fingers, but she wore a thick silver bangle on her left wrist.

Seemingly unaware of the scrutiny, Louise folded her hands on the table and looked at Rona expectantly. 'Now – tell me all about you!'

'There's not much to tell,' Rona fenced.

'Well, for a start, you're a journalist, aren't you? I saw one of your articles in a magazine.'

'I do some freelance work, yes.' There was a silence. Louise obviously expected more, so she added, 'And my husband's an artist.'

'Ah, so he *is* your husband? We wondered, as you have different surnames.'

Rona said a little stiffly, 'I kept my own because I use it professionally.'

'So what kind of things do you write about?'

She was chatty enough now she was asking the questions, Rona thought crossly. 'Whatever might be of interest,' she prevaricated.

'The one I read was about some local firm. It must have needed a lot of research.'

'Most of my work does.'

Louise looked at her thoughtfully from under thick black lashes. 'You must enjoy it.'

'Yes, I do. I like tracing threads backwards and seeing where they lead. It can be quite challenging.'

Their coffee arrived, and as she poured it, Rona prompted, 'You're from Canada, aren't you?' Louise's accent was, in fact, more pronounced than that of her parents.

She nodded.

'Though you're actually English, your mother said. How long were you out there?'

'Oh, several years.'

'It's somewhere I'd love to go. Whereabouts did you live?'

A look Rona couldn't analyse flickered across the other woman's face. If the idea hadn't been ludicrous, she'd have guessed it was alarm.

'I don't – Toronto.' Louise thrust a plate of biscuits towards her. 'How long have you lived here?'

'All my life, apart from university.'

'Lucky you.'

'Sometimes I feel I should have been more adventurous.'

Louise shook her head decidedly. 'You've been able to put down roots, establish your own place in society. In a town this size, you'll know a lot of people, and they'll know you, which must give a sense of security. I envy you.'

'I've never thought of it that way,' Rona admitted with a little laugh.

'You probably haven't needed to,' said Louise Franks.

The conversation had become less than comfortable, and by tacit consent, neither of them asked any more questions. In fact, Louise seemed to have retreated into her shell, leaving Rona to keep up a stream of inconsequential chat while they finished their coffee and started to walk home.

As they turned the corner into Lightbourne Avenue, Rona was startled to see Mrs Franks standing at her gate, looking agitatedly to left and right.

'Oh, God!' said Louise under her breath.

Catching sight of them, the woman stiffened and stood waiting until they reached her.

She gave Rona a brief nod, and turned to her daughter.

'Louise!' Her voice was shaking. 'Where on *earth* have you been? We've been worried to death. I *told* you not to go out! *Anything* could have—'

'Ah, there you are, love.' Keith Franks, the left side of his face swollen, came down the steps from the house. 'All safe and sound, as I was sure you would be.'

He put an arm round his wife, but she shook him off, turning back to Rona.

'Thank you for bringing her back, Mrs – Miss—'

'Rona,' Rona supplied. 'And I didn't actually bring her back; we went out together for a coffee.'

She was aware of Louise's quick flash of gratitude, but her mother was unconvinced.

'Well, it was very good of you,' she mumbled, and, taking Louise's arm, led her firmly up the path and into the house, leaving Keith and Rona eyeing each other uneasily.

Rona gave him a cautious smile and would have moved on, but he said quickly, 'I don't know what she told you – Louise, I mean – but it's not wise to take her too literally. She's been ill, you know, and she still gets – confused.'

Since she could think of no suitable reply, Rona smiled again and, tugging gently on Gus's lead, turned thankfully into her own gateway.

The afternoon in the garden wasn't as relaxing as she'd anticipated. Her eyes kept drifting from her book to the high wall on her left, aware of movement and occasional low voices behind it. From her position close to the house, she could not, she knew, be seen from next-door's windows, yet she felt curiously exposed.

What an odd family they were, she reflected: the parents reserved and, certainly on the face of it, over-protective; and Louise herself a complex mix, shying away from personal questions, yet seeming touchingly eager for some form of contact. Rona hoped fervently that they'd soon find a home of their own, preferably on the other side of Marsborough.

*   *   *

'What do you think was the matter with her?' she asked Max over the phone that evening, having regaled him with the morning's events.

'My dear girl, how in the world should I know? I've never even met the woman!'

'Her father said she was confused, but she seemed all right to me. Well, more or less all right.'

'Never mind, you're unlikely to be called on to give a diagnosis.'

'But I'm uneasy about them, Max. I didn't even enjoy being in the garden this afternoon.'

'Now you're being fanciful. As I told you, I talked to – Keith, I think he said his name was – and found him very affable. I can't see anything unusual about parents wanting to protect their daughter if she's been ill.'

'But not allowing her out by herself!'

'Perhaps she has epilepsy or something.'

'And they've been discussing us,' Rona added indignantly.

'Well, we've been discussing them!'

'They wondered if we were married, as we have different surnames.'

'Reasonable enough. When they've been there a bit longer, they'll notice I don't come home every evening, and they'll probably discuss that, too. Good luck to them!'

'I wish you were coming home tonight,' she said in a small voice.

'Sweetheart, for goodness' sake! You'll probably never come across them again. Think how seldom we saw all the other people who've taken that house.'

'I hope you're right,' said Rona.

There were no more sightings of their neighbours over the next two days, and Rona's initial discomfort eased. Perhaps Max was right, and there'd be no further contact. And now it was Friday evening at last, and they were about to meet the Willows.

As she was preparing to go out, it occurred to her that they mightn't agree to being researched. Her previous efforts had, after all, turned up several skeletons. As one of the Curzons had remarked, most long-established families had them; it was a question of whether or not they could be contained. Well, she decided philosophically, that was a bridge she could cross when she came to it.

'Ready?' Max enquired, looking into the bedroom.

'Ready!' she confirmed, picking up her bag.

'Then let's go and meet your next victims!' he said.

The Kingstons lived in a large modern house in Piper's Way, an executive development on the far side of Guild Street. There were already two cars in the driveway, and although there was room for another, Max parked on the road.

'In case we need a quick getaway!' he said.

Georgia and Patrick met them in the hall, gratefully accepted Max's bottle of wine, and exclaimed over the Provençal mats Rona had brought.

'If the table weren't already laid, I'd put them on straight away!' Georgia exclaimed. 'How clever of you – they're just the right colour. Now, come and meet our other guests.'

The two men in the sitting room rose as they entered. One of them was Simon Grant, who came forward to kiss Rona and shake Max's hand.

'I don't think you've met the Willows,' Georgia said. 'Julian and Felicity, Rona and Max.'

As the four of them nodded smilingly at each other, Rona and Max avoided each other's eyes. For Felicity Willow was not the woman they'd seen with Julian at the London restaurant. Here we go! Rona thought resignedly.

'I certainly know *of* you both,' Julian was saying, 'and I've a feeling Rona and I met once, many years ago.'

'That's right,' she said. 'I think it was at the tennis club.'

And he'd changed surprisingly little, she thought, as she sat down at Patrick's invitation and took the glass he handed her. He was still tall and thin, with a lean, clever-looking face and deep-set eyes. Only his hair was different. Fair and fine, it had flopped over his face in his youth; now it had receded, leaving him with a high and bony forehead.

Felicity Willow leaned forward with a smile. 'I've read some of your biographies,' she said to Rona, 'and enjoyed them very much. Have you any others in the pipeline?'

Max laughed. 'A leading question!'

Rona flushed, aware this could lead to the subject she'd hoped to postpone till later in the evening. Georgia came to her rescue.

'I loved the one about Sarah Siddons. What a life that woman had!'

The conversation turned to a discussion on the theatre, but Rona had barely relaxed when another potentially delicate subject arose, and again, to her annoyance, it was Max who precipitated it.

'It's ages since I saw a West End show,' Hilary was remarking. 'What's on at the moment?'

And Max replied, '*The Sound of Music,* for a start. We saw it on Saturday.'

'Of course – it was Rona's birthday. Did you get my card?'

'Yes; thanks very much.'

'And how was the show?'

'Very good; it was lovely to hear all those songs again.' Rona caught Max's eye, willing him not to mention their theatre supper, and thankfully he subsided.

In the event, it was Julian himself who raised the matter of the articles. Georgia had seated him next to Rona at dinner, so that she could, if she wished, bring up the subject, and it was as they were starting their dessert that he said without preamble, 'I've been enjoying your series in *Chiltern Life*. Someone said the Curzons have also received the treatment?'

'That's right,' Rona answered carefully, 'but we're holding publication to coincide with their anniversary.'

'That family tree must have been hell to work through. We go back further, but our lineage is much simpler – father to son right down the line.'

'Actually—' Rona began, and broke off, seeing the twinkle in his eye. 'You know what I'm going to ask, don't you?'

'I've a pretty good idea. I was wondering when you'd get round to us.'

'Would you mind?'

'I'd be honoured. We've lots of family documents, all filed chronologically and more or less on your doorstep. Though no doubt you'll want to go to Yorkshire at some stage, when you come to Lady Araminta.'

Lady Araminta, Rona noted. Not just 'Honourable', then; Georgia had demoted her.

'And you predate the Curzons?' she prompted.

'Yes, by nearly fifty years. But as I said, we've had the

good sense to have only one son per generation, which has spared us a lot of hassle.'

No doubt, like the Curzons, the Willow women had taken no interest in the business. Rona hoped they'd nonetheless received their due desserts.

Felicity, sitting opposite them, smiled across. 'Are you boring Rona with stories of the family?' she asked. 'I should warn you, Rona, once started, there's no stopping him.'

'We have received the accolade, darling,' Julian informed her. 'She wants to write us up for her series.'

'No doubt it was you who suggested it!'

'I might have nudged her a little.'

'Really,' Rona assured her, 'I was intending to ask him.'

'Well, if you're sure, we'd be glad to give you all the help you need, wouldn't we, darling?'

There was something immediately likeable about Felicity, though Rona, remembering the woman she presumed to be her rival, felt she could make more of herself. She wore minimal make-up, and her soft brown hair with its wispy fringe looked as though she'd washed it herself – very different from the chic stylishness of her husband's London companion. Moreover, though her dress was obviously expensive, it did little for her, being altogether too matronly. Rona longed to take her to one of Magda's boutiques.

'When are you hoping to embark on this?' Julian asked.

'Whenever's convenient; my desk is clear at the moment.'

'Shall we say Tuesday, then? All the papers are at the house, so you'd be working from there. As you'll appreciate, space at the store is at a premium, with everything being on the one floor.'

'Julian's grandfather tried to buy the walkway above,' Felicity put in, 'so we could expand upwards, but it caused an uproar. There was a Conservation Society, even then.'

'What are you all talking about so earnestly at your end of the table?' Simon demanded laughingly.

'My next project,' Rona told him. 'Willows' Fine Furniture, Past and Present.'

'And God bless all who sail in her!' Max added facetiously.

'You pulled it off, then,' he commented, in the car on the way home.

'Julian brought it up himself. Said he'd wondered when I'd get round to him. Barnie told me he'd had enquiries from local businesses, but he didn't mention the Willows. At least I'll be working close to home this time – in fact, actually in *their* home, though Julian was careful to point out I'll need to go to Yorkshire, to pay homage to their aristocratic roots.'

'Who,' Max remarked drily, 'probably won't thank you for reminding them they're related to trade.'

Dominic stood at his window, looking down over the town of Marsborough. He'd been damn lucky to find this place, he reflected. Not only was it fully serviced, with a first-class restaurant on the ground floor, but there was also a coffee lounge doubling as an informal club, which residents made use of to meet business colleagues. And to crown it all, Carla had a flat two floors below him, so was always on hand. It could not have been more convenient.

He glanced at his watch. Another fifteen minutes till the conference call. An important deal was under way, and he was running through the points he intended to make, when a tap on the door broke his train of thought.

'Not now, Carla,' he said testily. 'I need to keep my mind clear.'

'I'm sorry,' Carla sounded harassed. 'You have a visitor who insists on speaking to you.'

He turned angrily. 'I see no one without an appointment, you know that.'

'You'll see me,' said a voice behind her, and as she perforce moved aside, Lady Miranda Barrington-Selby, known colloquially as Dominic's heiress, came into the room.

He felt his heart jerk, surprise and guilt combining to wrong-foot him. 'Forgive me, Miranda,' he said gently, 'but I really can't talk to you now. I'm awaiting an important call.'

'I'm sorry if it's inconvenient, Dominic, but that's your fault, not mine. If you'd had the courtesy to return my calls, I shouldn't have had to seek you out.'

He said quietly, 'Five minutes, then,' and nodded dismissal at Carla who, having failed to preserve his privacy, was hovering uncertainly. She went out, closing the door quietly behind her.

He turned back to Miranda. God, why couldn't she accept

that what had been between them was over? It was an episode about which he'd always been uncomfortable, and latterly ashamed. She was so agonizingly *young*. How could he have let things get so far out of hand? Yet, in his defence, it had been she who'd initiated the affair, phoning almost daily to invite him to some function or ball or opening, until, flattered, he'd succumbed, accepting that she always got her way. She was also very beautiful, with her cascade of red-gold hair and her green eyes.

And those green eyes now challenged him from across the room. She was still by the door. He beckoned her closer, but she made no move.

'It's not a social call, Dominic. I've come to tell you I'm pregnant.'

He stared at her, his heart plummeting. 'You can't be,' he said ridiculously.

She ignored him. 'And Daddy isn't too happy about it.'

Dominic moistened his lips. 'Daddy', whom he'd met through business contacts, was a prominent member of the House of Lords. But God, what timing. Any minute . . .

'Miranda, I'm truly sorry, but I can't deal with this now. I've—'

'An important call. Yes, so you said.'

'Look, I'm not being dismissive, believe me, but it really is impossible. If you'd care to wait, I'll meet you down in the coffee lounge in an hour or so. It's not open to the public, so tell them you're meeting me. There's a supply of magazines in there, to help pass the time.'

And before she could protest, he took her arm and led her firmly out to Carla.

Back in his room, he rubbed a hand over his face. Oh, God, God, God, he could have done without this! How in hell could he remain focussed for the duration of this blasted call?

It seemed a very short space of time before the phone rang.

Five

Dominic's willpower being one of his strengths, the conference call had gone well, but he remained at his desk for a good ten minutes after it ended, wondering how best to approach Miranda.

Finally, deciding to play it by ear, he took the lift to the ground floor and made his way to the coffee lounge. He saw her at once, long legs crossed, hair screening her face as she flicked through a magazine; saw also that several of the businessmen grouped around the room were casting speculative glances in her direction.

She looked up as he approached, but didn't speak.

'Another coffee?' he asked, seating himself opposite her and noting her empty cup.

'No, thanks.'

Pity; it might have helped things along. He cleared his throat. 'Right; I'm sorry to have kept you waiting. Now, let's start again. You're sure you're pregnant?'

'Of course I am.'

'And – forgive me – it is mine?'

Her eyes flashed, but she merely said tightly, 'Yes.'

He waited for the inevitable claim that there'd been no one else, but surprisingly it didn't come; a glaring omission in the circumstances.

'How far on are you?'

'Twelve weeks.'

'Twelve weeks?' he repeated, his voice rising. 'You took your time telling me.'

'I wanted to be sure.'

He thought back three months. April. Easter in Paris. He'd intended the weekend to be their last together, during which he'd gently extricate himself from the affair. In the event, since she was enjoying it so much, he'd postponed doing so, finally broaching the subject over dinner at the Savoy a couple of weeks later.

With a pang, he remembered the blank shock on her face, the phone calls that had followed, during which she'd alternately wept and raged at him, refusing to accept that it was over. It had been the messiest and most painful ending of any of his affairs. And now this.

She was watching him, perhaps following the pattern of his thoughts.

'So what now?' he asked quietly.

She lifted her shoulders in a shrug.

'Miranda –' he was striving to be patient – 'you must have something in mind. Otherwise, why come to see me?'

Still she remained silent, studying him intently.

'Do you want to keep the baby?' he went on. 'If so, and if it is indeed mine, I shall, of course, support you. If you don't want it, I'll pay for the operation. I can't say fairer than that.'

'You could ask me to marry you,' she said.

He stared at her, wild thoughts of entrapment circling in his head. 'I trust you're not serious.'

'I'm very serious, Dominic. It's what I expected, right from the beginning. I thought you knew that. Daddy certainly did.'

The veiled threat again. He decided to ignore it. 'You must know it was never on the cards.'

'Why not? We're both free. We have a lot in common. We—'

'Miranda,' he said gently, 'we have *nothing* in common. Nothing. We'd a great time together – I admit that – and I'm fond of you. But with two failed marriages behind me, I've no intention of putting myself through another. This simply shouldn't have happened.'

His eyes narrowed. 'How *did* it happen? You told me you were on the pill.'

She looked away, and the answer hit him like a sluice of cold water.

'You stopped taking it,' he accused her. 'Didn't you?'

'I might have forgotten once or twice.'

Anger replaced his sympathy for her. 'You little fool! You meant this to happen! Didn't it occur to you that at my age, the last thing I'd want is another child? My youngest is nineteen, for God's sake – not much younger than you.'

He realized, to his annoyance, that their altercation, low-voiced though it had been, was attracting interest. Several heads had turned their way, and he forced himself to sit back in his chair, drawing a deep breath.

'That being the case,' he went on, a little more calmly, 'what do you propose to do? Will you keep the baby?'

But again she avoided a direct answer. 'Didn't you ever love me?' she asked.

'I was fond of you; I never pretended it was more than that.' A sense of injustice fuelled his anger. 'You might be young, but don't play the naive, wronged girl with me. It won't wash, and I refuse to be cast as the Big Bad Wolf. You told me yourself you'd had other affairs; how was I to know you were taking this one seriously?'

She didn't reply. He was wondering how to resolve the impasse, when she suddenly gathered up her handbag and rose to her feet.

'I have to go,' she said rapidly, and almost ran from the room. Taken by surprise, he half rose himself; then, as she hurried across the foyer and disappeared through the swing doors, he sank back in his chair, furiously aware that her exit had been observed by everyone in the room. An intensely private man, he swore fluently under his breath before reaching for his mobile.

'You want me to man the barricades?' Carla enquired, before he could speak.

'They've already been breached,' he answered shortly. 'Have you any plans for lunch?'

A surprised pause. Then, 'None that can't be altered. Why?'

'I'd be grateful if you'd join me. In the restaurant in ten minutes?'

'Yes, sir.'

He flicked his phone shut, slid it into his pocket, and, rising abruptly, went in search of a drink.

The afternoon was overcast, the air heavy. Rona had taken Gus to the park that sprawled up Furze Hill overlooking the town; if there was a breeze to be found, it was there that she'd find it. And, indeed, the air did seem fresher on the park's upper slopes, where Gus, freed from his lead, ran joyously ahead, searching for a stick for her to throw.

Her last day of freedom, Rona thought fancifully; tomorrow, she would begin working on the Willow story. She sighed, wishing she could summon up more excitement. Initially she'd been looking forward to the project, but from what Julian had said, the Willows' history was so meticulously annotated, it seemed there'd be little for her to do other than reproduce it. And, she thought ironically, travel to Yorkshire to pay her respects to the gentry.

Gus bounded up, a stick in his mouth, dropped it at her feet and looked up at her expectantly, his flag of a tail waving. Obediently, she bent and threw it for him. Perhaps, she told herself, the family had hidden depths; perhaps she'd discover some unknown facts that would add interest – though hopefully, this time any skeletons she might unearth would be of the strictly metaphorical kind.

She followed Gus up the steep, grassy slope, grateful for the breeze lifting her hair. At the top, where the ground levelled out, was a bench from where one could look over the roofs and chimneys of the town spread below, and Rona often paused there. She enjoyed the sense of perspective the view gave her, a distancing from the problems and questions that awaited her down in the town. Today, however, the bench was occupied, and she was about to walk on when something about the seated figure struck her as familiar and she realized, to her dismay, that it was Louise Franks.

She was tempted to continue, affecting not to have seen her, but, sensing someone behind her, Louise was already turning her head, and Rona, resigned to the inevitable, smiled and walked over.

'Hello, Louise. I thought it was you.'

'Rona. Come and join me.' She patted the bench beside her, and Rona sat down. 'Fantastic view, isn't it?'

'Yes; I often sit here for a while before starting back.' She flicked Louise a glance. 'Your father at the dentist's again?'

Louise smiled and shook her head. 'No; I've managed to persuade them I shan't collapse in a heap if I'm out alone.'

'Good for you.'

Gus, resenting the interruption to the game, deposited the stick at Rona's feet, and Louise scratched his ears. 'Thanks for not asking,' she said abruptly.

Rona turned to look at her. 'Asking what?'

'Why I'm kept wrapped in cotton wool.'

There was an awkward pause. 'Your father told me you'd been ill,' Rona ventured.

'It's a little more than that, as you must have gathered. Actually, I've lost my memory.'

'Oh, no!' Rona exclaimed involuntarily. 'How awful for you!'

'Yes, it is.'

'How did it happen?'

'As the result of a car crash, in Canada. I suffered severe head injuries, and was in a coma for two weeks. In all, I spent a couple of months in hospital.'

'I'm so sorry. Was anyone else in the car?'

'No, and there was no other vehicle involved. They never discovered what happened.'

'So – what *do* you remember?'

'Coming to in hospital. And, of course, everything that's happened since.'

'But nothing before?'

'Not even my name, or where I lived. When they handed me a mirror, I didn't recognize myself; it was a stranger staring back at me.'

Rona shuddered. 'What about your parents?'

'Well, obviously, I didn't know them. They had to convince me who they were, and try to fill in my background.'

'But it didn't help?'

Louise shook her head. 'No, it didn't. Or at least, it hasn't yet.' She leant forward, hands clasped, gazing unseeingly over the town below them. 'You know, the worst thing is the loss of – of self. It's hard to explain, but when you think about it, it's memories that make us who we are. They're unique to each one of us, and no two people have the same. Even shared memories are remembered from personal angles.'

'But – you didn't, for instance, have to learn how to speak again, or read, or walk?'

'No; they explained that there are different kinds of memory, and the type of amnesia you have depends on the head injury. The memory dealing with skills, like reading or driving, is called "procedural", and that, thank God, was unaffected in my case. Then there's "semantic memory", which is general knowledge – what year it is, who's the president of the USA, that kind of thing, and that did come back. But the intensely *personal* memory – about things you yourself experienced – is known as "episodic", and that's what I've lost.'

'But that might come back, too?' Rona suggested, trying to lighten the bleak picture Louise was painting.

'Possibly, but I was warned it could take years. In the meantime, I've no idea where I've been, who my friends were, or what ambitions I might have had. It sounds paradoxical, but without a past, you can't really have a future. I'm existing in a perpetual, disembodied present.'

'But your parents filled in some of the blanks?'

'Oh, they did their best. They told me, for instance, that I'd recently been through an acrimonious divorce, and reverted to my maiden name.'

Rona smiled. 'As I told you, I never gave mine up.'

'Good for you. They even think the stress of the divorce could have affected my driving and contributed to the accident.'

'Did your ex get in touch, to check how you were?'

'No, but he's in the Far East somewhere, so he wouldn't have heard about it. Other than that, I was apparently born and brought up in Yorkshire. I met Kevin when I was sixteen, and there was never anyone else. After university, he was offered a job in Toronto, so we got married and went out there.'

'Your parents too?'

'Not at first; they came when Father retired. I was all the family they had, and they wanted to be nearer.' She gave a harsh laugh. 'So I could look after them in their old age, I suppose. But as things turned out, they had to look after me.'

She stood up suddenly. 'God, I'm sorry, Rona. I didn't mean to saddle you with all this. It's just that you're the first person, other than medics or my parents, that I've actually spoken to.'

Rona also stood. 'I'm sorry you've had such a rotten time. If there's anything I can do . . .'

'Just put up with me letting off steam sometimes, if you can stand it. Every so often, the sheer frustration of it gets to me.'

'I'm not surprised.'

Gus was nudging her foot and she belatedly picked up the stick and threw it for him.

'Are you starting back now?'

Louise shook her head. 'I'll stay a bit longer. Thanks for being a good listener.'

'Any time,' Rona said awkwardly, and, as Gus came galloping back, she started to walk slowly down the slope towards home.

The address Julian had given her was in an area of Marsborough Rona didn't know well. Normally, she drove down Alban Road only en route for the station, and Oak Avenue was a turning some distance beyond it. The houses were all detached and stood in large gardens, but the styles varied, giving added interest to the road.

The Willow home was on the right hand side about halfway down. A gravelled drive swept in a semicircle from one gate to another further on, but since neither was open, Rona parked on the road. She then found the gates to be operated by remote control, and, feeling slightly annoyed, had to press the button to announce her presence. A disembodied voice said uninvitingly, 'Yes?'

Rona's irritation increased. She had an appointment, for God's sake. 'It's Rona Parish,' she said a little sharply. 'I *am* expected.'

'One minute, please.'

A consultation appeared to take place off air, as it were, after which the voice became more placatory. 'I'm sorry, Ms Parish. Please come in.' There was a loud buzz and the gate swung ponderously open.

It hadn't sounded like the friendly Felicity, Rona thought as, still disgruntled, she crunched her way up the drive. A secretary, perhaps, but if so it was inefficient not to know of the appointment. The front door opened as she approached and Felicity stood there, flushed and smiling.

'I'm so sorry, Rona, on two counts. First, Julian had to go out unexpectedly, though he should be back soon. And secondly, I was in the garden and didn't hear the buzzer. Do come in.'

She led the way through a spacious hall and an attractive

sitting room to a conservatory running along the back of the house.

'Tara's making coffee,' Felicity said, indicating a cushioned wicker sofa. 'I thought we could have a chat before you go up, and with luck Julian will be back by then.'

So the disembodied voice belonged to the absent Tara. Maid? Au pair? Or secretary, as she'd first thought? No explanation had been offered. Rona seated herself, leaning her briefcase against the leg of the sofa. Beyond the glass in front of her, a garden laid mostly to lawn stretched green and luxuriant, giving rise to ignoble doubts about adherence to the hosepipe ban.

'As we explained,' Felicity continued, 'all the archives are stored here, on the second floor. When Julian was young, the top of the house was converted into a flat for his grandparents, but now it's used as offices. The lift still comes in useful, though.' She smiled. 'The children spend many a rainy afternoon zooming up and down, though they're barred from it when Julian's working.'

'He works from home, then?'

'Occasionally. We have all the necessary, of course – fax, Internet, and so on – but he also has an office in London, which is more convenient for business contacts, and he spends a fair bit of time on the continent. Ah, here's coffee!'

Rona looked up at the sound of approaching footsteps, and experienced a jolt of surprise. For the young woman who'd come into the conservatory and was laying a tray on the table was none other than Julian's London companion.

Rona held her breath, wondering if she herself had been spotted there. To her relief, it seemed not. Seen at close quarters, Tara – as she presumably was – looked even more attractive than from across the restaurant floor. Tall and slim, her shining brown hair was cut in a style that screamed 'Mayfair', and she was dressed with careless elegance in a black silk shirt and white trousers. Seeing the two women together, Rona's heart sank, doubting if Felicity could hold her own against such competition.

'This is Julian's cousin, Tara Delaney,' Felicity was saying. 'Tara, meet Rona Parish, who's going to write the family history.'

Tara spared her a glance. 'Sorry to have treated you like a tradesman,' she said lightly. 'Flick hadn't mentioned you coming.'

'I thought Julian would be home.' Felicity glanced at the tray, noting it held only two cups. 'Aren't you joining us?'

'No, I really should get back. Love to Jools, and I'll call you at the weekend. Thanks for baling me out, as usual.' She bent and kissed Felicity's cheek 'Nice to have met you, Rona.' And she was gone. A minute later, they heard the front door close behind her.

'She's been having a bad time,' Felicity explained. 'A long-term love affair broke up about a month ago, and it knocked her sideways, poor love. When she feels particularly low, she comes here for a few days, for a bit of TLC.'

Rona smiled but made no comment. Was this seemingly lovelorn woman repaying Felicity's kindness by sleeping with her husband? It seemed more than likely.

'Now, what were we saying? Ah yes, the flat.' Felicity passed her a cup of coffee and a plate of shortbread biscuits. 'It hasn't a separate entrance – it didn't seem necessary with family – but the front door's always unlocked when someone's home. So when you're working here, don't bother to knock, just come straight in and take the lift. And I'll give you the code for the gate before you go.'

'Thank you. You say Julian's grandparents lived here; has it always been the family home?'

'Oh no; over the years, everyone had their own place, but by the time Julian was six or seven, old Albert was in his eighties and getting decidedly frail. He and his wife had a large house along Alban Road with a sizable garden, and it was obviously too much for them. So my parents-in-law offered to convert the top floor here, and they were glad to move in.' Felicity smiled. 'It gave Albert a new lease of life – he lived to be ninety-six.'

'But you and Julian took over the house when you married?'

'Yes. He'd always loved it, and reading between the lines, I don't think my mother-in-law was too fond of it. She's Swedish, and a lady of definite opinions. As soon as we became engaged, she nudged Graham into handing it over to us and moving to a modern house in Woodbourne, more suited to her Scandinavian tastes!'

Rona sipped her coffee. 'You mentioned your children; how old are they?'

'Minty's nine – named, as you'll gather, after Araminta – and

Robin's seven.' Felicity gave a little laugh. 'I think Julian told you about the one son per generation? I've always been thankful we had a girl first, or he mightn't have risked a second baby, in case it was another boy!'

'Surely he doesn't take it that seriously?'

'Fortunately, it wasn't put to the test.'

The sound of the front door reached them, followed by Julian's voice calling, 'Hello?'

'We're in the conservatory,' Felicity called back, and he came striding through to join them, holding his hand out to Rona.

'So sorry to keep you waiting. An unexpected emergency; there was a leak at the shop and no one could find where it was coming from.'

'Did it do any damage?' Felicity asked anxiously.

'No, fortunately, but we moved some of the stock just in case. We didn't want to close, obviously, so it was literally a question of all hands to the pump.'

'And now it's fixed?'

'Yes, and everything back in place.'

'Would you like some coffee, darling? This will be cold, but I could make some fresh.'

'No, thanks, I had some down there, to keep me going. Has Tara gone?'

'Yes, she sent her love.'

'Right. Well, if you're ready, Rona, I can show you around upstairs.'

As she followed him out to the hall, he said suddenly, 'On second thoughts, you might like to see this first.'

He pushed open the door of the room across the hallway, revealing a handsome dining suite, whose sideboard was resplendent with crystal and silver. But it was not that he wished to show her. As she entered the room, he gestured to the wall behind the door, on which hung a large portrait in a gold frame. Rona didn't need to be told who the sitter was, but she was certainly a striking-looking young woman. Her rich auburn hair was caught up in the fashion of the time, but the tilt of her chin and a glint in her eye gave some indication that this was no meek beauty, content to sit back and allow others to dictate her life. She had, as Rona knew, defied her family and run away to marry a humble craftsman.

Julian was looking at her expectantly, and she said, 'She's very beautiful, and brave, too, to do what she did for love.'

'It wasn't exactly riches to rags, you know,' Julian said, with a touch of impatience. 'Sebastian might not have been her social equal, but the business was already well-established and increasingly highly thought of.' He smiled ruefully. 'People tend to confuse Sebastian with the romantic story of John the barrow-boy who started the firm, but that was nearly eighty years before. Anyway, I thought you'd like to see her.'

He led the way back into the hall and round a corner to where a small lift had been installed.

'I usually make a point of walking up,' Julian said with a smile, 'but my secretary uses this, and I suggest you do, too. It's more convenient, and takes you straight to the second floor.'

Thereby preserving the privacy of their family quarters on the first, Rona noted.

They emerged on to a small landing, which had two doors at the front of the building and two at the back. The front rooms, Julian explained, had been his grandparents' bedroom and sitting room, though no traces remained of that former usage. The first room they entered was equipped with two desks, a computer, scanner, fax machine and all other necessities of the modern office. Shelves crammed with books lined the walls – most of them, from Rona's quick glance, on furniture – and two small filing cabinets stood behind the door.

'As I mentioned,' Julian continued, 'I have a secretary who works freelance, and whom I call on as need dictates. She usually comes in when I'm away, to deal with emails, queries and so on, and any work I've left for her. She could probably answer any questions you have, but if you need to speak to Felicity or myself, one of these phones is an intercom.'

He returned to the landing and opened the second door. 'And this is the archive room.'

Rona looked around in some awe. One wall was solid with filing cabinets, each drawer bearing a card meticulously listing its contents. Against the opposite wall were several glass display cabinets containing papers and various artefacts. There was also a comfortable-looking sofa and, under the window, an upright chair in front of a large table, where papers could be spread out.

'I presume you have a laptop?' Julian enquired.

'Yes.'

He nodded in satisfaction. 'The rooms at the back are a bathroom and kitchenette respectively. They've been left more or less as they were, and obviously still come in useful. Beryl makes tea and coffee, and if she's here over lunch, warms up food in the microwave – our one innovation.'

'It's all very compact,' Rona said admiringly. Remembering other family archives she'd studied, she added, 'Are the records mostly to do with the business, or is there also personal history? I admit I'm more interested in the human element.'

Julian gave a short laugh. 'Oh, we've had plenty of that! There are letters and photographs by the score. Make full use of them. All I would ask is that I have the chance to veto anything that's too sensitive.' He hesitated. 'Would you like to make a start now, or have you another engagement?'

'I'd like a preliminary look, if I may. Then I could make a proper start tomorrow.'

'Fine; I'll leave you to it, then. Just let yourself out when you've finished. Oh, and I'd better give you the security code for the gate.'

Rona took it down.

'We have a daily who's here nine till four every day, so the house should always be open. Good luck with your research! I'll be most interested to see what you produce.'

'I have Lord Roxford's Private Secretary on the line,' Carla said expressionlessly, 'enquiring if you'd be free to lunch with him tomorrow.'

'Oh God!' Dominic flung himself back in his chair. 'Dress code sackcloth and ashes, I presume?'

'He suggests his club,' Carla continued, 'and apologizes for the short notice, but the summer recess starts on Thursday.'

When he made no comment, she added, 'You've not much choice, have you?'

He ran a hand through his hair. 'This, I could do without. Why couldn't the silly girl do as I suggested, instead of running bleating to her father?'

'Probably thought he had more clout.'

'He's always seemed a laid-back sort of chap,' Dominic said reflectively, 'but admittedly that was before I toyed with his ewe lamb. You're right, though, I'll have to go.' He straightened, his face brightening. 'And when you've accepted with due thanks, see if you can get me a mid-morning appointment with Brocklehurst. No point in wasting a trip to London.'

The phone rang stridently, breaking Avril's concentration on the television programme she was watching. Pressing the mute button on the remote, she went to answer it.

'Mrs Parish? Guy Lacey here. Sorry to trouble you, but Sarah's mobile's switched off.'

'It would be,' Avril replied. 'She's gone to the cinema.'

'Then I wonder if you'd be kind enough to give her a message? She asked me to collect her music centre; she'll want it at home during the summer, and can't fit it into her car. I'd intended to come on Thursday, when she breaks up, but something's come up and I shan't be able to make it. So could you tell her I'll call round tomorrow instead, about seven thirty, if that's all right?'

'I'll tell her, yes.'

'And perhaps she could phone me, to confirm it's OK?'

'I'll see she gets the message.'

'Thanks very much.' A pause. 'Did you enjoy your lunch at the Clarendon?'

'I did, thank you. And you?'

'It was a good send-off for my colleague, but I have to confess I don't care for all-male occasions. Too much booze consumed, for one thing, and I'm getting too old for that; I always pay for it later. Was yours a special occasion?'

'My daughters' birthday.'

'Both of them, of course. I must say they're very alike.'

'On the surface, maybe.'

'But it's only skin deep? Well, that's what makes life interesting, isn't it? Not that I'd know, having only one.'

'Oh, life's been interesting, all right.'

He laughed. 'Right. Well, see you tomorrow, perhaps? And thanks for taking the message.'

See you tomorrow, perhaps? Avril repeated to herself as she restored sound to the television. Yes, she thought she could promise him that.

Six

Rona was in the archive room the next morning when her mobile rang, and she answered it to hear her sister's agitated voice. Unusually, they'd not spoken for over a week, when Lindsey had been so unforthcoming about her French trip.

'Can you meet me for lunch, Ro? I need to see you.'

Rona felt a wave of irritation. Another of Lindsey's crises, no doubt. 'Actually, Linz, it's not very convenient. I'm working at last, and—'

'You have to eat,' Lindsey said sharply.

Rona thought of the salad in the fridge across the landing. No doubt it would keep till tomorrow, and it wasn't as though she was paid on an hourly basis. In fact, the Willows weren't paying her at all, but she'd hoped for a clear day to start her research.

'Well?' Lindsey said impatiently. 'You're in Marsborough, aren't you?'

'Yes, off Alban Road.'

'For heaven's sake, that's just round the corner. The Bacchus at one?'

Rona sighed. Lindsey always wore her down. 'I'll be there,' she said.

Lindsey was already seated at an alcove table.

'Where's Gus?' she asked, as Rona joined her.

'Spending the day with Max. I can't cope with him when I'm working.'

'You fixed yourself up with the Willows, then?'

'Yes; I'm based at their home in Oak Avenue. Down past the station,' she added, in response to her twin's enquiring eyebrow.

Lindsey picked up the wine bottle and filled Rona's glass. 'It was arranged at the Kingstons' dinner party?'

Rona nodded. 'This is my first full day.'

'And I've scuppered it. Well, sorry and all that, but I wanted you to see this.'

She reached in her handbag, produced a page from a society magazine, and passed it across the table.

It was filled with photographs taken at some function, and Rona wondered what she was supposed to be looking at. Not recognizing anyone, she turned to the text for elucidation. And found it.

Under a shot of a smiling couple seated at a table ran the caption: *Lady Miranda Barrington-Selby and Mr Dominic Frayne.*

Rona studied the faces with interest. So this was the famous Dominic. The picture was too small to distinguish features, but her eyes moved critically over the thick hair, the confident smile. And the girl with her hand possessively on his arm looked young enough to be his daughter.

Unwillingly, Rona looked up to meet her sister's eyes.

'The magazine's dated the ninth of April,' Lindsey said unsteadily. 'That's after we met.'

'But you hadn't been out with him then,' Rona pointed out reasonably. 'Perhaps he dumped her after meeting you. You didn't think he'd been living in a monastery, did you?'

'Or perhaps he *hasn't* dumped her,' Lindsey said darkly, 'and that's how he spends all those weeks when I don't hear from him. *Lady* Miranda, for God's sake! I can't compete with that! And just *look* at her, Ro! She looks about twelve! If I'd seen that photo without knowing either of them, I'd have taken him for a dirty old man!'

'Oh, come on! He's not *that* old. Where did you find this?'

'At the dentist's, where else? I had my six-monthly check this morning.'

'Pity they don't update their magazines.'

'That wouldn't have changed anything. And don't say "What the eye doesn't see", because it won't wash.'

A waiter approached and they broke off to choose and order their meal.

'So what do you expect me to do?' Rona asked, when he'd gone.

'Advise me.'

'On what? Linz, there's only one option; forget you ever saw it.'

Lindsey stared moodily at the photograph. Then, very delib-
erately, she tore the page in half, then into quarters, then into
still smaller pieces, and stuffed them in the ashtray.

'Feel better?'

'Pity I can't do that to him!' Lindsey sighed. 'OK, maybe
I'm overreacting. But I can't help wondering if he took her
to France.'

'She was then and you are now,' Rona said firmly, hoping
she was right. 'Now, stop being evasive about your own trip,
and tell me everything that happened.'

While Rona and Lindsey were discussing him, Dominic was
being shown into the dining room of the London club. During
the journey, he'd been attempting to formulate the best
approach to Miranda's father. He could hardly claim she'd
made all the running, even though it was true. Better, he'd
decided, to sit tight and judge the prevailing mood.

At least his greeting was cordial enough.

'Frayne! Good of you to come.' Rupert Barrington-Selby,
ninth Earl of Roxford, came to his feet and reached for
Dominic's hand, grasping it firmly. 'Sit down, sit down.'

He was a large man in every sense, over six foot, with broad
shoulders and a heavy frame. In his fifties, he'd developed a
paunch, and his fair-to-sandy hair was thinning. Though on
the few occasions they'd met he'd been dressed formally,
Dominic had a mental image of him in tweed jacket and cords,
the archetypal country squire.

'First things first,' Roxford said firmly. 'I've ordered a good
claret – hope that suits you – and I'm going for duck pâté,
followed by Beef Wellington. I can strongly recommend both
dishes, but if something else takes your fancy, just say.' He
nodded towards the menu.

'Your choice sounds admirable, thank you.'

'Excellent. And an aperitif?'

With a clutch of anxiety, Dominic wondered if this affa-
bility stemmed from his host's belief that he was entertaining
his future son-in-law. What, exactly, had Miranda told her
father?

However, as the waiter moved away, Roxford came swiftly
to the point.

'Unfortunate business, with Mirrie.'

'Yes, indeed,' Dominic said soberly.

'I suggest we get the discussion over straight away, then we can enjoy our meal.' He paused, staring down at the snowy cloth. 'I was well aware she'd set her cap at you,' he continued, 'and, with due respect, I issued all the necessary warnings. Sadly, she chose to ignore them.'

Dominic began to breathe more easily. 'She said you knew she was serious,' he offered, hoping to scotch any misunderstanding.

The earl nodded, lifted his promptly-delivered aperitif in a silent toast, and drank. 'Knew,' he confirmed then, wiping his mouth on his napkin, 'and told her, in no uncertain terms, not to be a goose. I love her dearly, but I wonder sometimes if she's a sensible idea in her head. No offence intended, old chap.'

'I blame myself; I should have been more responsible—'

'My wife tells me Mirrie saw to that side of things,' Roxford said obliquely. 'She took a gamble, and lost. I trust she'll be wiser in the future.' He cleared his throat. 'Look, I'll come straight out with it. My main reason for meeting you is to ask if you'd have any objection to an abortion?'

Dominic, taken completely by surprise, reached hastily for his glass, gaining a much-needed moment's grace. 'Not if that's what she wants,' he said cautiously. 'In fact, when she came to see me . . .'

'Can you honestly see her as a mother? She can't even take care of herself. It's a sad, messy business all round, but this seems the best way, provided you agree. After all, it's your child, too.'

'I did say I'd support it, if—'

Roxford waved this away. 'Yes, yes, good of you, but that's not the solution.' He waited, eyeing Dominic from under beetle brows.

It was his child, too. Dominic surprised in himself a feeling of regret, realizing to his discomfort that he'd never considered the child itself. Its conception had been simply a mistake, to be rectified as quickly as possible, and he now felt a sense of guilt. Yet, to be realistic, there was no question of his having any future contact with it. It was an innocent victim, a means towards an end; and now that the gamble, as Roxford put it, had failed, it was neither wanted nor needed.

'How does Miranda feel?' he asked in a low voice.

'She's seen sense, at last.'

'Then – of course it's all right with me,' Dominic confirmed, feeling as though he'd signed a death warrant.

'Fine. Good chap.' Roxford sat back in his chair. 'And here, on cue, comes the pâté. Bon appétit!'

Rona returned to Oak Avenue, mulling over the conversation during lunch. Gavin's view that Dominic wasn't to be trusted weighed heavily on her; was his association with this girl proof of that, or had the relationship indeed ended before he began seeing Lindsey? *Tell her to watch her step.* She had not, of course, done so. Lindsey was prickly enough, and, if she sensed criticism, would clam up completely. The best Rona could hope for was that doubts raised by the photograph might put her on her guard, making her a little more cautious in her dealings with him.

Back at the window table, however, she dismissed her sister's problems, and, to ensure a swift return to the past, started to read some letters she'd come across before lunch. They were signed respectively by Charles, Frederick and James, each of them signing himself Araminta's loving brother. Immediately, the biographer in Rona wanted to know about them, which one had inherited the title, and who each of them had married. She started leafing through the file, only to pause in stunned disbelief as a name leapt out at her. Eyes still fixed on the papers, she reached for her mobile.

'Lindsey Parish.'

'Linz, you'll never believe—'

There was an irritated sigh. 'Ro, you know I don't like—'

'You'll want to hear this.' Rona took a deep breath. 'Like to hazard a guess as to who Lady Miranda's father is?'

'What on earth—?'

'None other than the Earl of Roxford.'

There was a silence, which Rona broke impatiently. 'Well? What do you think of that?'

'How the hell,' Lindsey said slowly, 'did you come up with that?'

'The Roxfords – family name Barrington-Selby – happen to be the upper-crust relatives the Willows are so proud of.'

'Good God!'

'I think the phrase is, "It's a small world."'

'You'll actually be interviewing them?'

'If Julian has anything to do with it.'

'Including Miranda?'

'Unlikely; she lives in London, and I'll be going to Yorkshire, to the family estate.'

'Ye gods. You're absolutely sure about this? That the present earl's her father?'

'Ninety per cent. At the very least, they must be closely related.'

'A title in the family would be quite a coup for Dominic.'

'You sound like Julian!' Rona scoffed, then glanced guiltily at the door. 'Come on, you don't seriously think he'd be swayed by that, do you?'

'It might tip the balance, if he's genuinely fond of her. We don't *know* they're not still an item.'

'If they were, where would you fit in?'

'That,' said Lindsey heavily, 'is the million dollar question.'

When she finished at five o'clock, Rona was pleased with her first day's work. Even without the Miranda connection, the archives looked more promising than she'd expected; the Willows had been inveterate letter-writers, and a surprising amount of personal correspondence survived. Together with the photographs, they should help her build up an interesting profile of the family.

Having garaged the car and walked home, she let herself into the house, resolving to open all the windows to dispel the day's stuffiness. Then, as she closed the front door, she saw a note lying on the mat, and stooped to retrieve it.

Rona, she read in a hasty scrawl, *please contact me. I must speak to you. Louise.*

Damn! She'd been looking forward to a leisurely shower before Max got back, but as she didn't know next door's phone number, the only way to contact Louise was by going to the house.

Five minutes later, armed with a book as an excuse for calling, she walked down her garden path and up the one next door. Her ring was answered by Mrs Franks, who looked at her in some surprise.

Rona smiled at her and held up the book she was carrying. 'Louise and I were discussing this the other day,' she said brightly. 'I thought she might like to borrow it.'

'That's kind of you,' Barbara Franks replied after a moment, and made a move to take the book from her.

'Is Louise around?' Rona asked quickly.

The woman hesitated, but a voice called from upstairs, 'Is that Rona? I'll be right down.' And she'd no choice but to invite her in.

Louise came running down the stairs, and Rona said quickly, 'This is the book I was telling you about. I think you'd enjoy it.'

'Thanks – it's good of you to bring it.'

Mrs Franks, forced into hospitality, offered a cup of tea, adding, 'Or would you prefer something cold?'

'There's home-made lemonade,' Louise said.

'That sounds perfect.'

At her gesture, Rona preceded Louise into the doorway on the right. Although she'd been in the house before, it was a strange sensation to walk into the room that corresponded to that in their own house, before she and Max had knocked down walls and turned two rooms into one. Used to the larger space, this sitting room seemed small and cluttered, and the furniture showed signs of wear and tear left by previous tenants. No attempt had been made to personalise it; the mantelpiece was bare of any kind of ornament, there were no books on the shelves, and the prevailing atmosphere struck Rona as depressing.

'Thanks for not letting on about the note,' Louise said in a low voice. 'I'm sorry to have dragged you over. I've calmed down a bit now.'

Before Rona could reply, Mrs Franks came in with a tray bearing a large glass jug of lemonade and two glasses.

'Tell you what,' Louise said quickly, 'let's take it outside; it's a pity to be indoors in this weather.'

And we can be sure of no one overhearing us, Rona thought.

They went together down the basement stairs to the kitchen and the door to the back garden. Rona hadn't been here before, and this room also was very different from their own, seeming old-fashioned with its free-standing units and dated cooker. She supposed that since the owners of the house didn't live here, there was no incentive to provide other than basic amenities.

Louise opened the glass-paned wooden door that, in their own house, they'd replaced with a full-length glass one, and led the way to the bench under the apple tree. A ginger cat that had been lazily washing itself on the stone terrace unfurled itself and followed them.

'So that's your cat,' Rona commented. 'I'm afraid Gus was chasing it the other day.'

Louise set the tray on the bench between them and scooped the cat on to her lap, where it turned round three times before settling down.

'We've christened her Amber,' she said, pouring the lemonade. 'Strictly speaking, she's not ours. She seems to have adopted us; every time we open a door, she darts inside. We've phoned the RSPCA and put notices up, but nobody's claimed her and I've grown quite fond of her.'

Rona gratefully accepted a glass of lemonade. 'So – what was worrying you?'

'I was frightened,' Louise said. The word seemed shockingly out-of-place in the sunlit garden.

'*Frightened?*' Rona repeated incredulously. 'What of?'

'My parents, I suppose. If they *are* my parents.'

And as Rona stared at her, she added, 'You see, I – don't think I'm who they say I am. I mightn't even be their daughter.'

'But—'

'They've never shown me any proof,' Louise went on quickly, 'and would you believe, I've not even seen my passport? When I began to have doubts I asked for it; but they said they'd put everything of value in the bank for safekeeping, till we have our own house. Though why that should be any safer than rented accommodation, heaven knows.'

'It does sound excessively cautious,' Rona agreed.

'And another thing: there are no photos of me as a child, no family groups. Everyone has photographs, don't they?'

Rona thought of the corner table in her mother's sitting room, crammed with baby snaps of herself and Lindsey, graduation and wedding portraits, holiday photos.

'I'm not even sure I was married.' Louise glanced at her left hand. 'I don't *feel* as though I was, and I've seen nothing

relating to any husband. In fact, I'm starting to question everything they've told me.'

'But why?'

Louise shrugged, and did not reply.

'Did you ask to see photographs?'

'Yes; they had some implausible story about a fire having
destroyed everything. Very convenient, isn't it?'

Rona struggled to be objective. 'But why would they go to
such lengths? What have they to gain by pretending you're
their daughter and bringing you back to this country?'

'That's what I've been trying to work out.' She gave a mirth-
less laugh. 'Perhaps I'm heir to a great fortune!'

'But you couldn't claim it if you were supposed to be their
daughter.'

'That's true.'

Rona was silent, trying to think of some way to reassure
her, to dispel what was surely an impossible scenario. 'How
long ago was the divorce?' she asked.

'Again, I've only their word for it, and thinking back, they
were pretty vague. It was a quickie, apparently, and if it came
through just before the accident, as they implied, it would
have been about six months ago.'

'You could check on the Internet; it must be on record.'

Louise brightened. 'I never thought of that. Only trouble
is, I don't have access.'

'There's an Internet Café in Guild Street.' Rona pursued
another line of thought. 'Where did you go when you came
out of hospital?'

'Briefly to a rented flat they were living in, where they
told me they'd decided I needed a completely fresh start,
and we were moving back to the UK. We flew here about
a week later, and stayed in London while Father sorted out
this house.'

They were both silent, thinking over what had been said.
Louise was absentmindedly stroking the cat, its fur glistening
orange and gold in the sunshine. After a while, she looked
up, meeting Rona's concerned eyes.

'A bit extreme, wasn't it? After all, Canada's the second-
largest country in the world; you'd think they could have found
somewhere over there for my "fresh start" without having to
cross the Atlantic.' Her eyes fell. 'That's what made me wonder

if they were running away from something – if someone was after them.'

'But you *are* all British,' Rona said after a moment. 'Perhaps, after the fire, then the crash, then your loss of memory and long stay in hospital, they simply wanted to come home.'

'I could have understood that, but they didn't *go* home – at least, not to Harrogate, which was where they'd lived before and presumably still have friends. Instead we came here, to a town two hundred miles away, where we don't know a soul. Why?'

'Have you asked them?'

'Oh, I get a variety of reasons, but none of them convincing.' Louise finished her lemonade and put the glass back on the tray. 'God, Rona, I should never have dragged you into this. You must think I'm a complete nutcase.'

'Of course not. It's a horrible position to be in, unable to remember anything; it's no wonder your imagination works overtime.'

Louise smiled crookedly. 'Imagination?'

Rona flushed. 'I didn't mean that, exactly, but it would be easy to get the wrong slant on things. There's probably a perfectly simple explanation.' She put down her own glass. 'I haven't been much help, I'm afraid, and I really have to go now. Max will be back any minute.'

'Of course.' Louise stood up at once, tipping the cat on to the grass. 'Thanks for responding to my *cri de coeur*. I really appreciate it.'

'Keep asking questions,' Rona suggested, as they walked back across the grass. 'Perhaps things will start to fall into place.'

'Off her chump,' Max said flatly, when Rona had relayed the conversation. 'I should steer well clear of her.'

'I think she's really frightened, Max,' Rona replied, sipping her vodka. 'Imagine not knowing anything about your past life. It must be terrifying.'

'I grant you that. It's the bit about not being their daughter and suspecting them of God knows what that I can't stomach.' He transferred the chicken breasts on to plates and sprinkled them with toasted pine nuts. 'Are the trays ready?'

'Actually, I think I'd rather eat inside this evening,' Rona said diffidently. She nodded to the table, where she'd already laid out glasses and cutlery.

Max turned to glare at her. 'So now this mad woman stops us from sitting in our own garden?'

'No, I—'

'Don't give me that, Rona. This is the first time you've not wanted to eat outdoors.'

'I'm not sure how far our voices might carry,' she said feebly.

'And we'll be discussing government secrets, will we?'

'Please, Max. I know I'm being silly – just humour me.'

He sighed gustily. 'The sooner those people find their own house, the better I'll be pleased. Are we allowed to have the door open?'

'Of course.'

'I suppose that's something,' he said.

When Avril returned from the charity shop, there was a note from Sarah saying she'd not be in for a meal, and would Avril mind seeing to her father when he called for the music centre. As she hung up her jacket, she glanced in the mirror and, catching herself smiling, made a mocking little face at her reflection.

Normally, she'd have begun preparations for supper, but it was Maureen's birthday, and she'd brought in a cake to have at their tea break. It had taken the edge off Avril's appetite, and she decided to wait till Guy Lacey had been before making a start on her meal.

He arrived promptly at seven thirty. 'Sorry to impose on you like this,' he said, as she showed him in. 'I hope Sarah cleared it with you?'

'Well, there was a note asking me to do the necessary.'

'She didn't check with you in advance? I'm so sorry; I hope this hasn't put you out at all?'

'No, no; I've no plans for this evening.'

Guy grinned ruefully. 'I'd intended taking her for a meal – I'll certainly need something before starting back – but I've been stood up in favour of the boyfriend.' He paused, looking at her with a raised eyebrow. 'I suppose you've already eaten?'

To her annoyance, Avril felt herself flush. 'Actually, no; I was just about—'

'You wouldn't consider taking pity on me? I eat alone too often these days, and I can't say I enjoy it.'

'Well, I . . .'

'Please. I assure you I know which knife and fork to use, and don't talk with my mouth full.'

She laughed. 'In that case, fine. I was going to make a fish pie; there'd be plenty for two.'

'Absolutely not. I'm putting you out as it is. And as it happens, I discovered an interesting-looking pub last time I was over. They've a reputation for good food, and I've been wanting to try it. Are you game?'

'Well, if you're sure . . .'

'Excellent. And I warn you, I don't intend to address you as Mrs Parish all evening.'

'It's Avril.'

'And as you know, I'm Guy. Right, let's find something to eat.'

'Olivia?'

'Dad? Is that you?

'It is indeed. How are you, sweetie?'

'I'm fine. Did you get my text?'

'I did, but I much prefer speaking to you.'

'Dinosaur!' she said affectionately.

'I was wondering if I could pop up to see you?'

There was a pause, and when she spoke her voice had hardened. 'Has Mum put you up to this?'

'Up to what?'

'This isn't about talking me into staying on at uni?'

He sighed. 'Obviously that's what we'd both like, but it's not the reason for seeing you.'

'It's just that it's a bit sudden. Usually your visits have to be booked in advance.'

'Don't make me feel guiltier than I do, Livvie.'

'Ah, so you admit to guilt!' she teased.

But he could not respond. Guilt was indeed lying heavy on him. Roxford's words – *It's your child too* – continued to reverberate round his head. Suppose, between them, they'd thoughtlessly disposed of another Olivia, or Crispin, or Dougal? He closed his eyes on a wave of almost physical pain.

'Dad?' Concern touched her voice. 'Are you OK?'

He made an effort to appear so. 'Yes, yes; a little tired, that's all.'

'Have you seen the boys recently?'

'No, but I've left them both messages.'

'Checking up on the clan?'

'Something like that. How about I come up this weekend?'

'That'd be great. Give me a ring when you get here.'

'Will do. Bye, sweetie. Love you.' And he rang off, feeling slightly easier in his mind.

The Mulberry Bush was about five miles from Marsborough, on the Cricklehurst road. Avril must have driven past countless times, without noticing it. On this warm July evening, the garden alongside, screened from the road by high hedges, was crammed with a lively clientele, enjoying the late sunshine. A couple were leaving as she and Guy arrived, and they were able to claim the table.

'I'll get a menu,' Guy said, as she sat down. 'What would you like to drink?'

Avril drew a deep breath. 'Could I possibly have a Pimm's?'

'Excellent choice for a summer evening. I might even join you.'

She watched him as he threaded his way between the tables, a tall, lithe figure in cream cords and tan-coloured shirt. Incredibly, this was only the third time they'd met, but she felt totally relaxed with him, with none of the tension she usually experienced on meeting new people. No doubt his own ease of manner was a contributory factor.

It was some minutes before he returned, carrying two brimming glasses and with a menu tucked under his arm.

'It's chaos in there,' he reported. 'We might have quite a wait for our food. Not in any hurry, are you?'

She shook her head. 'I'm not the one with a long drive home.'

'Oh, that won't worry me. Just remind me not to leave without that music centre.'

She glanced at his coke. 'I see you changed your mind about the Pimm's.'

He nodded. 'It was a nice thought, but non-alcoholic seemed wiser, with that drive in mind. Cheers, anyway. Here's to a pleasant evening.'

They read through the menu together, impressed by its wide range, made their choices, and Guy went back to place their order. Gradually the evening darkened around them, and candles on tables all over the garden glowed like a host of fireflies.

'You're still in touch with your ex, then?' Guy said at one point.

'On occasion; and he's not actually "ex" yet.'

'It's good you can meet amicably.'

'Yes; it wasn't always the case.'

She knew he was watching her, but kept her gaze down, twirling the swizzle stick with its slices of fruit. And since he had broached the personal, she deftly turned the tables on him.

'Sarah said your wife died when she was a baby.'

'Yes, barely a year old. She was killed in a car crash.'

Had he been in the car? she wondered, but dared not ask. 'How appalling for you. However did you cope?'

He smiled crookedly. 'With difficulty, and the help of several good women. And before you raise your eyebrows at me, I'm referring to fully trained nannies in the early days, followed by equally competent housekeepers.'

A voice from the pub doorway called out a number, and Guy stood up, signalling his whereabouts. 'At last! I'm dying of starvation!'

The plates set before them certainly looked appetizing; Avril had chosen Thai fishcakes with a side salad, and Guy home-made steak and mushroom pie. For a few minutes they ate in silence. Avril stole a glance at his face, lit by the flickering candle, thought it looked rather sad, and blamed herself for mentioning his wife.

However, seeming to feel there was more to be said on the subject, he added, as though there'd been no break in their conversation, 'I worry about Sarah sometimes. It was a difficult childhood for her, never knowing her mother. I even wondered whether I should marry again, for her sake, but was never sufficiently tempted. Perhaps that was selfish of me.'

'I think you did an amazing job,' Avril said sincerely. 'She's a bright girl, full of self-confidence.'

'Oh, she has plenty of that,' her father agreed. 'A bit too much at times!'

Avril smiled. 'She has decided opinions, certainly.'

'She told me you were kind to her the other day. Gave her some good advice. Thank you for that.'

Avril was taken aback. 'It was only what I'd have advised my own daughters.'

'Exactly. That's why she appreciated it, and I do, too. And while we're exchanging compliments, I was impressed with your two. Very attractive young women. One of them's a journalist, I seem to remember?'

Avril bit her lip; when Sarah first arrived to lodge with her, accompanied by Guy, she'd been obliged to explain the press reports about Rona's involvement in a murder case.

'She is at the moment,' she answered him, 'though she has several biographies to her name.'

'Very impressive. And your other daughter?'

'A partner in a local firm of solicitors.'

'You must be proud of them both.'

'I am, yes. As you are of Sarah.'

He smiled. 'Parents! Let's hope we're not deceiving ourselves!'

The conversation moved to more general topics – books, the theatre, travelling – and they found they had several tastes in common. Eventually, the meal came to an end; around them most of the tables were now empty as diners made their way back to their cars, and by mutual consent they also rose. Guy put a hand under her elbow to guide her through the dark garden and round the side of the pub to the car park. The car, when she slid inside, was still warm from the day's sunshine. It had been a perfect evening, and she was sorry it was over.

They drove in companionable silence back to Belmont, the suburb where Avril lived, and she went ahead to open the front door while Guy rearranged the seating to accommodate the music centre. As she stepped into the hall, she found herself face to face with Sarah.

'Didn't you get my note?' she demanded, with a touch of irritation. 'Dad hasn't—'

'Don't panic, honey, I'm here now.' Guy came up the path towards them, and Sarah stared from one of them to the other.

'Since you stood me up for supper,' he went on easily, 'Avril here kindly kept me company. Now, have you unplugged everything for me?'

Sarah, for once at a loss for words, nodded, and he went past her up the stairs. After a minute she followed him uncertainly. Avril, opting for diplomacy, went into the dining room and began to lay the table for Sarah's breakfast. She heard them come downstairs, Sarah talking in a low voice, and go out to the car. Then, as she stood back to check everything was in place, Guy appeared in the doorway.

'I'm off now,' he said. 'Thanks so much for your company this evening.'

'I enjoyed it,' Avril answered primly. 'Thank *you* for inviting me.'

'Have a good summer.'

'You, too.'

And then he was gone, the front door closing behind him, and she felt suddenly flat.

'Goodnight,' Sarah said, as she passed the dining-room door.

Avril turned. 'Oh – goodnight.'

She'd have said more, but the girl had already started up the stairs. Avril, pulling a little face, turned off the light and went to lock up.

Seven

During the next few days, Louise's doubts about her identity continued to prey on Rona's mind. *Was* she simply deluded, as Max maintained, or was there some substance in her suspicions? The absence of photographs, the watchfulness of the Franks and their seeming unwillingness for a friendship to develop all fuelled her unease.

Having wished for no further contact, she was now eager to speak to Louise, though aware, to her shame, that her change of heart wasn't wholly due to concern. The curiosity that drove her working life, in both biographical and journalistic research, was a force to be reckoned with, a primeval need-to-know that would not easily be gainsaid. But even if Louise wished to contact her, it would be difficult now she herself was out of the house between nine and five. And Louise wasn't to know she didn't spend every evening in Max's company.

Meanwhile the weekend came and went, and though from time to time voices were heard in the next-door garden, Max's patent scepticism prevented Rona from following them up.

On the Monday morning, immersed in some old files, Rona was surprised to be interrupted by the intercom. She lifted it to hear Felicity on the line.

'How's it going?' she enquired.

'Fine, thanks. There's some really interesting stuff.'

'Do you take a break for lunch?'

'Not really; I bring sandwiches.'

'It just struck me as rather silly that we're both eating in solitary splendour, you upstairs and me down. Would you care to join me, or would it interrupt the flow? I'm making a cheese quiche, if that carries any weight!'

Rona laughed. 'I'm easily persuaded where food's concerned. Thanks very much, I'd love to.'

'One o'clock suit you?'
'Fine.'
'See you then.'

Felicity had set up a card table in the conservatory, covered
it with a white cloth and put a jug of roses in the centre. The
doors to the garden were open, and its sounds drifted in to
them – birdsong, and the hum of bees.

Rona leant forward to smell the flowers. 'Why is it I love
the scent of roses, but don't care for rose perfume? I find it
altogether too cloying.'

Felicity glanced at the blooms, a blend of cream, pink and
deep, dusky red. 'They're from the garden; I picked them this
morning.' She held up a bottle. 'Wine?' And at Rona's accept-
ance, poured out two glasses before bringing in the quiche
and a large wooden bowl of dressed salad.

'This is certainly an improvement on tuna sandwiches!'
Rona commented.

'And for my part, it's nice to have company.'

'Isn't Julian ever in for lunch?'

'Very seldom, during the week. Even if he's working from
home, he likes to get out for a break and meet his pals in the
pub.'

Rona wondered cynically if it was only his pals he met.
Following on from the thought, she said tentatively, 'Last time
I was here, I met – your cousin, was it?'

'Julian's; they've known each other for ever, and even had
a boy-and-girl thing going in their teens. Rather sweet, really.'

Had she and Max jumped to the wrong conclusion? Rona
wondered. Their closeness in the restaurant, Julian's hand over
Tara's, hadn't *looked* cousinly, but he might simply have been
offering comfort.

'You said she split up with someone; was that quite recent?'

'A couple of months ago. They'd been together for eight
years.'

'Married?'

'No; she'd already tried that, it hadn't worked, and she
swore she wouldn't go through it again.' Felicity sipped her
wine. 'Though it's my opinion Simon got through her defences,
and she'd have married him if he'd asked her. Instead, he
called time and moved on.'

'That's hard luck.'

'Yes; she took it badly, poor love.'

'I presume she's not one of the blue-bloodied cousins?' Rona queried with a half-smile.

Felicity laughed. 'No, merely the daughter of Graham's sister Nancy. As to the Yorkshire lot, Julian hangs on to the connection, bless him, but it's a very tenuous one. All right, Lady Araminta was his great-grandmother, but I honestly can't see how we're related to them now. I get lost in the maze of second and third cousins, Lord knows how many times removed.'

'I came across some of her letters,' Rona commented. 'They're from members of her family, all deploring her choice of husband!'

'I don't doubt it! Well, at least that'll give you an entrée when you go up to see them. Oh, and I almost forgot: my mother-in-law has invited you to coffee.'

'Oh.' Rona was taken aback; she'd have preferred to sort out the background before beginning interviews. 'That's kind of her,' she added hastily.

'I warn you, she'll give you the third degree. Don't be put off, though; she can seem quite fierce, but it's all show.'

'When—?'

'She gave me a few dates for you to choose from.'

Felicity rose and went into the sitting room, returning with a slip of paper. 'Thursday or Friday this week, Monday or Wednesday next.'

'Actually, I could make any of them: I kept a couple of weeks free, in case Julian wanted me to go to Yorkshire.'

'Then pick whichever you like.'

Rona opted for the following Monday, which should give her sufficient time to prepare for the interview, and Felicity jotted down the address.

'It's in Woodbourne, but quite easy to find,' she said. 'A development of Scandinavian houses, just past the bus station.'

The meal came to an end, and at Rona's insistence, Felicity allowed her to help to clear the table and carry the dishes to the kitchen.

'Thanks very much,' Rona said, watching her load plates into the dishwasher. 'I really enjoyed that.'

'So did I. We must do it again.'

As Rona took the lift to the second floor, her thoughts

reverted to the chic and seemingly self-possessed Tara. It was difficult to imagine her with a broken heart.

Having collected Gus from Max on her way home, Rona garaged the car in Charlton Road and, instead of going on to the house, turned instead into the slipway leading up to the park. The day had clouded over, making it marginally cooler, and walking Gus now would absolve her from having to go out later.

Unlike the lower lawns, which, like the flowerbeds, benefited from regular watering, the grass on the upper slopes was scorched and dry, crunching under her feet. It was, as usual, populated by other dog-walkers and mothers with toddlers and pushchairs. Rona knew several of them by sight, and they exchanged smiles or brief comments as they passed. Gus, also as usual, had found a stick, which she was expected to keep throwing for him.

An advantage of these walks was that they provided a chance for her to sort out plans or problems, and that afternoon her mind was occupied with Julian's Scandinavian mother, whom she'd be meeting the following week. She wondered if his father would also be there.

As the ground levelled off, she glanced towards the bench where, last time, she had seen Louise. Today it was unoccupied, but the sight of it switched her thoughts seamlessly to her next-door neighbours and the various question marks they generated. She paused, gazing out across the rooftops below, and as Gus once more panted hopefully up to her, a voice behind her said, 'I didn't know you had a dog.'

Rona turned, to see a man half-smiling at her.

She smiled cautiously back, wondering if this was a new chat-up line. 'Is there any reason why you should?'

His smile faltered and his eyes, a very dark blue, narrowed as they went over her face. Then he said questioningly, 'Lindsey?'

Rona breathed more freely. Not an importunate stranger, then. 'Rona,' she corrected.

'My God! It's amazing how alike you are! It's only when—' He broke off, laughing, and held out his hand. 'Forgive me – I'm Dominic Frayne.'

It was Rona's turn to stare. This man was not at all like the mental picture she'd built up, and which the minute photo in the magazine had done nothing to dispel. Admittedly he conformed to Lindsey's various descriptions of him – tall, in his late forties, hair streaked with grey – yet to her eyes he looked more like a poet than a ruthless tycoon, with his slightly over-long hair, his sensitive mouth and seemingly far-sighted eyes.

'I suppose you get this all the time,' he was saying. 'Do you resent being recognized not as yourself, but as someone else?'

'It comes with the territory,' Rona answered, reflecting it was the second time recently that one of Lindsey's swains had mistaken her for her twin.

'So you're the biographer? I'm delighted to meet you.' He bent to pick up the stick Gus was guarding, threw it for him, and fell into step beside her as she resumed walking. 'I've read all three, but I particularly enjoyed Pitt the Elder, a man who's always interested me.' He smiled. 'I often think he must be spinning in his grave, now that we're part of the EU!'

'Having lost the empire he helped us acquire.'

'Exactly.' He flicked her a sideways glance. 'It would be interesting, sometime, to have a discussion on how time has dealt with his accomplishments.'

Gus lolloped back and deposited his stick at the feet not of Rona but of Dominic. They both laughed.

'A sure sign of favour!' Rona declared, as he threw it again.

He glanced at his watch. 'I must be getting back; I'm expecting a call.' He nodded towards the row of houses opposite the top entrance to the park. 'I live just across the road, so I'm lucky to have all this on my doorstep.'

'Is it your main home?' Rona asked, on Lindsey's behalf.

He smiled wryly. 'At the moment, it is; I've left two "family homes" behind me in my chequered career, but actually this suits me very well. It's amply big enough for my needs, and there's no garden to be responsible for during my frequent absences.'

They came to a halt, having reached the parting of the ways.

'Are you working on a biography now?' Dominic enquired.

'No; I got my fingers burned on the last one I started, and haven't geared myself up to try again.'

'You should. You have a real talent for them.' He smiled. 'I hope that didn't sound patronizing; it wasn't meant to.'

'I'll take it as a compliment, then.' She sighed. 'Yes, I know I should get down to it. The trouble is, it's such a long-term project.'

'Most worthwhile things are.' He held out a hand. 'Goodbye, Rona. I've enjoyed meeting you. I hope our paths cross again.'

Rona watched him cross the last short stretch of grass to the park gates, trying to sum up her impressions. She'd imagined him to be arrogant and self-opinionated, but that hadn't come across at all, and the adjectives that now came to mind were far more positive: charming, self-assured, attractive. Yes, she could understand Lindsey falling for him, and, for that matter, young Lady Miranda being bowled over. All the same, she told herself, as Gus rejoined her and they turned to retrace their steps, she mustn't lose sight of the fact that he was causing her sister sleepless nights with his apparent lack of commitment. Whether this was deliberate or not, she had no way of knowing.

'I met Dominic in the park,' she told Lindsey on the phone that evening. 'He mistook me for you.'

'Some people have all the luck! Did he ask after me?'

Rona thought back, realizing, with a slight sense of guilt, that once the correct identity had been established, Lindsey's name hadn't been mentioned.

'It was all very general,' she hedged.

'He didn't bring up the French trip?'

'No; as I said, it was—'

'Very general.' Lindsey sighed. 'Well, at least tell me what you thought of him?'

'Actually, he was much nicer than I expected.'

'Damned with faint praise.'

'Well, I've always resented his offhandedness with you.'

'And now you forgive him?'

'No, but I can see why you do.'

'He didn't say he'd be getting in touch with me, or anything?'

Could hoping his and Rona's paths crossed again be interpreted that way? 'Not in so many words.'

'Your exchanges,' Lindsey said acidly, 'seem to have been not only general, but positively abstract. Still, perhaps seeing you might remind him it's time he phoned me. We can but hope.'

And Rona was relieved to leave it there.

* * *

When Rona arrived in Oak Avenue the next morning, it was to find Julian in the office with a middle-aged lady he introduced as Beryl, his part-time secretary.

'I was hoping to see you, Rona; I've been in touch with Rupert Roxford. The House has gone into recess and he's off to Scotland at the end of next week, in time for the twelfth. Will it be possible for you to get to Yorkshire before then?'

'Yes, of course.'

'Today's Tuesday: I suggest you go up on Thursday, if that suits you, and stay overnight, returning on Friday. How would that be? Would it give you enough time?'

'If it's convenient for the Roxfords.'

'It is; I checked. The estate's at Ottersby, just north of Harrogate. There's a nice little pub in the village, which I'm sure would put you up for the night. The Roxford Arms, no less!'

'Very appropriate.'

'Fine; that's fixed, then. Let me know if there's any more information you'd like before you set off.'

It occurred to Rona that, unlike her previous family researches, it seemed to be the Willows rather than herself who were directing procedures. Not that it mattered, as long as she continued to have their cooperation.

Back in the archive room, she decided to concentrate on the Yorkshire connection, so any questions that might arise could be answered while she was there. In fact, she could find very little reference to the Roxford family, which seemed to confirm Felicity's theory that there was now – and had for some time – been virtually no link between them. Araminta's parents appeared to have had no interest in their Willow grandchildren – bearing out her disinheritance – and apart from a few further letters from her brothers, more and more widely spaced as time went by, there was little else on record. Which, snobbery apart, was sad.

'I'm off to Yorkshire for a couple of days on Thursday,' Rona told Max on the phone that evening. 'I'll have to polish my tiara in readiness!'

'Just the one night?'

'Yes; I'll be spending it, would you believe, at the Roxford Arms. And as it's Thursday to Friday, it won't interfere with your evenings at home.'

'If we'd not been away so recently, I'd have come with you, and taken the chance of some landscape painting. It's a while since I did any.'

'That would have been great. Is there no way you could manage it?'

'Afraid not; I'm still making up for lost time on the holiday.'

After her salad supper – an easy option during the summer months – Rona went up to her study to make a few notes for the Yorkshire trip. The room felt stuffy, and as she pushed open the window, she saw Louise in the garden next door, and, on impulse, called down to her.

Louise started on hearing her name, looking first towards the back door of the house, before, as Rona called again, locating her.

'I've been wanting to speak to you.' Rona lowered her voice slightly as Louise moved nearer. 'Could you come round for a few minutes?'

'Well, I . . .' Louise looked about her, as though seeking an excuse.

'For a glass of wine, perhaps?'

'I don't really—'

Inspiration suddenly came. 'I've something to tell you.'

Louise looked up at her for a long minute, before nodding and going into the house.

Rona ran downstairs, and had the front door open by the time she turned in the gateway. She still had an oddly detached air about her, but her skin was faintly sun-burned, contrasting with the whiteness of their first meeting. She dropped the cigarette she was holding on to the path, and ground it out before coming into the house.

'How are things?' Rona asked her, gesturing her towards the sitting room.

'Much as before.' Louise paused on the threshold. 'What a lovely room! I can't believe this house is the same as ours!'

'We knocked down dividing walls,' Rona said. 'On three floors, actually. Now, sit down and I'll get the wine.'

When she returned with a chilled bottle and two glasses, Louise was studying the paintings on the wall.

'Are these your husband's?' she asked. 'He's an artist, isn't he?'

'He's an artist, and they're his paintings in that he chose them, but he didn't paint them. He doesn't like displaying his own work, and most of it is commissioned anyway, or else sells pretty quickly. We have one in our bedroom, but that's all.'

'It must be wonderful to have a gift like that.'

She sat down and took the glass Rona offered her. 'Is he home? I wouldn't want to intrude.'

'No, he won't be back tonight.'

'He's away?' Louise seemed surprised. 'I thought I saw him in town at lunchtime.'

Rona sighed; yet again an explanation was called for. 'He's not away, but he has a studio nearby, and when he has evening classes, he sleeps over. It's easier that way.'

Louise didn't look convinced, and Rona expanded her explanation. 'When we both worked from home, it was like Jack Spratt and his wife. Max likes to listen to music at full volume while he paints; I need complete quiet when I write. Then there were students and sitters always coming round, and as the studio's on the top floor, I was the one who had to keep breaking off what I was doing to let them in.'

She raised her shoulders in a shrug of resignation. 'So, in the interests of preserving our marriage, we bought the cottage, where he can make as much noise as he likes. And, as I said, on the evenings he teaches – three times a week – he stays over there.'

Louise offered no comment. Instead, abandoning the subject, she said, 'You have something to tell me?'

'Yes, but first, I was wondering if you'd been able to find out anything about your earlier life?'

The other woman's fingers tightened on the glass. 'I said too much the other day; please forget it.'

Rona ignored that. 'You were going to try the Internet?'

'I didn't have any luck,' Louise said briefly.

'The records weren't there? I thought—'

'Oh, I found the right website. I'd asked my parents – casually, of course – the date of our wedding, and presumed it would have taken place where we'd lived, but I drew a complete blank. So then I tried dates before and after, but still with no luck. There was absolutely no record of either Louise Franks or Kevin Stacey, under either marriage or divorce.'

Rona sipped her wine, her mind racing. 'What about your birth certificate?'

Louise shook her head, not meeting her eyes.

'A blank there, too?'

'I didn't look,' Louise said in a low voice.

'But why not? If you could—'

Louise flung her head back, making Rona jump. 'Don't you *see*, Rona? I'm *frightened* to look for it! If there's no record of that either, it might mean—'

'Mean what?' Rona prompted, when she didn't go on.

'That I don't exist,' Louise said in a whisper.

Rona leant forward quickly and put a hand on hers. 'That's nonsense, and you know it.' She paused. 'Haven't your parents got a copy?'

'It was conveniently lost in the fire, along with everything else. So – what did you want to tell me?'

Rona reflected a moment. Did she really want to become further embroiled in this? Her momentary inspiration of a few minutes ago now seemed the height of foolishness.

'Well?' Louise demanded impatiently.

Rona took the plunge. 'I'm going up to Harrogate on Thursday.'

Louise stared at her speechlessly.

'It's to do with the research I'm working on, but I wondered if, while I'm there, you'd like me to have a look round, see if I can find out anything?'

A smile flooded Louise's face, totally altering her appearance. 'Oh, Rona, would you? That would be wonderful.'

'I can look in the electoral registers – I did that for one of my other projects – but I'd need to know the road you lived in. The records are arranged by districts, not by names.'

She looked at Louise expectantly, but her momentary joy had faded, to be replaced by doubt. 'I'd have to ask them, and give some sort of reason for doing so.'

'Surely you can think of something; say you're trying to exercise your memory.'

They were interrupted by the phone ringing in the hall, and immediately Louise stood up, setting her half-empty glass on the coffee table.

'I won't keep you,' she said quickly. 'Obviously, I'd be very grateful for anything you can find out in Harrogate.

Thursday, you said? I'll do my best to get the address before you go.'

And before Rona had time to do more than nod, Louise had preceded her into the hall, and disappeared out of the front door. An abrupt end to the conversation, Rona reflected as she picked up the phone, but at least she'd made the offer. And really, if Louise chose to ignore it, so much the better.

'Hi there, honey-bun.' It was her father.

'Hello, Pops.' Rona struggled to detach her thoughts from Louise. 'How are you?'

'Fine, but it seems a while since we touched base. Not since your birthday, in fact.'

'Oh, Pops, I'm sorry. Time seems to rush past. You'll be pleased to hear I've started work again.'

'That's splendid. Who have you got under the knife this time?'

She laughed protestingly. 'I'm not that bad! Actually, it's the Willow family.'

'Ah! The descendants of the barrow-boy!' It was a well-known Marsborough legend.

'Not to mention the landed gentry.'

'Oh, yes; there's a title there somewhere, isn't there?'

'Indeed there is, and to make sure it's not overlooked, I have to go up to Harrogate on Thursday, to interview them.'

'Really? I'd have thought any family links would be lost in the sands of time.'

'They are, to everyone except Julian Willow, who's clinging to them by his fingernails.'

'You'll be back by the weekend, though? Catherine and I were hoping you, Max and Lindsey could join us for Sunday lunch.'

'I can't speak for Linz, but as far as I know, Max and I are free, and we'd love to come.'

'Catherine's inviting her family, too, so it will be quite a gathering.'

The baby-worship session Lindsey was dreading.

'That'll be good; I look forward to seeing Daniel and Jenny again. And little Alice, of course.'

'Twelve thirty at Catherine's, then, unless I hear from you. We can catch up then.'

He rang off, and Rona, her intentions of note-making going

by the board, went back into the sitting room, where her eyes instantly fell on Louise's half-full glass. She stood looking at it for a moment, then, with a sigh, poured more wine into her own, and turned on the television.

Eight

Julian had made the appointment for her, and although the Roxfords wouldn't be free to see her till four, Rona decided to make an early start, to give herself a chance to look round before meeting the family. She'd learned that the house was open to the public, which seemed an ideal way of gleaning some background information.

It was a humid, hazy day, with no direct sunshine to make driving difficult. The traffic was fairly light, and she made good time. She stopped somewhere on the Yorkshire borders for a sandwich, and reached the village of Ottersby at one thirty. By her reckoning, it was roughly ten miles north of Harrogate, and some two miles from Roxford Hall.

Having registered at the Roxford Arms and been shown to her room, she changed from her casual travelling clothes into a dress she felt more suitable for interviewing a lord and lady, and, on returning downstairs, asked the friendly landlady for directions to the Hall.

'You can't miss it, love,' she was told, in a comfortable Yorkshire accent. 'Straight up the road out of the village, and after a mile you'll see the walls of the estate. The gates are a mile or two further on.'

She looked at the clock above the bar. 'They don't open till two, but it'll be after that by the time you get there.'

Rona, who'd no intention of admitting she'd be interviewing the owners, thanked her and went back to the car. This was a lovely spot, she thought, looking about her, and Max would have had difficulty choosing which aspect to paint, had he been able to accompany her. Rolling moorland stretched away on either side, and the baaing of sheep reached her on the still air. Momentarily, she wished Gus was here, and they could have set off together to explore this new terrain. Another time, perhaps, but this trip was strictly business, and she had work to do.

With a sigh, she got back in the car and set off up the road towards the Hall. As she'd been told, high grey stone walls soon appeared on her left, running alongside the road for a couple of miles before they were broken by a pair of wrought-iron gates which, to her relief, stood open.

Rona turned into them and followed a winding drive between copper beech trees until the house came into view, a large, rambling stone building with an impressive tower at one end. A signpost directed her to the right, in the direction of the car park, where a kiosk guarded its entrance.

'House and gardens, or gardens only?' she was asked.

'Both, please.' She handed over her money, was given a ticket and a plan of the gardens in exchange, and directed to a place in the car park, which was already filling up. As she got out, she realized to her annoyance that since she wouldn't be returning to the car till after the interview, she'd have to take her briefcase with her.

Feeling slightly overdressed in this rural setting, Rona set off along the gravel path, following the groups of twos and threes who were heading in the same direction. As they approached the house, they were being shepherded together by an efficient-looking woman with a clipboard.

'I'd like to tell you a few facts about the house before you go in,' she was saying, as Rona joined the fringes of the group. 'It was built in 1560 by Sir Jasper Harris for the first Lord Roxford, and the same family have lived here ever since. It's still a family home, and the private apartments are in the east wing.'

She moved on to architectural details of the exterior, including the tower, the windows, and the motto carved over the main door, and the small group obediently looked upwards, to the right or to the left, attempting to follow the various points described.

'The Great Hall might look familiar,' the guide continued, 'as it's been used as the background to several recent films and television adaptations. A notable feature of the house is the superb wood carving throughout, particularly on the front of the minstrel gallery, the door lintels and fireplace surrounds, some of which is attributed to Grinling Gibbons.'

The woman smiled as she looked round the group. 'You won't be surprised to hear Queen Elizabeth the First visited

Roxford on several occasions, and the room still known as the Queen's Bedchamber contains the four-poster in which she slept.

'There are fine collections of porcelain, furniture and portraits, to which succeeding generations have contributed, and the wedding dress of Lady Georgina Roxford, wife of the fourth Earl, is on display in one of the bedrooms. So, ladies and gentlemen, you are now free to take your time going through the house. There are attendants in every room, and they'll be happy to answer any queries you might have. It only remains for me to say that snacks and afternoon teas are served in the old tithe barn, which you'll find signposted when you leave the house.'

She nodded at them in benign dismissal. 'Enjoy your visit.'

Rona followed the slow-moving group up the steps and into a marble-floored lobby, where they were required to show their admission tickets. A smiling attendant held out her hand for Rona's briefcase.

'We ask visitors to leave umbrellas and larger items in our lobby room,' she explained, and Rona was relieved rather than otherwise not to have to carry it around with her.

The first room they came to was the Great Hall, which was approached under an ornate marble archway, guarded on the right by the statue of a young girl leading a goose. The large space was taken up by grouped furniture, several sets of brocaded sofas and chairs, with notices requesting that no one sit on them. There were occasional tables bearing ornaments and bric-a-brac, a magnificent inlaid bureau about six feet high, and a pair of cabinets displaying collections of what Rona guessed to be Meissen china. A minstrels' gallery ran along one end, and a huge marble fireplace had pride of place on the opposite wall.

To her surprise, no areas were roped off, and visitors were free to walk round at their own pace, to look at whatever interested them. She moved through another archway to find herself in the library, whose walls were completely covered by bookcases packed with books that, by their shabby condition, looked to be well-read. She glanced at some of the titles and found a widely varying taste, from Tolstoy, Pushkin and the complete works of Shakespeare, to journals on agriculture, science and religion. A large desk stood under the window, bearing a silver inkwell and leather blotter and pen-holder.

The dining room, a superbly panelled room displaying the carving they'd been told to look out for, contained a long table fully laid for a banquet, with exquisite glass and silver. By contrast, the walls of the drawing room were hung with several large portraits, presumably of ancestors and, from their modes of dress, from different periods of the family's history. Many of the men were in uniform, and Rona guessed it had been a family tradition to serve in the armed forces.

A lady in one of the portraits looked familiar, and she stopped to look more closely, just as a woman behind her asked the room attendant who the sitter was.

'Oh, that's Lady Araminta,' she was informed. 'You might say she's the black sheep of the family. She ran away to marry a carpenter.'

'What happened to her?' the visitor asked curiously.

'Fortunately, it turned out to be a happy marriage, and though there's no record of it, we believe she and the family were eventually reconciled, because she was left a small legacy in her father's will.'

That was news to Rona, and she stored it gratefully away. She continued her walk round the room, finding that the old portraits on the walls were counterbalanced by photographs of the present family, on the piano and on side tables dotted about the room. She examined them with interest. There were several of the younger generation, mostly taken outdoors, including one of the daughter – presumably Miranda – on horseback, a copper-haired girl laughing at the camera. Studying it, Rona fancied she could see a resemblance to her Titian-haired ancestress. In another picture, Miranda was standing between her two brothers, one seeming older and one younger than herself, cheerfully grinning young men in open-necked sports shirts.

A more formal photograph was of Lord and Lady Roxford, presumably commemorating some event, since Roxford was in his robes, and his wife in evening dress, complete with elbow-length gloves and, Rona was delighted to note, a diamond tiara.

She followed the now steady stream of visitors up a magnificent staircase and through the various bedrooms, including the one with the wedding dress on display, and that in which Queen Elizabeth I had reputedly slept. And in

glass cabinets along the corridors were displayed collections
of porcelain of varying manufacture, of snuff boxes, of mini-
atures, even of shells.

And as she walked, steeped in family history going back
over 400 years, Rona couldn't help wondering what the present
Roxfords had made of their only daughter's association with
Dominic Frayne. Though unlikely to have taken such drastic
action as their forebears, it was doubtful they would have
welcomed the alliance.

After descending to the basement and wandering through
the maze of kitchens, still-rooms and dairies, Rona collected
her briefcase from the foyer and emerged in need of a supple-
ment to her meagre lunch. She made her way to the tithe barn,
where she was able to enjoy a pot of tea and two warm scones
topped with strawberry jam and clotted cream.

It was now after three thirty, and she took the opportunity
of a last glance at the notes she'd made ready for the now
imminent interview. And she wondered, with a touch of appre-
hension, whether the Roxfords, with their illustrious past,
would be happy to feature in the annals of the Willow family
history.

She had been told to make her way to a private entrance
in the east wing, and this she now did, pressing the bell and
hearing it clang portentously inside. The door was opened by
a young woman in tailored blouse and skirt.

'Good afternoon. I'm Rona Parish, and I have an—'

'Please come in, Miss Parish. Lady Roxford is expecting
you.'

The hall, like the lobby in the main house, was chequered
in white and honey-coloured marble. Though on a smaller
scale, it was beautifully proportioned, and a graceful staircase
led up to a gallery that circled the hall and off which the
bedrooms presumably led.

The young woman knocked on one of the panelled doors,
opened it, and announced, 'Miss Parish to see you, Lady
Roxford.'

Cecilia, Countess of Roxford, had been removing some
fallen petals from the top of the piano, and she turned to
survey Rona from across the room. She was a tall woman,
dressed in a plain blue linen dress; her hair was short and
neat, her eyes keen and her mouth slightly pursed. Fleetingly,

Rona wondered from whom Miranda had inherited her beauty.

'Come in and sit down, Miss Parish.' Lady Roxford dropped the fallen petals into a waste basket and took her seat opposite that to which she'd directed Rona.

'It's very good of you to see me,' Rona began a little nervously. 'You probably know that I'm researching the Willow family?'

'So I believe, from my husband; though I confess I'm at a loss to see how we can help you.'

'Julian – Mr Willow – is anxious that it should be as full a history as possible of both family and firm, and there was, of course, a point at which their history impinged on yours.'

A smile touched the countess's face. 'Tactfully put, Miss Parish. Yes, we were brought up on tales of the scandalous Araminta. However, it's a tenuous link, and I shouldn't have thought warranted dragging you all the way up here to see us.'

Rona, unaware of any special etiquette to be observed, decided to relax and be herself. 'Actually, I've been enjoying myself,' she said frankly. 'I've just been on a tour of the house. It's magnificent, isn't it?'

Lady Roxford thawed slightly. 'Indeed it is. We love it dearly, and frequently use the downstairs rooms for entertaining. So, what would you like to ask me?'

'You've already answered part of it. I wondered how your family regards the Willow episode; you referred to Araminta as scandalous.'

'I wasn't entirely serious, of course. I think quite a few of us over the years have admired her for her pluck. She'd always been headstrong, but she must have been very much in love to act as she did, in the face of such severe disapproval. But exaggeration, as you must know, plays a large part in family legend. For instance, the Willows were a respectable and respected family, even in her day, and references to Sebastian as a simple carpenter are certainly spurious.'

'How exactly did they meet?'

'I don't know if you're aware of it, but not only was he the son of the firm, he was also a skilled and highly regarded furniture-maker. It happened that the wife of one of Araminta's brothers was expecting a child, and, having seen some of his work at an exhibition, they commissioned a carved cradle. Sebastian delivered it himself, offering to make any alterations they might wish, but they were so delighted with it that Charles persuaded him to stay on and do some more work for him. In all, he was up here for two or three months, during which he and Araminta inevitably came into contact – and the damage, if such it was, was done. The attraction was on both sides, but to his credit, Sebastian made no attempt to prolong it. It was she who insisted on leaving with him when the time came.'

'And was disinherited?'

'So the story goes, though I think it was done in a fit of temper, and her father later regretted it. She was his only daughter, and had always been the apple of his eye. It was only natural he should hope for an advantageous marriage for her.'

'And I learned today he left her a small legacy.'

'Yes. Altogether, a happy enough ending, considering the circumstances.'

'Are you still in touch with the Willows?' Rona asked, with assumed innocence.

'Not personally, though I believe my husband and Julian occasionally lunch together.'

They heard voices in the hall, and she added, 'There's my husband now. He was hoping to get back in time to meet you.'

The door burst open and a larger-than-life figure exploded into the room. He was dressed in a check shirt and riding breeches, and his face was red with sunburn and exertion. Rona rose hastily to her feet in time to take the hand thrust towards her.

'Apologies for being late, my dear,' he said breezily. 'Miranda's horse lost a shoe, and that delayed us. Delighted to meet you.'

Belatedly, Rona saw that his daughter had followed him into the room. Though recognizable as the girl in the photograph, Miranda Barrington-Selby was a pale copy of her former self. In contrast to her father's ruddy features, there was no colour in her face other than the purple shadows under her eyes. She, too, was dressed in riding clothes, and carrying her hat by its strap.

'This is Miss Parish, my dear,' Lord Roxford introduced, and, to Rona, 'My daughter, Miranda.'

The two young women nodded cautiously at each other.

'No doubt my wife has been able to answer your questions?'

'Yes, thank you. She's been very helpful.'

'Splendid, splendid. Not sure that we've much to offer that's of interest, but Julian was determined we should see you. You've covered the story of Araminta, then?'

'Yes, I – have a much clearer idea of events now.'

'She's also been over the house,' Lady Roxford put in.

Lord Roxford nodded approvingly. 'Good move. Give you some idea of the background.'

His wife's glance moved to their silent daughter. 'I hope you've not overdone things, dear,' she said anxiously. 'It might be wise to go upstairs and have a rest before dinner.'

The girl nodded, smiled wanly in response to a paternal pat on the arm, and went out of the room.

There was a brief silence, then, by way of excuse or explanation, Rona wasn't sure which, Lady Roxford remarked, 'She's been a little under the weather lately.'

'I'm sorry,' Rona said inadequately. Feeling her welcome was coming to an end, she went on, 'I won't take up any more of your time. I'm extremely grateful to you both for agreeing to see me and answer some questions, and I'm delighted to have had the chance to see round your lovely home.'

They both smiled at her, as though she were a child who'd said the right thing.

'Regards to Julian and his wife,' Roxford said, as, in response to a bell rung by his wife, the young woman who'd admitted Rona appeared and, after appropriate words of farewell, escorted her back to the door.

Outside on the gravel, Rona stood uncertainly for a moment. She had, she realized, paid to see the gardens, and had not yet done so. It would do her good, after the long drive and somewhat tricky interview, to have a walk and clear her head. Returning briefly to the car, she locked her briefcase in the boot, and took the path leading to the lake.

On her return to her room at the pub, Rona took out her laptop and typed up notes on her visit to the Hall. As Lady Roxford had remarked, there'd been no need for her to come to Yorkshire; everything she had learned here could have been accessed from other sources, but Julian had wanted to show off his connections. In retrospect, though, Rona was glad to have met the Roxfords – not to mention their daughter – and seen where they lived. Also, she was looking forward to satisfying her curiosity about the Franks the following day.

Before going down for supper in the pub restaurant, she phoned Lindsey.

'I was about to ring you,' her sister exclaimed, before Rona could speak. 'You'll never guess who's just been on the phone?'

'Then you'd better tell me.'

'Adele Yarborough! She's finished her psychiatric treatment or whatever it was, and is back home.'

'Oh Linz, I'm sorry. Max did tell me, and I meant to warn you.'

'Well, thanks a bunch! I got the shock of my life. And you'll never believe it, but she's had the gall to invite us to a drinks party they're giving next week – you and Max, as well as the neighbours here.'

The Yarboroughs lived in the same cul-de-sac as Lindsey, some fifteen minutes' drive out of Marsborough, and before her temporary removal to Norfolk, Adele, a student of Max's, had claimed he'd molested her, an accusation that had resulted in an uncomfortable few hours with the police.

'I doubt if Max will go within fifty yards of her.'

'That's what I thought. To be fair, though, she *was* genuinely ill during all that fracas. I think I'll go along, and I can report back to you on how she seems. Sorry, though, this is your call; did you want something?'

'To tell you that you in turn will never guess who I met today.'

'Surprise me.'

'None other than Lady Miranda.'

She heard Lindsey's indrawn breath. 'Where the hell are you?'

'The far-flung north. Ottersby, to be precise, a couple of miles from Roxford Hall.'

'She was at the house?'

'Yes; I only met her briefly. She'd been riding with her father, and I must say she looked pretty washed out. Her mother said she'd been "under the weather", whatever that meant.'

'Lovelorn, would you say?'

'Could be.'

'What was she like?'

'Difficult to say. She didn't open her mouth.'

'Well, if she's up there, at least she's not with Dominic.'

'No one can argue with that,' Rona said.

Max's call came as she was preparing for bed.

'Did you remember your curtsey?' he asked her.

'You'd have been proud of me.'

'Seriously, did it go OK?'

'Yes, they were pleasant enough, but as Lord Roxford remarked, there was no need whatsoever for me to come up here.'

'Massaging Julian's ego, that's all.'

She paused. 'Have you been back to the house?'

'No, why?'

'I wondered if there was any post.' She paused again. 'Lindsey's had an invitation from the Yarboroughs, and says we're also on the guest list.'

This time the pause was on his side. 'An invitation to what?'

'A cocktail party. For next week, I think.'

'Well, you go if you like, but I shan't.'

'That's what I thought. In that case, neither shall I.'

'We can make some plausible excuse.'

'No doubt. Well, see you tomorrow, darling. Goodnight.'

'Goodnight,' he said.

The following morning, she settled up with the pub, put her case in the boot, and set off for Harrogate. The last time she'd had to search the records, it had required making an appointment at the archive centre and booking a reading table. However, when she'd phoned to do so, she was told past copies of the electoral rolls were available in the local library. No appointment was necessary, and, even better from Rona's viewpoint, the rolls were in volumes rather than on microfiche.

Through indirect questioning, Louise had found out the address of the Franks' old home – 26 Rawsdon Drive – and also the date on which she herself had left for Canada. On arrival at the library, therefore, Rona's first task was to check in which district or parish the road fell, then unearth the volume for the year 2000, which would have been Louise's last entry. Having done so, she settled at a table with a feeling of anticipation. If she could provide evidence that Louise had indeed lived with her parents prior to moving to Canada, it should do a lot to restore some sense of identity.

Which did not, however, prove to be the case. There was no difficulty in tracing the listing for the Franks, but the names recorded were Barbara M., Karen E. and Keith G. There was no mention at all of Louise.

Rona frowned and leafed both backwards and forwards in case she'd made some mistake. But the address tallied – 26 Rawsdon Drive – and the year was the one she'd been given. She sat back, studying the page in bewilderment. Could it be that the Franks had, either intentionally or otherwise, given Louise the wrong date? Perhaps she'd left for Canada a year earlier? As to who Karen might be, Rona had no idea. There'd been no mention of a younger sister. Could she, then, have been an unmarried aunt, who'd been living with them? Even Keith's mother? There was no way of knowing.

Not to be defeated, Rona collected several back volumes, but each gave the same information. When, however, she consulted the 2001 records, interestingly enough, only Barbara and Keith's names appeared. Whoever Karen was, she seemed to have moved away at the same time as Louise. Was this significant?

Rona stared at the pile of volumes in frustration. There must be a logical explanation, but try as she might, she couldn't detect it. Remembering her previous experience, she then looked up the names of the neighbours on either side of the Franks' house and directly opposite, then checked them against the latest roll. Two of the names were the same.

She glanced at her watch. Ten to eleven. She wanted to be home by six, and it was a four-hour drive – possibly more on a Friday evening. She'd just have time to drive out to Rawsdon Drive in the hope of catching at least one of the couples at home. With luck, they might be able to solve the mystery.

She bought a map of Harrogate, located the road she wanted, and, after a couple of wrong turns, found her way there. Parking the car outside number twenty-six, she glanced up at the house, wondering if the people who now lived there had bought it from the Franks, or whether there'd been an intervening sale. It was worth enquiring.

Her heart sank when the woman who answered her knock was in her twenties, and holding a baby in her arms. It was no surprise to learn they'd moved in only six months ago, and had no knowledge of previous owners.

Rona walked down the drive and up that of the next-door house, but when her ring resulted only in the distant barking of a dog, it was obvious no one was home. Which left the house opposite, whose occupants had also been there during the time of the Franks.

This time, a woman of about sixty opened the door, and Rona's spirits rose, guessing her to be the Susan J. Griffiths who'd been listed at this address. She launched into her prepared speech.

'I'm sorry to trouble you, but I wonder if you can help me? I'm trying to trace Mr and Mrs Franks, who used to live opposite. Have you any idea how I can get in touch with them?'

'Goodness me, no,' Mrs Griffiths replied. 'The last I heard of them was when they left about three years ago, to join their daughter out in Canada.'

'That would be . . .' Rona frowned, as though trying to remember.

'Karen,' supplied Mrs Griffiths promptly. 'She'd been courting a local lad, David Swann, and when his firm transferred him to Toronto, they got married and she went with him. Barbara and Keith visited them a couple of times, then, when Keith took early retirement, they moved out there permanently.'

Rona was now totally confused. So Karen had been their daughter, and married David Swann. Then where did Louise, who'd married Kevin Stacey, come into the picture?

She said tentatively, 'They had another daughter, didn't they? Louise?'

Mrs Griffiths shook her head. 'No, just the one.' She looked at Rona more closely. 'I thought you said you knew them?'

'Not personally,' Rona back-tracked. 'They're friends of friends. I heard they'd recently moved back to the UK, and wondered if you might know their new address?'

'Sorry, can't help you there. We lost touch when they left.'

'My friends certainly spoke of a Louise,' Rona persisted. 'Could she have been a niece, or something?'

'It's possible, I suppose' Mrs Griffiths said doubtfully, 'but I never heard of her.'

In desperation, Rona added, 'I called at number twenty-four, but no one was in. Might they . . .?'

'I really couldn't say; they keep to themselves.' Mrs Griffiths was becoming less forthcoming, and Rona feared her suspicions had been aroused. She felt in her handbag and extracted a card. 'I'm only here for the day, but if they do know anything, could you possibly ask them to phone me? My friends would be so grateful.'

She held out the card, and after a moment, the woman took it.

'Thanks so much for your help,' Rona continued, remembering just in time not to add the woman's name, which she should not have known. Her quick smile elicited no response, and she made her way down the path and across the road to her car, hearing the door close behind her.

As she was about to drive off, she glanced back at the house, in time to see one of the net curtains twitch. With luck, curiosity would prompt Mrs Griffiths to pass on the card. If not, well, Rona had done all she could.

It would have been wiser, she reflected as she turned out of Rawsdon Drive, not to have offered to make these enquiries; their result would only add to Louise's uncertainties.

'Cal! Hi, there! Good to hear from you! How are things?'

'Fine, fine. You too?'

'Great, yes. I've got a new job, did you hear? Finally made the move, and so far, I haven't regretted it. Still in IT, but a different line.'

'Good for you. And Susie?'

'Blooming. Literally. We're expecting an addition to the family in October.'

'Congratulations, that's great. Look, the reason I'm phoning is I thought you'd like to know a woman has been sniffing around, making enquiries about the Franks.'

The hairs rose on the back of his neck. 'When was this?'

'Yesterday, I think. The folks were out, but the old biddy across the road came over with a card she'd left, asking them to get in touch if they knew where the Franks are now.'

'Toronto, isn't it?' he said slowly.

'She seemed to think they were back in this country.'

His grip tightened on the phone. 'Who—' His voice was hoarse, and he cleared his throat. 'Who is this woman?'

'According to Dad, the name on the card was Rona Parish, and she lives down your way. It might be worth looking her up, finding out how much she knows.'

'It might indeed,' he said slowly. 'You don't happen to have her address?'

'Yep; I thought you'd want it, so I jotted it down. Nineteen, Lightbourne Avenue, Marsborough. It *is* your neck of the woods, isn't it?'

'Yes, only a few miles away. Did she say *why* she wanted to contact them?'

'On behalf of friends, but Ma Griffiths had her suspicions, not least because she seemed to think they had a daughter called Louise.'

'Could be a different family altogether.'

'Always possible, of course.'

'I'll check, naturally. Thanks, Cal.'

'Let me know how you get on.'

'You can bet on it.'

He put down the phone and sat staring into space. Perhaps, after all, justice might be done.

Nine

Rona was grateful for the respite that the weekend gave her. Not only would Louise not approach her for news while Max was home, but she needed time to decide how to impart her findings.

'Can you make any sense of it?' she asked Max yet again, as they sat over Saturday lunch. '*Why* isn't Louise listed, and where is Karen?'

Max shrugged. 'I did warn you to keep out of it.'

'But it gives credence to her story, doesn't it? That she mightn't be their daughter?'

'Then why would they say she was? And if she isn't, who the hell is she?'

'I don't *know*!' Rona put her head in her hands. 'Oh, I *wish* I'd never looked her up! At least there was some doubt before.'

'If you ask me, there's plenty now,' Max returned. 'Forget it, and concentrate on the Willows. In all probability, the lot next door will be moving out soon, and taking their problems with them.'

'I suppose I could approach it from another angle, and track down Kevin Stacey.'

Max pushed back his chair and got to his feet. 'I don't know why you ask my advice. You never take it.'

'Sorry! It's just—'

'I know, I know. It always is.' He dropped a kiss on the top of her head. 'Come on, let's go down to the club and watch some tennis. The tournament's on today.'

'You should have entered for it,' Rona said, starting to clear the table.

He grinned. 'Only fair to give someone else a chance!' he said.

*   *   *

That evening they went to Dino's, the Italian restaurant she'd mentioned to Louise. It was a home-from-home for Rona, since, with her dislike of cooking, she frequently came here for supper when Max had his evening classes.

As often happened, several of their friends were also there, and the obliging Dino set up a larger table so they could sit together.

'I presume the Willow introduction bore fruit?' Georgia asked at one point, winding her pasta round her fork.

'Oh Georgie, I'm sorry – I meant to report back to you. Yes, I started work there last week. In fact, I'm just back from Yorkshire, after paying my respects to His Lordship!'

Georgia looked blank, and Rona explained, 'Araminta's descendant, Lord Roxford.'

Georgia put her fork down. 'Good grief! I thought Julian was exaggerating, and it was some country squire they were related to! I never imagined—'

'Oh, it's the real thing, believe me. They live in a stately home that's open to the public, and are shortly off to Scotland for the grouse-shooting.'

'I shall look on Julian in a new light!' Georgia declared, amid general laughter.

'Did Lindsey enjoy her day-trip to France?' Magda enquired, as their plates were removed.

'Very much, thanks.'

'Odd, that you should have come across the Roxfords,' Gavin commented. 'It's their daughter Dominic Frayne was involved with.'

'So I believe,' Rona said steadily.

Magda shot her a glance. 'Does Lindsey know?'

'Of course.' She made it sound as though Dominic had told her. 'As a matter of fact,' she went on quickly, 'I met him myself, quite by chance, in the park.'

Gavin raised an eyebrow. 'Did you warn him off?'

'Certainly not. I thought he was charming.'

'Oh, he's charming, all right. That's half the trouble.'

Magda put her hand on his sleeve. 'That's enough, darling. You can't go round blackening people's characters! I'm sure Lindsey knows what she's doing.'

That would be a first, Rona thought silently, and was glad when the conversation turned to other matters.

As she and Max walked home through the warm darkness, the anxieties that her friends' company had held at bay again reached out for her. It was almost midnight, but there was a light behind one of the upstairs windows next door. Rona wondered whose room it was, and if Louise was lying awake up there. Max, seeing her upward glance, pulled her against him.

'Sufficient unto the day,' he said, and though Rona realized a new one was just beginning, she merely nodded agreement as they went together into the house.

Lindsey replaced her coffee cup on the bedside table and picked up the newspaper. It was a habit she'd acquired during her marriage to Hugh, to retrieve the Sunday papers from the mat, make a cup of coffee, and take them back to bed. In the early days, Hugh had later gone down to make breakfast, and brought it up on a tray. Nowadays, Lindsey omitted breakfast altogether. Today, in particular, she'd no desire to eat, since she'd no doubt be having a large lunch at Catherine's.

She sighed deeply, hoping she wouldn't be expected to coo over the baby. She hadn't a maternal bone in her body, and made no secret of the fact. Just as well, considering the chaotic state of her love life. Moodily, she reviewed it. Jonathan, with whom she was still having a half-hearted, on/off affair, had been in Spain with his family for the last fortnight, and was due back today. Hugh, encouraged by the night they'd spent together, was still very much to the fore, but she'd no wish to see him. And Dominic, despite his meeting with Rona, still hadn't been in touch. And there was no doubt, she thought miserably, that it was Dominic she wanted. It was now three weeks since their day in France, which at the time she'd felt had marked a step forward in their relationship. They'd seemed easier with each other, more relaxed in each other's company, and then there was that single, casual kiss on which, foolishly, she'd built so much. Had it meant nothing at all?

Her thoughts turned to Miranda Barrington-Selby. Rona had thought she didn't look well. Was that why she was at the family home in the middle of a working week? Lindsey was aware – since she'd made enquiries –that she *did* work, in some obscure art gallery near Covent Garden. Perhaps, she thought uncharitably, she drifted in and out as she chose, taking time off whenever she felt like it. But the fact remained that her name had been linked with Dominic for several months, and for all Lindsey knew, he still cared for her.

Oh, damn, damn, *damn*! she thought, pounding her fist on the duvet. Perhaps she should get away for a while; she'd not had a holiday this year, foolishly postponing plans in the hope that Dominic might suggest something. Which, she thought now, was unlikely in the extreme, and she was damned if she'd wait any longer. The only drawback was that since all her friends were married, she'd no one to go with. Admittedly Hugh would be glad to take her, but that was a commitment too far. There were singles holidays, of course; perhaps she should look into them.

Dispiritedly, she again picked up the newspaper, and this time began to read it.

It was a warm, sunny day, and they were having drinks on Catherine's patio, while baby Alice, now four months old, slept peacefully in her carry-cot under the cherry tree, and Gus, equally peacefully, lay under Max's chair.

As always, Rona was struck by how natural her father and Catherine were together – like a married couple already, starting to say the same thing, and breaking off with a laugh, seeming to anticipate each other's needs. Tom looked years younger than during the last stressful year before his retirement, when his marriage had gone into terminal decline; while Catherine seemed to have blossomed under this new love. Although she could still not be called pretty, there was a bloom about her, a glow, that added considerably to her attractiveness.

Rona's eyes moved on to meet those of Catherine's son, Daniel, who had smilingly observed her study of their parents. She smiled back, knowing he shared her pleasure in their happiness. Though she barely knew him, she liked Daniel and would be glad to welcome him as her step-brother, despite Lindsey's dark forebodings on the enlargement of the family.

She looked across at her twin, and her contentedness diminished. Though Lindsey's sunglasses afforded some concealment, it was obvious to Rona that she wasn't happy. She'd not taken to Catherine and her family as Rona had, blaming her for the break-up of their parents' marriage, and though she was considerably more amenable than she had been, the reserve was still there. But the root of Lindsey's malaise was, as Rona well knew, the ambiguity of Dominic Frayne. Why couldn't the wretched man put her out of her misery, either by ending the association altogether, or making it more stable, so that at least her sister knew where she stood?

'A penny for them, Rona!' Tom said laughingly. 'You're looking positively fierce!'

'Sorry! I've one or two things on my mind, but I shouldn't have brought them with me.'

'Anything it might help to discuss?'

Rona hesitated, and Max said, 'She's weaving a mystery about the family who've moved in next door.'

Lindsey looked up. 'Family? Ro said it was an elderly couple.'

'That's what we thought at first,' Rona replied, throwing Max an irritated glance. 'But it turns out they have a daughter. Or at least, they might have.'

Tom leant forward interestedly. 'Now, that *does* require explanation.'

So Rona related the story, starting with her first meeting with Louise, going on to explain her loss of memory and consequent loss of identity, and finishing with the fact that her own researches in Harrogate had shown no trace of her.

'I feel very sorry for her,' she finished, 'and I'm dreading having to see her tomorrow, and tell her the result of my search.'

'But how intriguing!' Daniel said. 'The couple *did* have a daughter, and she did go to Canada, but her name wasn't Louise.'

'That's about the size of it. Nor was the man she married Kevin Stacey.'

'The woman who never was,' mused Jenny.

'And they themselves have no family photographs or certificates?' Tom confirmed.

'That's right, because of this alleged fire.'

Catherine laughed. 'Alleged? You don't believe in it?'

'As Louise said, it seems very convenient.' Rona looked round challengingly. 'Well, come on, then. We have mystery readers and puzzle enthusiasts among us – surely someone can come up with an explanation?'

They debated the matter for the next fifteen minutes, tossing ideas back and forth while Catherine put the finishing touches to the meal, but when they all went in to eat, they'd reached no conclusion. Which, Rona thought, was pretty much what she'd expected.

The afternoon was spent lazily in the garden, chatting, looking at the papers, and, in the case of Catherine and Jenny, playing with the baby, who lay kicking on a rug. Occasionally the conversation veered back to Louise, but no one had any further insights to offer.

At about six, Daniel and Jenny loaded the car with baby things, and the three of them left for the drive back to Cricklehurst. The others, urged by Catherine and Tom, stayed on. As the shadows lengthened, drinks were brought out, together with little salty biscuits, which attracted Gus's attention.

'We must go soon,' Rona said, laughing as he caught one in his mouth. 'Those probably aren't very good for him, but it's past his supper time.'

'He ought to have a walk, too,' Max remarked, stretching. 'He's had as lazy a day as the rest of us.'

'Speak for yourself!' Catherine protested.

'Which reminds me,' Rona said, 'let us help you to clear up.'

'Not a bit of it!' Tom cut in. 'What do you think I'm here for?'

'But at least we can take things through to the kitchen.'

'Definitely not. We enjoy setting things to rights and talking over the day.'

Lindsey was the first to unfurl herself from her chair. 'I must go; there are some papers I really should look at before tomorrow. Thank you so much, Catherine, for a lovely day.'

Rona breathed a sigh of relief, and Catherine and Tom looked pleased. 'Thank you for coming. We've loved having all of you.'

Now that the sun was low in the sky, a chilliness was beginning to invade the warmth, and Rona shivered. 'We must be on our way, too. As Linz said, it's been a lovely day. Thank you.'

'Let us know if you make any progress on your mystery,' Catherine said, as she and Tom saw them off.

* * *

Max garaged the car in Charlton Road. 'You go on home, and I'll take Gus for a brisk run round the park. I could do with some exercise myself.'

'Will you want any supper?' Rona asked.

'Cheese and biscuits will be fine.'

They walked together as far as the slipway, then Rona continued to the corner, turned briefly into Fullers Walk, and left again into Lightbourne Avenue. As she rounded the second corner, she almost collided with a man lighting a cigarette, and murmured an apology before walking on down the road and into her gateway.

The house was welcomingly warm, and she ran down the basement stairs to the kitchen, to prepare a supper tray they could carry upstairs. With the advance of evening, it was dark below street level, and she switched on the lights, remembering as she did so that the dishwasher needed emptying. Her mind on the afternoon behind her, she set about the task, methodically stacking plates on the counter under the window, prior to carrying them to the appropriate cupboard.

She couldn't have said what alerted her – possibly a primeval sense of being watched – but she looked up suddenly, seeing beyond the eye-level black railings a pair of stationary trousers, and as her eyes flew upwards, they met those of the man she had recently passed on the corner. For a long minute they stared at each other, Rona frozen with a plate in her hand, he motionless on the street. Then, abruptly, he turned and walked briskly away.

Convulsively, Rona leant forward and dragged the blind down over the window. Her heart was clattering against her ribs. He must have followed her, she thought distractedly. But why? She'd never seen him in her life.

Sudden fear seized her: she'd left the front door on the latch for Max! She flew up the stairs, hurled herself against the door, and pulled down the catch. Illogical, she told herself, struggling for breath; she'd seen him walk away. But perhaps he'd gone only a yard or two, and was intending to return? Oh God, Max, come home! Gus doesn't need *that* long a walk! Thank God this hadn't happened on an evening when he was holding classes, and wasn't due back at all.

Slowly, she went back downstairs and finished unloading the dishwasher, putting everything away in its appointed place.

Then she laid a tray with biscuits, butter and cheese, two glasses and a bottle of white wine from the fridge. Finally, carrying the tray, she returned to the ground floor. The last blue light of day was seeping into the sitting room through its uncurtained windows. Rona set the tray on the coffee table and moved cautiously to the windows, looking up and down the road. It was deserted, though as she stood there, a car drove past, its headlights cutting a golden swathe in front of it. She drew the curtains across, making sure there were no chinks, then switched on the lamps and perched on the edge of a chair to await Max's return, ears straining for the sound of footsteps on the pavement outside.

Minutes later she heard them and stiffened, listening as they turned to come up the path towards her. There was a rattle at the door handle, then an irritated ring of the bell. Rona went to answer it and, about to open the door, paused. She *knew* it was Max, but . . .

'Who is it?' she called.

'Who the hell do you think it is?' came Max's testy reply. 'Why did you lock the door?'

She pulled it open, and his annoyance faded as he saw her pale face.

'What's the matter, love?' he asked quickly. 'What's happened?'

Gus nosed her hand, and she bent to unclip his lead before replying.

'Rona?'

'A man followed me home,' she said unsteadily. 'I was in the kitchen, and I saw him staring in at me.'

Max frowned. 'What man?' Then, 'You say he followed you; where from?'

'The corner. I almost bumped into him – he was lighting a cigarette. I didn't think any more of it, till I saw him watching me.'

'You're sure it was the same man?'

'Yes; I didn't pay much attention the first time, but I did notice he was wearing a pink shirt, because it was very like one of yours.'

'Can you describe him?'

'Average height, brown hair, pink shirt, as I said. And light-coloured trousers.'

'Age?'

'Mid-thirties, I'd say.'

'What did he do when you looked up and saw him?'

'Stared at me a moment longer, then walked quickly away.'

'In which direction?'

'Further on down the road, so you wouldn't have passed him. Anyway, it was some time ago now.'

'Well,' Max said after a pause, 'I shouldn't let it worry you. He could merely have been walking in the same direction, and the light from the kitchen caught his eye.'

'But he didn't just glance inside, Max. He was standing still, facing me.'

'Never mind, he's long gone now. I'll have a quick wash, then I'll pour you some wine. That'll calm your nerves.'

Though she said no more, Rona wasn't reassured. Had the man been waiting for her on the corner, or was his being there pure chance? Had he, as Max suggested, merely paused to light his cigarette, then continued on his intended route? Even if that were the case, he'd stopped to stare in at her – not, surely, normal behaviour. A disturbing thought lodged in her head: whether or not the meeting was accidental, the fact remained that this stranger now knew where she lived.

Rona didn't go to Oak Avenue the next morning, since she'd an appointment in Woodbourne at ten thirty. She spent the time in her study, sorting out her notes and hoping Louise wouldn't realize she was at home. She'd have to see her this evening, though, and she'd still not decided on the best way of breaking the news.

Had Mrs Griffiths passed her card to the Johnsons, who'd been the Franks' next-door neighbours? And, even supposing she had, would they bother contacting her? She very much doubted it. It seemed that for all their joint efforts, she and Louise would never have proof, one way or the other, of her true identity, and whereas the passing of time would put the matter out of her own head, it would remain a life sentence for Louise.

Beset by such thoughts, Rona was glad when it was time to leave for her appointment. Max had taken Gus with him when he left that morning, since after seeing Mrs Willow, she would go straight to Oak Avenue. She'd have welcomed him at her side as she approached the corner of Fullers Walk, but today the only people around were an elderly couple some yards ahead of her, and a mother wheeling a pushchair, a dancing child at her side.

The drive to Woodbourne took about half an hour, and Rona settled down to enjoy it. The last time she'd been there, she reflected, she had seen the display of Curzon china in the window of the de Salis Gallery, and gone inside. Remembering the events that followed, she repressed a shudder, and switched her mind back to the present.

As Felicity had told her, the address was easy to find. Just past the bus station, a road led off the main thoroughfare, threading its way through a development of Scandinavian-style wooden houses, about a dozen in all, each standing on a fairly large plot. The front gardens were open-plan, those at the rear enclosed by fences to afford privacy. Rona remembered reading that they boasted what, at the time they were built, had been revolutionary features in the English housing market – triple glazing, wood-burning stoves and solar panels. The whole development was surrounded by trees, underlining the impression of a corner of Sweden, set down in the middle of an English market town.

And Erika Willow looked to be the archetypal resident. Tall and well-built, she had an abundance of flaxen hair that, held in a low ponytail, hung down her back. In her tanned face, her eyes were a disconcertingly light blue. Though she must have been in her sixties, she looked at least ten years younger.

'Mrs Willow, I'm Rona Parish; you kindly invited me to see you.'

Erika nodded. 'Please, come in.'

Even after all the years she'd lived in the UK, her voice had a Swedish intonation. She led the way into the house, and Rona looked about her with interest. The ground floor was open-plan, and floors, walls and ceilings were composed of rich, golden pine. The comfortable-looking sofas and chairs were upholstered in light blue, with darker blue scatter cushions, and the curtains hanging at the long windows were patterned in blue and white. The overall impression was of space, comfort and, somehow, cleanliness.

Erika Willow watched her reaction with a slight smile. 'It is different from Oak Avenue, yes?'

Rona laughed. 'Indeed it is.'

'For my poor husband, it took some getting used to. Now, he loves it as much as I do.'

'It's a charming house,' Rona said warmly.

'Thank you.'

Coffee was served in thick blue mugs, with a jug of cream alongside.

'How did you meet your husband?' Rona enquired, accepting one of the sweet biscuits passed to her.

'He came to Sweden to inspect our furniture. The two families, you see, have a long-standing business association, and in the days when Sebastian Willow made furniture, it was we who supplied the timber. After the last war, my father decided the time was right for us to branch into furniture-making ourselves. You won't remember, but in the fifties and sixties, Scandinavian furniture was all the rage in Britain, and the business thrived. We are still the main suppliers for Willows', as well as for many other, better-known, stores.'

Rona noted that she bracketed herself with the Swedish side of the family. 'Did any of Sebastian's descendants try their hands at furniture-making?'

Erika shook her head. 'He was a one-off. The others were all interested in the business, rather than the creative, side. For which, of course, we're grateful; if they'd continued to manufacture themselves, they'd have had no need of us.'

'Julian was saying how lucky it was there's been only one son per generation.'

Erika made a sound of impatience. 'He has this *idée fixe* that the family is unique in that. True, it has meant the business hasn't had to be divided, but other sons would not have been a problem. Quite the reverse, in fact. Many of his forebears would have welcomed another – "the heir and the spare" theory, particularly in the days of high infant mortality. Which is no doubt why they went on to have several other children, who –' she raised her shoulders in a shrug – 'either fortunately or unfortunately, turned out to be girls.'

She smiled indulgently. 'Did he also tell you he's unearthed myths of second sons being secreted out of birthing rooms and baby girls substituted? If he hasn't, he will. Of course, no one else believes a word of it.'

'May I use that story?' Rona asked eagerly. 'It would add colour to the article.'

'Of course.'

'Did you have only one child yourself?'

'No, we have a daughter, and to prove my point, she is younger than Julian. We wanted a second child; boy or girl would have made no difference.'

'Is she married?'

'Imogen? No, she's a career girl – an interior designer, so in tune with the family business. She has a flat in London, and that seeming requisite nowadays, a live-in lover, who, I am told, is "something in the City".'

Erika threw her a glance. 'Why? Will you want to see her?'

Rona shook her head. 'I don't think it'll be necessary, since she's nothing to do with the firm.'

'Julian told me you were equally interested in the family?'

'That's true, but mainly where there's some business connection.' Rona paused, and added diffidently, 'Will there be a chance to meet your husband?'

'Oh indeed, he'd like to see you. I offered to fill in the background while he finishes what he was doing in the garden.'

She walked to the sliding glass door, and called his name. Minutes later, he appeared and, rubbing his hand down his trousers, held it out to Rona.

'Not as clean as it might be,' he apologized. 'I've been doing some weeding.'

Graham Willow was of the same slight build as his son, and seemed somewhat dwarfed by the imposing figure of his wife. Like Julian's, his hair had receded, and there were hollows under his high cheekbones. Nonetheless, he looked healthy enough, and seemed in good spirits.

'I've been following your series with interest,' he said, 'and learned a lot about my neighbours in the process. Fascinating histories, some of them.'

'Not many have featured a runaway heiress!' Rona smiled.

Willow laughed. 'I hear my son had you traipsing up to Yorkshire. Quite unnecessary, of course.'

'I enjoyed the trip. Lord and Lady Roxford were very kind, and I had a tour of the house. There's a portrait of Araminta, similar to the one in the dining room at Oak Avenue. She was your grandmother, wasn't she? Do you remember her at all?'

'Oh yes, quite well. She lived into her eighties, and as children, my sisters and I used to go to her house for Sunday tea. We're a long-lived bunch, Miss Parish. My father lived to be almost a hundred.'

'So I heard. You had the flat made for him and your mother, didn't you?'

'That's right. In some ways I was sorry to leave the family home, though handing it over to Julian on his marriage made sense, and Erika here couldn't wait to move out.'

'It was a good family home,' Erika said firmly, 'and it still is. It is a house that needs children, and when we had ours, it suited us well. Now it's Julian and Felicity's turn.'

'How are you doing with your research?' Graham asked, seating himself in one of the chairs. 'Are you working chronologically?'

'No; I knew Julian wanted me to see Lord Roxford, so I've been concentrating on your grandparents.'

'And now that's under your belt, what will you turn to?'

'I'll start at the beginning, which is what I'd normally have done in the first place.'

'With John the barrow-boy? The sublime to the ridiculous?'

'I don't think either term applies,' Rona said tactfully.

'You're right, of course. In our heart of hearts, we're proud of both of them. I can give you facts and figures about the shop, incidentally, when you're ready for them – how much was paid for it, and when the various extensions were added.'

'Did they never consider opening other branches?'

'They did try once, but their timing couldn't have been worse. It was in the twenties, and the Depression put paid to them. After that, they decided to stick to the flag ship.' He stood up. 'Well, if there's nothing I can help you with at the moment, I'll return to my gardening. But call me anytime you need some answers; I'll be glad to oblige.'

'Thank you. I must go, too.' Rona turned to Erika. 'Thanks for the coffee and the information. Perhaps I could come back if I have more questions?'

'Of course.'

Erika showed her to the door. 'My love to the family.'

'I'll pass it on.'

It was only as she was driving home that Rona remembered Felicity's warning that Erika could be fierce. She'd seen no sign of it. Perhaps, she thought with amusement, it was a side of herself she kept for her daughter-in-law.

Ten

As previously arranged, Felicity had prepared lunch for them both, and was eager to hear how Rona had fared with her parents-in-law. There wasn't much to tell, but Rona outlined the gist of their conversation, omitting the references to Julian's *idée fixe*.

'It's a fabulous house, isn't it?' she ended. 'It must be very cosy in winter, with the wood stove burning.'

'Yes, it's attractive, but too sparse and modern for me,' Felicity replied. 'I'm not into minimalism; I reckon we came off best!'

Rona smiled. 'Then everyone's satisfied. And now,' she said, folding her napkin, 'I must return to work, and this time "start at the very beginning".' She helped to clear the table. 'Thanks so much for lunch, Felicity. Tomorrow, I'd like to take you to the Bacchus, if you're free?'

'There's no need for that,' Felicity protested. 'I love cooking, and as I said, I'm glad of the company.'

'All the same, I'd like to.'

'Then as long as you don't regard it as repayment, thanks, I'd enjoy it.'

Rona worked steadily till five o'clock, going back, as she'd said, to the earliest records and the famous John Willow. But to her disappointment, extensive though the archives were, a lot of the material was technical and business-orientated, and would be of little interest to the readers of *Chiltern Life*. The most interesting find, to Rona's mind, had been the letters following Araminta's defection. It seemed that tracing the progress of the firm from its small beginnings to its present eminence would not take as long as she'd expected.

She switched off her laptop and closed it, aware that she

was delaying her return home and the inevitable meeting with Louise. She hoped she could break the news without it sounding as if they'd come to the end of the line, even though, in her opinion, they had.

She collected Gus from Farthings and drove home, trying to work out the best approach and realizing with irritation that since she still had no note of Louise's phone number, it would again mean calling at the house. Which could be awkward, if Barbara or Keith were there; she couldn't keep escaping to the garden with Louise, without it looking pointed and arousing their suspicions: though what suspicions they might have, Rona couldn't imagine.

In the event, the decision was taken out of her hands. As she drew level with the Franks' house, the front door opened and Louise came hurrying down the steps.

'I was watching out for you coming home,' she said. 'How did it go in Harrogate? I've been on edge all weekend, wondering what you found out.'

Rona had continued to her own gate, Louise falling into step with her. 'Come in and have a drink, and I'll tell you about it,' she invited resignedly.

This time, apparently anxious not to waste a second, Louise didn't comply with Rona's nod towards the sitting room, but followed her down the basement steps, where she was sufficiently distracted from her anxiety to exclaim at the light and airy room.

'You really have done wonders with the house!' she enthused. 'It makes ours look desperately staid and old-fashioned.'

'Any luck finding somewhere of your own?' Rona asked, taking a bottle of wine from the fridge.

'Not really. We've been to see dozens, but nothing's quite right. Either the location's wrong, or the rooms are too small, or there's no garden. The trouble is, though the house we're in can't hold a candle to yours, it's still very handsome, with high ceilings and lots of character, and it's spoiling us for anything else.'

Louise took the glass Rona handed her, and they sat down at the kitchen table.

'Now,' she said eagerly, leaning forward with her hands clasped, 'tell me how you got on.'

'Not very well, I'm afraid.'

Louise sat back, dismay on her face. 'There's no trace of us?'

Rona kept her eyes on her glass. 'I found your parents, listed under twenty-six Rawsdon Drive, as you said.'

'But?'

'But the only other person at that address was a Karen E. Franks.'

Louise stared at her blankly. 'I don't understand.'

'Believe me, neither do I.'

'So who was she, this Karen?'

'Well, I wondered if she could have been an aunt, even your grandmother – there was no indication of her age or relationship to your parents. So I went to Rawsdon Drive and spoke to a woman who'd lived there when – when you did.'

'And?' Louise demanded impatiently.

'And,' Rona said, slowly and unwillingly, 'she said they'd had a daughter who'd emigrated to Canada, but – her name was Karen.'

Louise moistened dry lips. 'That's just – not possible.'

'And she married someone called David Swann,' Rona ended in a rush, eager to get it all over.

'But – what about Kevin?'

Rona shrugged helplessly.

'Not to mention me!' Louise added, her voice rising hysterically. She put both hands to her mouth. 'I was so sure this would make it all right,' she said tremulously. 'If I could *know* I'd actually lived there with my parents, then it would prove I'm who they say I am. But now where are we?'

She seemed on the verge of tears.

'I'm so sorry, Louise. I wish I'd never suggested looking.'

'In fact,' Louise continued, as though Rona had not spoken, 'it seems to prove the opposite – that I'm *not* their daughter. Suppose . . .' She paused, thinking furiously. 'Suppose this Karen died, and her parents – Keith and Barbara – couldn't accept it. Then they read in the papers about this unknown woman much the same age, who was found after a car crash, and had lost her memory. They put things like that in the paper, don't they? "Does anyone know this woman?" kind of thing. And if no one came forward to claim me, they might have thought I'd be a good substitute. That's certainly possible, isn't it?'

'I don't know,' Rona said uncertainly.

'I mean, women steal other people's babies after losing their own. This is the same idea, only with someone older. And it would explain why there was no record of my marriage or divorce,' she went on, the idea gaining ground. 'After all, *Louise* Franks never existed.'

'And Kevin Stacey?'

Louise lifted her shoulders helplessly. 'They might have invented him, to make it all more plausible. He probably doesn't exist, either.'

Rona leaned forward, covering Louise's hands with her own. 'There's no "either" about it, Louise. *You* exist, in your own right, whatever people choose to call you. Don't ever forget that.'

Louise said shakily, 'I suppose that's true. God, I'm glad I met you, Rona. You're the only thing that's keeping me sane.' She paused, pursuing her line of thought. 'It could be David Swann, Karen's husband, who's working in the Far East; in which case, he wouldn't know anything about the substitution.'

Rona shrugged helplessly. 'Look, let me give you my mobile number, then you can contact me at any time. Have you got one yourself?'

Louise shook her head.

'Then give me your home number.'

They each made a note, then Louise looked up, meeting Rona's concerned eyes. 'What should I do?' she asked simply.

'Can't you speak to your parents? If they knew how upset you are—'

But Louise was shaking her head. 'It would show I didn't believe what they'd told me.'

'You could ask them who Karen is; say the name suddenly came into your head.'

Louise stared at her. 'It would be interesting to see their reaction,' she said slowly. 'I might just do that.'

'She's gone next door again,' Barbara Franks said worriedly. 'I don't like it, Keith. That girl's a journalist; she must be good at ferreting things out.'

'But there's nothing to find, is there? Not over here – that's why we came back.'

'All the same, I'll be glad to get away from this house. Perhaps we should reconsider the Alban Road one.'

Keith said patiently, 'Moving across town won't interrupt their friendship, if that's what it is. We'd have to leave the area altogether, and to be honest, I'm heartily sick of moving. Lord knows, we've done enough of it in the last year.'

Barbara was staring unseeingly out of the window. 'What I can't help thinking,' she said, 'is, suppose her memory comes back?'

'It was ghastly,' Rona said to Max on the phone. 'I felt as if I'd slapped her in the face. She was so excited when she came round, but what I'd discovered was worse than a complete blank. It seems to deny her very existence.'

'Why the hell doesn't she come straight out and ask her parents?' Max demanded impatiently. 'They're not ogres. What does she think they'd do to her?'

'That's what I advised,' Rona agreed. 'She didn't want to, so I suggested she asked them who Karen was – the name that was on the electoral roll. The whole thing's completely bizarre. What was it Jenny called her yesterday? *The woman who never was*? That seems horribly apposite.'

'That's ridiculous, and you know it. There has to be a logical explanation.'

'Then will you kindly tell me what it is?'

There was a pause. Max said heavily, 'It's too late to start an argument. Go to bed, love, and stop worrying. It's really not your problem.'

'I've a feeling I've made it mine,' Rona replied.

She didn't sleep well that night, and the dreams that lingered on her frequent awakenings were filled with faceless strangers, car crashes, and a sense of impending danger. At six, she gave up all thought of further sleep, had a shower, and went down for an early breakfast. Gus greeted her with pleased surprise, and when she'd eaten, she took him for a brisk walk round the block. There was a freshness about the early morning that dissipated in the sluggish heat of day and which, in her unsettled state, she found very welcome.

Max had said Louise's problem wasn't hers, but she'd underlined her involvement by passing on her mobile number. She might well come to regret that.

*   *   *

Julian was in the hall at Oak Avenue when Rona arrived.

'I've been thinking,' he said, 'that you might like to have a look round the shop to get an idea of how it's run. We could show you the storerooms, explain which items are manufactured in the UK and which imported, where they've come from, and so on. It might help to put some of the earlier stock lists into perspective.'

'Thank you, I'd like that. Your mother was saying her family firm is one of your main suppliers.'

'That's true. I pay regular visits to Sweden; perhaps you should accompany me next time.'

Felicity, who'd come downstairs in time to hear this last remark, said warningly, 'That's not half as much fun as it sounds, Rona. I went once, and was bored out of my mind. There's no time for sight-seeing on these business trips – all I saw was a succession of timber yards and warehouses. And I don't even like herrings!'

Julian shook his head despairingly. 'Anyway, there's time enough to think about that, but regarding a visit to the store, how about going down this afternoon? I shan't be there, but I can arrange for Giles Stanton, the manager, to show you round.'

'We're lunching together at the Bacchus,' Felicity put in. 'She could go straight on from there.'

'Excellent. About two thirty, then?'

'Thank you,' Rona said, 'I'll be there.'

That morning, she was glad to bury herself in the Willow papers and push all thoughts of Louise from her mind. She also made a list of questions to ask the store manager, looking forward to increasing her knowledge of furniture in general.

At twelve thirty she went downstairs to find Felicity waiting for her. It was a twenty-minute walk to the Bacchus from Oak Avenue, and as Felicity was going straight on to visit friends in Chilswood, they took the car and parked in Market Street car park, almost alongside the wine bar.

Knowing its popularity, Rona had booked a table, and they were led to one of the booths against the far wall, whose shoulder-high partitions afforded the illusion of privacy.

'I've never been here at lunchtime,' Felicity said. 'It's quite a different clientele – a mixture of business people and shoppers, by the look of them. In the evenings, it's mainly couples,

many of them having a pre-theatre supper before going to the
Darcy Hall down the road.'

'Or a late one after the show,' Rona said, recalling visits of
her own.

She took the menu a waiter was handing her, and ran her
eyes down it.

'What do you fancy?' she asked Felicity. 'You probably
know what's on offer as well as I do.'

'I'll be having afternoon tea, so nothing too filling. Actually,
what I'd really like is a selection of tapas.'

'Good choice. I'll join you.'

She relayed their order to the waiter, and as he turned away,
her eyes moved to two men seating themselves at a centre
table. With a jolt of surprise, she recognized one of them as
Dominic Frayne.

Perhaps aware of her gaze, he turned, and she saw his
momentary hesitation as he attempted to establish whether or
not she was Lindsey. She smiled, and he half-rose in his seat,
returning her smile with a slight inclination of his head.

Felicity, who had seen the exchange, murmured, 'Very nice
too! Who is that charmer?'

'Dominic Frayne,' Rona answered, 'a friend of my sister's.'

'So *that's* Dominic Frayne! I've heard a lot about him, from
both Julian and Tara.'

'Oh?'

'Julian met him at the golf club, though his reputation had
gone before. Businessman of the Year, and all that. They say
he can be pretty ruthless, but having seen him, I doubt if he'd
need to be. I'd say charm is his most powerful weapon.'

Rona smiled. 'Possibly more with women than with men.'

'You have a point, I suppose, though Julian was very
impressed with him, and he doesn't impress easily.'

'And Tara?'

'Oh, they met at some reception in London. She was quite
smitten, I think, but at the time his name was linked with the
Roxford girl.'

'He's been linked with quite a few people, I believe,' Rona
said, suddenly unwilling to discuss Dominic Frayne.

Felicity picked up something of her reserve. 'Sorry, I'm
being tactless. He's a friend of your sister's, and of course
you don't want to gossip about him.'

Luckily, the arrival of their wine obviated the need of a reply.

'Talking of Tara,' Felicity went on, 'she phoned last night. She's attending a reunion dinner at Farnbridge on Thursday, and wants to spend a few days with us on her way home. Which I'm afraid will mean suspending our lunches.'

'Just as well for my waistline! Seriously, don't give it a thought. You've done more than enough already, and in any case I shan't be coming in every day from now on. I've enough to make a start on the article, and will just be looking in from time to time to check things, if that's all right?'

'Of course; whatever suits you.' Felicity sipped her wine. 'Though I hope, when you've finished, we'll still keep in touch.'

'I hope so, too.'

As she spoke, Rona realized her response wasn't mere politeness. There was an openness about Felicity, almost a naïveté, that was endearing, and Rona hoped fiercely that the predatory Tara would do nothing to hurt her.

Their tapas arrived, and conversation stayed on a more general level for the rest of the meal. As they rose to leave, Dominic came to his feet.

'I hope you've enjoyed your meal? May I introduce my business colleague, Neville Barclay? Neville, this is Rona Parish, renowned biographer.'

'Oh, please!' Rona protested laughingly, as his companion half rose to acknowledge her. 'Felicity, meet Dominic Frayne, and – Mr Barclay. Felicity Willow,' she added to the two men.

Dominic took Felicity's hand. 'I'm delighted to meet you. I've had some good games of golf with your husband.'

'So I believe,' Felicity smiled, flushing with pleasure.

They chatted lightly for a couple more minutes, then, niceties over, Rona and Felicity continued on their way to the door.

'Thanks so much for lunch,' Felicity said, as they parted on the pavement outside. 'Not to mention the introduction to Dominic Frayne!'

'Any time,' Rona smiled.

'Will you be in tomorrow?'

'Yes, I'll want to write up what I've learned at the shop.'

'See you then, and I hope you enjoy your tour.'

As Rona started down Market Street, her mobile rang in

her handbag, and she stopped, moving to one side of the pavement to answer it.

'Rona?' It was Louise's voice, highly pitched.

'What's the matter?' Rona asked quickly.

'You're not going to believe this, but my parents have put a private detective on to me!'

Rona frowned. 'What makes you think—?'

'He followed me from home. At first I thought I was being neurotic, but I tested him, going into one shop after another, and each time he was waiting outside, pretending to look in the window. Then I went to the café where you took me that time, and he came and sat at the next table, and kept staring at me.' Her voice rose in a wail. 'What can I *do*?'

'Where are you now?' Rona asked sharply.

'Back home.'

'Are your parents there?'

'They're in the garden. Rona—'

'What did he look like, this man?'

'Nothing out of the ordinary. I suppose that's one of the requirements for the job.'

'Can you describe him?'

'In his thirties, medium height, grey eyes.'

Rona's heart began to pound. 'What was he wearing?'

'Wearing?' Louise sounded distracted.

'You must have noticed, if he was sitting opposite you.'

'Well, he had on a short-sleeved sports shirt and light-coloured trousers.'

'What colour was his shirt?'

'*Colour?* What does that matter? I'm—'

'Humour me, Louise.'

'Light blue, if it's so important.'

It was little comfort; the pink one would be in the wash by now.

'He didn't make any attempt to speak to you?'

'No.'

'Or follow you, when you left the café?'

'Surprisingly, no.'

'Did you mention this to your parents?'

'Of course not. They—'

'I think you should, Louise. This could be very important.'

There was a pause. 'You mean—?'

'I mean that I don't think this man is anything to do with them. I saw him myself on Sunday evening, staring into my kitchen window.'

Louise sounded bewildered. 'He's some kind of stalker?'

'I don't know what he is, but I think he should be reported.'

'To the police, you mean? But he didn't actually *do* anything, and I can't *prove* he was following me.'

No, Rona reflected, that was the trouble. The police would be unlikely to pay attention to such vague accusations, no doubt taking the same line as Max had done. She sighed with frustration.

'Even if we can't report him, tell your parents. They'll know what to do.'

'What they'll do,' Louise said bitterly, 'is go back to not allowing me out on my own.'

'That might be no bad thing, for the moment. Please, Louise, do as I say. It's your safety that counts, not your independence.'

'Safety?' Her voice rose again. 'You think he might be dangerous?'

'I don't know what to think, but I'll do my best to get to the bottom of this, I promise. In the meantime, speak to your parents about it.' She paused. 'Did you mention Karen?'

'No, I haven't plucked up the courage so far.'

'I think you should. Look, I must go – I've an appointment in ten minutes. Take care, and I'll be in touch.'

She rang off, dropped her phone back into her bag, and, glancing at her watch, hurried on down the road, waiting with impatience until the traffic lights changed, and she could cross into Guild Street. Who *was* this man, and was it Louise or herself in whom he was interested? She caught herself glancing over her shoulder, and swore softly under her breath. She would *not* allow herself to feel vulnerable in her own home town.

Head high and shoulders back, she walked briskly down Guild Street to Willows' Fine Furniture.

The tour was interesting, and Giles Stanton a pleasant and knowledgeable guide, but to her annoyance, Rona's attention kept slipping. Time and again, she forced it back to what he was saying, reminding herself to ask the questions she'd prepared, and save the answers on her pocket recorder.

At her request, he pointed out items of furniture that had been supplied by Erika's family firm, Gustavsson of Örebro, several of which resembled pieces in Erika's home. The quality of the wood and attractiveness of design made them very desirable, and Rona was not surprised to see the high prices asked for them.

As Julian had requested, Stanton took her to the storerooms, where items were kept until there was space for them in the showroom, and produced order books and the latest brochures, one of which he gave her to take away.

'Have you come across the old brochures in the archives?' he asked, and she confessed she had not.

'Make sure you look them out. They're proof that furniture doesn't exist in a vacuum, but is a constantly changing mirror of its times – delicate, spindly chair-legs reflecting the elegance of the Regency period, for instance. And of course Art Deco swept all before it – not only furniture, but fashions, ceramics, architecture and much else.'

He glanced at her sheepishly. 'Sorry, I didn't mean to lecture you.'

'Please don't apologize. It's a fascinating subject, and I'd like to follow up several of the points you've made, for my own interest. May I come back some time, even after I've finished the article?'

'Of course, I'd be delighted.' He smiled. 'Even more delighted if you're tempted to buy some of the pieces you've seen!'

Rona laughed. 'I'll have to sweet-talk my husband,' she said.

She decided against returning to Oak Avenue. Neither Felicity nor Julian would be there, and she doubted if she herself would get much work done, with her mind on other matters. Instead, she'd collect Gus from Max's and take him for a walk. Perhaps Furze Hill Park would work its usual magic, and clarify things for her.

Unusually, she found Max in the kitchen at Farthings, making a cup of tea.

'I've finished the bit I'm working on,' he told her, 'and waiting for the paint to dry. So sit down and keep me company for a while. What have you been up to today?'

'Felicity and I had lunch at the Bacchus,' Rona began.

'All right for some!'

'And Dominic Frayne was there.'

'Not, I trust, with some glamorous blonde?'

'No, with a business colleague. I introduced him to Felicity, and she was very taken with him.'

'One of these days I must meet this male paragon.'

'I think you'd like him. Perhaps, when things are more settled with Linz, we could have them both to dinner.'

Max grunted. '*If* things become settled. Gavin said he has a reputation, remember.'

'And I've spent the last hour or so at Willows', being instructed in the intricacies of the furniture trade.'

'With Julian?'

'No, the manager. It was very interesting.' She paused, gazing at the cup of tea in front of her.

After a minute, Max said, 'Come on, then. What is it you're not telling me?'

'I had a phone call from Louise.'

He groaned. 'Not that again.'

'She said she was followed this morning, when she left the house.'

'And you believed her?'

'Yes. What's more, her stalker sounded exactly like the man I saw on Sunday.'

Max frowned. 'He's still hanging around, then?'

'It would seem so.' She looked up. 'I don't like it, Max. I've a nasty feeling about him.'

'You've no way of knowing it's the same man. Don't tell me the pink shirt was in evidence again?'

'No, but her description tallied pretty closely.'

'As, if I'm not mistaken, it would with half the male population.' He put a hand on her arm. 'All right, I admit I don't like this any more than you do; it might be wise for me to sleep at home for the time being.'

She looked up gratefully. 'Would you, Max? I'm probably being silly, but I really think there's something behind all this.'

'Then for God's sake don't take any chances. Keep to well-populated places, don't go out after dark, and I'll be home about ten. Now, take your trusty hound and let me get back to work.'

She leant across the table to kiss him. 'My hero,' she said.

*　　*　　*

As she'd planned, Rona took Gus to the park, but she was careful not to isolate herself from the other dog-walkers, and kept a careful eye on those around her. Nothing untoward occurred, and it was with a sigh of relief that she put her key into the front door of number nineteen.

But, as once before, as she pushed it open, she saw a note lying on the mat. Louise? she thought, bending to pick it up and unfold it. But it was not from Louise.

If you want to hear the truth about the Franks, she read, *phone me on* – and a mobile number followed. There was no signature.

Rona hastily closed the door and leant against it, her mouth dry, unsure, as a multitude of thoughts and questions collided in her head, whether it was the note itself or its message that worried her the most.

Eleven

Max said, 'For God's sake, don't phone that number.'
'I wasn't going to – at least, not yet. But it might at least throw some light on things. He obviously has some connection with the Franks, and he seems to know I've been asking about them. That's creepy.'

'What gets *me* is that he knows where you live.'

'But we knew that; I told you, he was looking in at me.'

'You think it's the same man?'

She gave a shaky laugh. 'I certainly hope so; I shouldn't like to think there's an army of psychos roaming the streets.'

'God, I wish I hadn't got this bloody class this evening.'

'At least you'll be home later.'

'But will you *promise* me not to try to contact him? At least before we've had a chance to discuss it properly?'

'All right, I promise.'

'And in the meantime, don't answer the door without looking through the spy-hole.'

Alarm quickened her voice. 'You think he'll come back?'

'God knows what he'll do. Just lock the doors and keep away from the front windows. I'll be home the minute I can get away. OK?'

'OK,' she echoed numbly. She put the phone down, glanced across the kitchen at the window giving on to the street, and, walking over to it, pulled down the blind. The evening sunshine, scarcely diminished, seeped through it into the room.

Gus licked her hand uncertainly, and she patted him, wondering how good a guard dog he would be, if put to the test. Then she shuddered at even having to consider it. This house had always been her refuge, her bolt-hole when things got tough. Now, it felt more like a trap, and herself a sitting duck. A stranger had watched her as she'd stood on this very spot, later returning with this ambiguous message. Why? And did his connection with the Franks make their proximity in the next house another cause for concern? What, if anything, did this man know about them, that he felt he should pass on?

Rona moved back to the note on the counter and, without touching it, studied it more closely. It was written in neat capitals on lined paper torn off a pad. There was nothing whatever to suggest what kind of person had sent it.

Beside her, the phone shrilled suddenly, making her jump. For a moment she froze, then she snatched it up and waited.

'Hello?' said an impatient voice. 'Rona? Are you there?'

'Oh, Linz!' Relief flooded her in an enervating wave and, clasping the phone, she moved to the table and sat down.

'I'm ringing for a chat, really, since we didn't get much chance on Sunday. How are things?'

'All right,' Rona said cautiously.

'Any developments on the people next door?'

'Not really.' Lindsey didn't know about the stranger, and at the moment Rona didn't feel up to telling her.

'How did Louise or whatever her name is take the result of your search?'

'She was upset, of course. I suggested she should ask her parents who Karen was, and see how they reacted.'

'It's all very odd, isn't it?

'Yes.' Rona seized with relief on a change of subject. 'I saw Dominic again today,' she said. 'He was at the Bacchus, where I had lunch.'

'Alone?' Lindsey asked sharply, and Rona felt a surge of pity for her insecurity.

'With a business colleague.'

'I suppose he didn't mention me?'

'He hardly mentioned anything. I was with Felicity, and we only paused for a second or two as we were leaving.'

'Well, I've decided he's a lost cause, and booked myself a singles holiday to go to Italy. Perhaps I'll meet someone interesting.'

'Good move, but I shouldn't write him off completely.'

'Give me three good reasons why not.'

Rona tried without success to think of them, but apparently the remark was rhetorical, because Lindsey was saying, 'Anyway, it seems I haven't lost my touch: believe it or not, I almost got picked up today! I was walking back to the office and came face to face with this guy, who nearly jumped out of his skin. Honestly, I thought he was about to have a heart attack. He started to say something, but Jonathan came up, and he shot off.'

Rona went hot and then cold. Had this man mistaken Lindsey for her? And if so, what had he tried to say? 'What did he look like?' she asked, forcing herself to speak lightly.

'Oh, nothing special, though admittedly I wasn't seeing him at his best. Not a patch on Dominic, but then, who is?'

'Well, if he shows up again, ignore him. Remember, Mum told us not to speak to strange men.'

'Sister dear, that was when we were six.'

'All the same,' said Rona weakly, 'there are some weird people about.'

'So you don't think it was my outstanding beauty that affected him?'

'I doubt it.'

Should she tell Lindsey? she agonized, but before she could reach a decision, her twin said, 'How about lunch tomorrow? The Bacchus again? Who knows, we might see the elusive Dominic.'

So much for her professed lack of interest. 'Yes, let's do that,' Rona said. Surely no harm could come before tomorrow lunchtime.

Harm? she repeated to herself, having rung off. Was that the way her mind was working, that this man wished her harm? Might it not be that he was concerned for her, knowing what he did about the Franks?

She'd been the first to see him, then Louise, now Lindsey. He was becoming ubiquitous. Who, in this complicated affair, were the good guys, and who the bad? She could only hope she'd find out before it was too late.

Nor, on Max's return, could he come up with any ideas, though they discussed the matter till nearly midnight.

'I agree the police wouldn't take it seriously,' he said finally, switching off the bedside light, 'but I think I'll have a word with Archie, and ask him to keep an unofficial lookout.'

Archie Duncan, a detective constable with the Marsborough force, was an erstwhile student of Max's, and had discreetly helped them out before.

'That would be best,' Rona agreed sleepily, and nestled down as his arm came round her.

When Rona left for work the next morning, there'd been no further call from Louise, for which she was grateful.

Once in the archive room, she searched for, and eventually found, the old brochures Giles Stanton had mentioned, and studied them with more knowledge and interest than would have been the case before her talk with him. She also replayed the recording, making notes as she listened. Yes, she thought with satisfaction as it came to an end, she reckoned she now had enough material to write an interesting and informative article that should please both Barnie and the Willow family. Which, after all, was the point of the exercise.

Dominic was not, of course, at the Bacchus, and though Lindsey didn't mention him, Rona noticed that she looked up every time someone entered the wine bar.

'Linz, about that man who almost accosted you,' she began, when a waiter had filled their glasses and moved away.

'Accosted? That's rather strong!'

'Just listen: I think I know who he is. Or at least, I don't, but I think he's the same man who's been following me.'

Lindsey frowned. 'What man? This is the first—'

'Just listen.' Rona related her own encounters, ending with Louise's frightened phone call of the previous day.

'And you think he mistook me for you?' Lindsey exclaimed. 'My God! The times fit; he must have just left the Gallery when I saw him. And he knows something about your neighbours?'

'That's what the note implies, wouldn't you say?'

'Perhaps they're a gang of terrorists!'

'In which case, he'd surely have gone to the police. And talking of the police, Max is going to have a word with Archie Duncan. Look, I'm probably overreacting wildly about the whole thing, and I'm only telling you so you can take avoiding action if you meet this man again.'

'Believe me, he won't see me for dust. Take care, though, Ro; you're more in the firing line than I am.'

'Max is coming home every night till it's sorted out.' Rona drew a deep breath. 'Anyway, that's quite enough on the subject. Here comes our lunch. Let's enjoy it.'

Lindsey hesitated, unwilling to let the matter drop, but in view of her sister's obvious reluctance, acquiesced.

'How's it going with the Willows?' she asked instead, as they embarked on their warm chicken salad.

'Almost finished, actually – the research, that is. Now I have to write it up, but I can do that at home.'

'And you get on OK with Julian and his wife?'

'Yes; Felicity's great. She's insisted on my joining her for lunch when I'm there, which is why I repaid her by bringing her here yesterday.'

'Well, you certainly fell on your feet, having lunch cooked for you! I should hang on in there as long as you can!'

Rona's dislike of cooking, which Lindsey, an accomplished chef, was at a loss to understand, led to frequent badinage.

Rona smiled. 'They'd have been suspended in any case; Julian's cousin is descending on them for a few days. Actually, I shan't be sorry to miss her.'

'Oh?'

'I think she imposes on Felicity, who's too sweet to notice. Also –' Rona dropped her voice – 'when Max and I were in London, we saw her and Julian having dinner together, and they were all over each other.'

Lindsey raised an eyebrow. 'Not in a cousinly way?'

'Possibly a kissing-cousinly. Felicity told me that in their teens, they'd had a boy-and-girl thing going. Tara's just ended a longish relationship – or had it ended for her – and is reportedly in need of some TLC. Which Julian seems only too ready to provide.'

She gave an embarrassed laugh. 'All of which is highly slanderous. I wouldn't have dreamed of saying it to anyone else.'

'Fear not, talking to me is like talking to yourself. What's she like, this Tara?'

'Chic, sophisticated, glamorous. Everything Felicity, bless her, is not.'

Lindsey ate in silence for a minute. Then she said, 'And what's your opinion of Julian? Apart from suspecting him of adultery?'

'Hush!' Rona looked quickly round, but to her relief no one was within earshot, and those at the nearest tables were engaged in conversations of their own.

'He's all right; he's been very nice to me. I may be wrong, but I get the impression he's rather weak. Susceptible to flattery, perhaps.'

'Well, sadly there's nothing you can do. Felicity will have to stand on her own two feet – sink or swim.'

Rona smiled. 'Any more metaphors you can mix?'

'And presumably, since you'll only be in contact with them short-term, you'll never know the outcome.'

'I just hope there isn't one,' Rona said.

The only person Rona saw on her return to Oak Avenue was the daily help, a large, red-faced woman in an overall. They nodded to each other in the hall as Rona made her way to the lift. She worked steadily all afternoon, tidying such loose ends as she could and going through the relevant archives for what might well be the final time.

When she left at five thirty, she removed her teabags from the little kitchen and her bottle of milk from the fridge, unsure when or if she'd be back. She'd enjoyed working here, even without Felicity's friendship, and no one had disturbed her. That wasn't always the case at home, where her phone rang frequently and people came to the door. And as the thought entered her head, she wondered if the note had been left only because its author had received no answer to his knock. Lindsey's experience seemed to indicate he was anxious to speak to her. He might well be back.

Louise did not, as Rona had half-expected, come to meet her again when she reached home. Though relieved, she would have welcomed the assurance that there'd been no further sighting. Still, they had each other's phone numbers now, and if she was worried, Louise would no doubt contact her.

It was Wednesday, so Max would in any case have been coming home after his afternoon classes. He usually arrived about seven, and Rona, temporarily denied access to the sitting room window, awaited his return with impatience. She no longer felt at ease when alone in the house, and bitterly resented it.

But no one either phoned or came knocking at the door, and Max's return brought an easing of tension. She greeted him in the hall, and they went down to the kitchen.

'Nothing further to report?' he asked, emptying the ingredients for their meal out of a succession of carrier bags.

'No, thank heaven. I met Linz for lunch, and put her in the picture, in case he approaches her again.'

'And no further word from next door?'

'No.'

'Well, I spoke to Archie, but as I suspected, he didn't think there's much in it. He says the most likely thing is that this guy has a grudge against the Franks, and is out to make trouble for them. Apparently that's quite common, and without anything criminal occurring, it's hard for him to get involved.'

'Oh, fine. So he'd rather we were banged on the head or something?'

Max leant over and kissed her lightly. 'Let's try to keep this in perspective,' he said. 'Discussing it with Archie made me feel a lot easier. As he pointed out, if this bloke had contacted you in Yorkshire, you'd have been glad to hear from him. You were, after all, *asking* for information about these people.'

'It was you who told me under no circumstances to call him,' Rona pointed out indignantly.

'I know; I overreacted, too. But looked at objectively, it's because he's down here rather than up there that you were spooked.'

'That, and the fact that he's been following me, and Lindsey, thinking she's me. Not to mention Louise.'

'But has he? We don't know for a fact that the man you saw is the same one that Louise – or Lindsey, for that matter – came across. They could be three separate people.'

'Too much of a coincidence,' Rona said shortly.

'Possibly. But even if he's the same guy, he's not done anything *wrong*.'

'Well, I just wish he'd go and not do anything wrong somewhere else,' she said.

When Max left after breakfast, Rona seriously considered going to Oak Avenue, if only to get out of the house. But that, she felt, would be giving in to paranoia.

Halfway through the morning, she almost changed her mind. When the phone rang, she was totally focussed on John Willow and his slow but steady rise from barrow-boy to office boy, to manager, to shop-owner. Could such a thing happen nowadays, she wondered, with the present emphasis on quali-fications and training?

She reached for the phone and tucked it between her ear and shoulder, eyes still on the computer screen. 'Hello?'

'Is that Rona Parish?'

The present and its perceived perils rushed back into her consciousness. It was a man's voice, and one she didn't recog-nize.

'Who's speaking?' she asked sharply.

'You don't know me, but I must speak to you. It's very important.'

'Was it you who left the note?' she interrupted.

'Yes; I apologize for not signing it, but my name wouldn't have meant anything, and I'd much prefer to explain in person.'

'I'm sorry, I have nothing to say to you, and I'd be grateful if you didn't contact me again.'

'But it really is—'

Rona dropped the phone back on its cradle and sat staring at it, willing it not to ring again. It didn't, and after a minute she dialled 1471. As she'd expected, the number given was the same as that on the note. As the trembling set in, she called Max.

'He's been on the phone,' she said without preamble.

Max swore. 'What did he want?'

'To speak to me, about something very important.'

'You didn't agree to meet him?'

'Of course I didn't. I told him not to contact me again.' She paused. 'Do you still think I'm making too much of this?'

'What did he sound like?'

She thought back. 'It was quite an educated voice.'

'I meant, did he seem – disturbed in any way? Another of Archie's suggestions was that he might be a fan, of either your books or articles. They sometimes get obsessive, and stalk the people they admire.'

'Archie's full of bright ideas, isn't he?' Her voice shook slightly. 'Do you think he'll come here again?'

'No, I don't. He'll have got the message now, and will prob-ably try to enlist someone else.' Max hesitated. 'Do you want me to come back?'

She knew he didn't want to, that he'd been looking forward to a day's productive painting before his evening class.

'No, I'm OK. I won't open the door, and I'll let the answer-phone take any more calls. If I'd been thinking clearly, I'd have done it this time.'

'Good girl.' He sounded relieved. 'Let me know if there are any problems, and failing that, I'll see you about ten.'

'See you,' she repeated, and rang off. But John Willow had lost his fascination, and it was some time before she could dig herself back into the article.

The rest of the day passed without incident. The phone didn't ring again, and no one came to the door. Rona forced herself to concentrate on her work, and by the end of the afternoon, was quite pleased with what she'd achieved.

She went downstairs, made a cup of tea, and settled in the sitting room – away from the windows – with a library book. At seven, she phoned for a take-away from a firm she frequently used, and checked through the spy-hole that it was the usual delivery boy. She ate her meal at the kitchen table – blind across the window – then returned upstairs to watch television. Only a couple of hours till Max came home.

Then, at nine forty-five, as she was beginning to expect him, the phone did ring. She went into the hall and waited for the answerphone to cut in. Max's voice reached her.

'Pick up, darling, it's me. Look, I'm sorry, but I'm going to be late. One of the students is having trouble with her car; she can't get it to start, and nor, for that matter, can I. I don't know if you've noticed, but it's raining heavily and she lives out at Shellswick. Everyone else has gone, so I've no option but to run her home.'

'Oh, Max!' Rona glanced at her watch. 'That's a good twenty-minute drive each way!'

'I know, love, and I'm very sorry. You go to bed. I'll give you a ring when I'm on the way back. On your mobile, so you'll know it's me. See you soon.'

Dejectedly, Rona returned to the sitting room, only half-concentrating on the end of the programme she'd been watching. She then sat through the whole of the news, and at ten thirty took Gus down to the kitchen and gave him his bedtime biscuits. Without television to mask the sound, the rain now impinged on her consciousness. It was sluicing down the glass door and bouncing off the patio outside. Not a good night to be driving down narrow country lanes, she thought with a shiver.

She watched Gus finish his biscuits and contentedly climb into his basket, taking his usual time to settle himself. Then she switched off the light and went upstairs, collecting her library book from the sitting room en route. She'd follow Max's suggestion about going to bed, but she wouldn't sleep until he was home.

The bedroom curtains were blowing out through the open window, and Rona pulled them back inside. They were soaking wet, and she had a surge of longing for Greece. If only they were still there, making love in the warm, still nights with the cicadas on the veranda outside. In Greece, there had been no disturbed people who'd lost their memory and possibly their identity, no silent strangers staring in out of the darkness.

Rona pulled her T-shirt over her head and was reaching for her nightdress when the bedside phone rang. A shaft of hope went through her. Max, on his way home already? Then, with a clutch of fear, she realized it was the landline, and he'd promised to call her mobile.

Bare-footed and heart pounding, she raced down two flights of stairs to the kitchen, crossed the room in the semi-darkness, and reached the answerphone as it kicked in. In the still room, Felicity's urgent voice sounded unnaturally loud.

'Rona? Oh, please, please be there!'

Rona caught up the phone. 'I'm here, Felicity. Whatever's the matter?'

'Oh, thank God!' It came on a sob. 'It's Julian; he's been in an accident. He's seriously hurt, and my car's being serviced. I know it's a huge thing to ask, but could you take me to him?'

Rona glanced at the streaming rain outside. 'Where is he?' In Marsborough, please God; though if he were at the Royal County, Felicity could have run there in ten minutes.

'That's what I don't understand; he's at the Princess Royal, in Farnbridge.'

'*Farnbridge?*' It was at least twenty miles away.

'I know; I'm dreadfully sorry. I – I can give you directions.'

'I know the way,' Rona said slowly. 'I went to university there.'

'That's a relief. Rona, I know it's late and everything, and I hate having to ask you, but – but he could die!'

Her voice broke, and Rona heard herself say, 'I'll be there in ten minutes.'

She pulled her T-shirt back on and rang Max's mobile. *Answer it!* she screamed silently, as the dialling tone rang in her ears. But it was the voicemail that replied.

'Max, I have to take Felicity to Farnbridge. Julian's been in an accident. God knows when I'll be home. Phone me when you can.'

Only as she ran downstairs did she remember his instructions not to go out in the dark, and the reason for them. But surely no one would wait outside on the off-chance of seeing her on a night like this.

'Gus!' she called, as she struggled into her waterproof. 'Come here! Good boy!'

After a surprised pause, he came loping up the basement stairs and submitted to having his lead clipped on. Oh, *how* she didn't want to go! Rona thought. And surely Felicity had closer friends than herself, whom it would have been more natural to have called on?

But with Julian's life in the balance, there was no time for questions. With a resigned sigh, she opened the front door, put up her umbrella, and set off through the wet darkness, the dog trotting at her side.

Felicity was waiting for her at the gate, and opened the passenger door before Rona had a chance to do so.

'I can't tell you how grateful I am,' she said, pulling it shut behind her and fumbling for the seat belt. 'I've brought a flask of coffee. You're sure you know the way?'

'I'm sure.' The windows steamed up anew from Felicity's wet clothes, and Rona turned up the fan.

'Fortunately, the girl next door was able to come in,' Felicity said jerkily, as they set off. 'She often babysits for us, and if we're going to be late, stays overnight.'

A stream of cars passed the end of Oak Avenue before Rona was able to turn on to Alban Road. 'You said you don't know why Julian's in Farnbridge,' she prompted gently.

There was a long silence, and Rona wondered if, her mind elsewhere, Felicity hadn't heard her. But then she said steadily,

'There are quite a few things I don't understand, Rona. And until I have a clearer picture, I'd rather not broadcast them; which is why – unfairly, I know – I called on you. In our circle, rumours fly like wildfire.'

They had passed Market Street, and were now driving up the northern stretch of Alban Road, their windscreen wipers, though working frenetically, unable to keep the glass clear. On the pavements, crowds, just out of the theatre or cinema, struggled with umbrellas, and streetlights threw great globules of light on to the wet road. It was slow going in the heavy traffic, and Rona could feel Felicity's desperate frustration.

Then, in a flat voice, Felicity said, 'I'm sorry; you deserve an explanation, and I know you'll be discreet. Julian went to London this morning, by train. His car's at the station. At least, I assume it is. That's the point, you see; I can't think why he was in a car at all, let alone up in Farnbridge. He told me he'd several meetings, would stay on for a business dinner, and spend the night at his club.'

Rona, with a sideways glance at her set face, remained silent.

'A parallel story, which I keep assuring myself has no connection,' Felicity continued, 'is that, as I told you, Tara's attending a reunion dinner in Farnbridge this evening.'

Oh God, Rona thought, on a wave of pity. As if her husband's accident wasn't enough, Felicity had this additional burden.

Instead of making any comment – and what could she say? – she asked, 'What exactly did the hospital say, when they phoned you?'

'That there'd been a serious accident just outside the town. An RTA, they called it. No other vehicle was involved; apparently the car had skidded on the wet road and gone into a tree.' She added inconsequentially, 'The roads are always dangerous when it rains after a long dry spell. There's oil on the surface, I think.'

'Did they say where he was hurt?'

'Severe facial cuts and – and internal injuries.'

She was quiet for a while, and Rona saw she was crying. She switched on the radio, tuned to Classic FM, in a silent gesture of sympathy.

They were turning on to the ring-road when Max phoned.

Rona plugged in her hands-free device, desperate to hear his voice.

'Where are you?' he asked at once. 'Are you all right?'

Conscious of Felicity beside her, Rona answered as briefly and concisely as she could.

'And where are you?' she asked then.

'Almost home. I tried to phone earlier, but couldn't get a signal. Driving conditions are appalling, aren't they? For God's sake take care, darling, and I hope things aren't as bad as you fear at the hospital. You'll keep me informed?'

'I'll try, but I shan't be able to use my mobile. If I don't manage it, I'll ring you as we're leaving.'

As she used the plural pronoun, she wondered whether in fact Felicity would be spending the night at the hospital. It seemed more than likely.

'Do that, and if you can give me an idea of when you'll get back, I'll meet you at the garage.'

As she rang off, Felicity took out her own mobile. 'I'll see if there's any more news,' she said tremulously.

Apparently there wasn't; Julian was still in the operating theatre. Felicity told whoever it was that she'd be there in about twenty minutes – an optimistic estimate, Rona feared – and broke the connection. The rain was easing off slightly, and she reduced the speed of the windscreen wipers. Their wheels hissed along the wet ground, and, without the benefit of streetlights, they were dependent on the gold path carved out by their headlights. Rona prayed they wouldn't meet any oncoming traffic on the narrow roads.

It was like a nightmare, she thought, driving through the wet darkness, not knowing what awaited them at their destination. On the back seat, Gus stirred sleepily, then settled down again. Houses began to appear, and streetlights, and at last they were approaching Farnbridge.

It was only as, having left Gus in the car, they were hurrying across the hospital forecourt, that Rona remembered Felicity's flask of coffee, never opened. She'd have welcomed it now.

Twelve

A hospital at night is not the most cheerful of places. Having announced themselves at Reception, Rona and Felicity were led down long, dimly-lit corridors to the relatives' room. There was no one inside, though the cushions on the sofa were dented, and there were polystyrene cups half-full of coffee. Rona couldn't help wondering what news had awaited those previous occupants.

After about five minutes, a white-coated doctor came in and smiled at them gravely.

'Mrs Willow?'

Felicity sprang to her feet. 'Yes; how's my husband?'

Her eyes begged him for good news, but he answered quietly, 'It's still too early to tell. I can, however, report that the operation went well, which is a step in the right direction.' He paused. 'I don't know whether you realize, Mrs Willow, that your husband wasn't the driver of the car?'

Felicity stared at him, moistening her lips. 'I – hadn't really thought about it,' she stammered. Then, with rising urgency, 'Was someone else hurt?'

'Yes, the woman with him. We've established her identity, but so far have been unable to trace any next of kin. I was wondering—'

'Tara?' whispered Felicity fearfully.

The doctor looked relieved. 'You do know her; that's what we hoped. Perhaps you can tell us whom we could contact?'

There was a long silence, and the doctor looked at her enquiringly. 'Mrs Willow?' Then, more gently, 'Perhaps you'd like to sit down again?'

Carefully, Felicity lowered herself to a chair. 'She's my husband's cousin,' she said with an effort.

'Excellent. Then if I send someone along, you'll be able to supply all the necessary details?'

'How badly hurt is she?'

'She has chest injuries from the steering wheel, but, unlike your husband's, they're not life-threatening. Shall I take you to her?'

'No,' Felicity said sharply. 'I want to see my husband.'

'I understand that, but he's not yet regained consciousness; and your cousin is very distressed. She feels responsible for the accident, and keeps asking after your husband. She's not been told of his condition.'

Felicity's hands knotted in her lap. 'Is his life still in danger?'

'The next few hours are crucial,' the doctor said, with professional caution, 'but the signs are hopeful. That's really all I can say at this stage. If you'd like to see him now, I'll find someone to take you to him. And after that, perhaps . . .?'

His voice tailed off enquiringly, but Felicity gave no assurances, and after a moment, he nodded and left the room.

Into the sudden silence, Rona said, 'She probably wanted a partner at the dinner.'

'Then why did they both make a secret of it? And where were they planning to spend the night? They must have just left the university.' Felicity caught her breath as another thought struck her. 'If she'd been drinking, I'll kill her,' she said.

There was a tap on the door and a nurse came in, smiling brightly. 'I'll take you to your husband now, Mrs Willow.'

Felicity rose quickly, but at the door she stopped and looked back. 'You will stay, won't you, Rona? At least until I know he's going to be all right?'

'Of course I will,' Rona said.

Knowing Felicity, she felt pretty sure she would go to Tara, after satisfying herself on Julian's condition. Though hurt and deceived, there was no vindictiveness in her. In the meantime, Rona ventured out into the corridor in search of the coffee machine.

Dominic said lazily, 'I'd almost forgotten how good we are together.'

Carla laughed and lay back on the pillows. 'You mean I'm an adequate enough stop-gap, while you're between lovers.'

He smiled, smoothing back her damp hair. 'You underestimate yourself. But between lovers is where I'll be remaining for the foreseeable future. After the Miranda scare, I shall take things very slowly for a very long time.'

'What of the fair Lindsey?'

'We'll have to wait and see, shan't we? I met her sister, did I tell you? A highly intelligent young woman. As to Lindsey, no doubt she'll be at the Yarborough drinks party tomorrow.'

'So you'll take her?'

'She won't need an escort; she lives only a hundred yards down the road.'

'That's not the point, though, is it?'

'Are you trying to push me into the arms of another woman?' he demanded, mock-seriously. 'Don't tell me you're already tiring of my attentions!'

'I've a feeling you might lose that one, if you're too offhand. As I said, she has other irons in the fire.'

'I'll bear that in mind,' he said.

As Rona had expected, Felicity opted to remain at the hospital. She returned after some forty minutes to renew her thanks and let Rona know her decision.

'He's just come round, but he's very groggy. He – was able to squeeze my hand.'

Tara was not mentioned, and Rona dared not enquire.

'I'm so very sorry to have dragged you into this, Rona. You've been a true friend, and I'm extremely grateful. I only hope you're not too tired, now, to drive home.'

'I'll be fine. I had as strong a coffee as I could get out of the machine. But what a relief, that he seems to have turned the corner.'

Felicity gave her a quick hug. 'I'll phone you tomorrow, with an update.'

The rain had stopped by the time she left, and she released Gus from the car and walked with him round the perimeter of the car park, pausing halfway to phone Max.

'Yes?' His voice was thick with sleep.

'It's me,' she said ungrammatically. 'I'm just about to set off.'

'What time is it?'

'Five past one. I should be back by two.'

'How's the patient?'

Now wasn't the time to explain about Tara. 'Out of the woods, I think. At any rate, he's regained consciousness.'

'That's good news. And what about you? You must be exhausted.'

'Not too bad. I'm walking Gus round the car park, and the fresh air's helped. It's stopped raining, thank goodness.'

'Well, drive carefully, and give me a ring as you're coming into Marsborough. I'll meet you at the garage.'

'You don't have to,' she protested, not very convincingly.

'Yes, I do. I'm not having my wife walking the streets alone in the night watches.'

'Bless you, then. See you soon.'

By the time the car was garaged and they'd walked home, both Max and Rona felt wide awake.

'Would you like something to drink?' he asked, closing and locking the front door.

'Yes, please; something hot, I think; it seems more appropriate at this time of night.'

'Appropriate nothing,' Max retorted. 'You have your cocoa by all means, but I'm ready for a nightcap.'

Gus disappeared the moment his lead was unclipped, and by the time they reached the kitchen, he was curled up in his basket. They both laughed.

'He doesn't approve of unsociable hours,' Max said. 'Now, fill me in with the details. What was Julian doing in that neck of the woods?'

So, seated at the kitchen table, Rona told him the full story – or as much as she knew of it.

'We were right, then,' Max commented, holding his whisky to the light to admire its richness of colour. 'They *were* playing away from home.'

'It looks like it. I feel dreadfully sorry for Felicity. She's so sweet and trusting – she doesn't deserve this.'

'What do you think will happen?'

'Oh, she'll forgive him. I'm quite sure he's no intention of leaving her; he just wanted to have his cake and eat it.'

'But presumably Tara will be persona non grata from now on.'

'I'm not even sure of that; once the dust has settled, I wouldn't be surprised if she's back.'

Max shook his head wonderingly. 'Would you be so understanding, if I went off the rails?'

'You'd better not believe it. I'd tear you limb from limb,' she said.

Fortunately, Friday was the one day Max had no commitments. With the alarm switched off, it was after ten when they awoke, and they were still in their dressing gowns when Felicity phoned from the hospital.

'He's out of danger,' she said at once, 'but they'll be keeping him in for a while. I've booked into a local B and B, at least for the weekend. My parents-in-law are holding the fort at home.'

'And Tara?' Rona asked.

'Is also making good progress.'

'That's good,' she said lamely.

'There are one or two things you should know,' Felicity went on, her tone neutral, 'but they can wait till I see you. In the meantime, I know I can trust your discretion.'

'Of course. Give Julian my best wishes, and I'm so glad he's improving.'

After an improvised brunch, Max went to Farthings for an afternoon's painting and Rona worked on her article. Once or twice, she looked out of the window to see if any of the Franks were in their garden, but despite the return of the sunshine, there was no sign of them. Only the ginger cat lay basking on the warm stone.

Had Louise mentioned Karen? Rona wondered. Perhaps she'd been the key to the whole mystery, harmony was now restored, and in the general relief, Louise had omitted to tell her. But her curiosity could only be contained for so long; if there was still no word by Sunday evening, Rona resolved either to phone her or call round.

From her first-floor flat, Lindsey watched the succession of cars drawing up at the Yarboroughs' house on the corner. Fairhaven, the cul-de-sac where they lived, was a fifteen-minute drive from the centre of Marsborough, and contained only eight detached houses. The original intention had been to build more, together with a school and a parade of shops, but money ran out and the plans fell through. Designed to appeal to all members of the community, the houses were of different sizes and styles, Lindsey's and one other being built as two flats.

She sighed, wishing she hadn't accepted this invitation and unsure how many, apart from immediate neighbours, she would know. It was a pity, if understandable, that Rona and Max had declined.

Still idly watching the arrivals, she thought over her last conversation with her sister, about the strange man she'd met outside the office. Was he really a stalker, and what was his connection with Rona's neighbours? It was a constant surprise to Lindsey that Rona's unexceptional line of work should so often bring her into contact with unsavoury characters.

She glanced at her watch. No point in delaying any further. Picking up her handbag, the bottle of wine and the potted plant, she set off, with mixed feelings, for the house at the end of the road.

At first sight, Adele Yarborough looked no different from the last time Lindsey had seen her, shortly before her breakdown. Her pointed little face was as pretty as ever, enhanced only by the lightest application of lipstick; the ash-blonde hair was still in its gamine style, and the large, slate-grey eyes met Lindsey's only briefly before, as always, shying away. Moreover, Lindsey noted with unease that the dress she wore had the long sleeves that had so worried Max, concealing, as they then did, unexplained bruises and cuts that later proved to have been self-inflicted.

She hoped the psychiatric treatment had indeed been successful, and that the long sleeves were now simply habit. Nonetheless, they seemed incongruous in the warmth of the August evening.

Adele was exclaiming with delight over the proffered plant, as, still avoiding eye-contact, she ushered Lindsey into a surprisingly empty room. Then Philip came through the patio doors, and was handed the bottle of wine.

'So glad you could come, Lindsey,' he greeted her. 'Everyone seems to have drifted outside, if you'd like to join them. What can I get you? There's Pimm's, red, white or rosé wine, or soft drinks.'

'Pimm's would be lovely, thanks.'

'Right; you go on, and I'll bring it out to you.'

Lindsey moved across the room, from where she could see groups of people standing chatting on the lawn. Hoping to spot a face she recognized, she stepped outside, to find her wish immediately granted: the first person she saw was Jonathan Hurst.

His face lit up at the sight of her, and, excusing himself from the people he was with, he hurried over and kissed her cheek.

'I wasn't expecting to see you,' she told him.

'Oh, Philip and I go way back. We knew each other in Stokely, in the old days.'

Of course; she remembered now. Incredible though it seemed, at one time Rona had suspected both Jonathan and Philip of murder, another example of her sister's topsy-turvy world.

'Your wife not with you?' she asked casually, her eyes searching the various groups.

'No; Tamar's running a slight temperature, and although she'd have been fine with the babysitter, Carol elected to stay home. She's like a mother hen if the kids aren't well.' He smiled. 'As things have turned out, though, it's all for the best.'

Philip appeared with Lindsey's Pimm's. 'I'm sorry Rona and Max couldn't make it,' he said, 'but I think you'll know quite a few people. Most of the neighbours are here, for a start.'

Lindsey nodded, recognizing the Sinclairs from number five, and Barry and Brian, the gay couple from the flat below her own. Barry, catching her eye across the lawn, gave her a cheerful wave.

Lindsey hadn't been out here before, and saw that, being a corner site, the garden was fairly large. At the far end, partially screened by a couple of fruit trees, she could make out a swing and climbing frame, bringing unwelcome memories of her traumatic meetings with the Yarborough children. She could only hope they bore no scars from their mother's illness.

'Well, well,' Jonathan said softly, breaking into her reflections, 'look who's here.'

And she turned, to see Dominic standing in the doorway.

He smiled and came towards them, shaking hands formally with first Lindsey, then Jonathan. So that's how he wants to play it, Lindsey thought; fine by me.

'Carla not with you?' Jonathan asked.

'No; nor Carol with you?'

Jonathan shook his head. 'One of the kids is ill.'

Unreasonably, Lindsey felt her irritation rising. Well, she'd told Rona she'd given up on Dominic; now was the time to suit her action to her words, and, seeing a familiar face across the garden, she seized her chance. 'Will you excuse me?' she broke in. 'I want a word with Rosemary.'

Threading her way between the groups, she felt a fierce satisfaction at the surprise she'd glimpsed on both their faces. Now, she thought savagely, they could talk about their women to their hearts' content.

Rosemary Shaw, Head of English at Marsborough High, lived in one of the other flats. Lindsey knew her only slightly, but she was pleasant and friendly, and at the moment served her purpose well.

During the next half-hour or so, the groups formed and reformed as people moved about, greeting friends and being introduced to strangers, and Lindsey, careful to keep her eyes on those closest to her, was consequently unaware of Dominic's steady and continuing attention.

Her abrupt departure as soon as he'd joined them had left him baffled. Granted, it was a while since he'd been in touch, but there'd been similar intervals before. Perhaps, he thought, with a touch of unease, Carla was right, and he'd overplayed his hand. He was surprised, and not a little disconcerted, to discover how much the possibility disturbed him. He'd also noted that his companion seemed equally put out, and Hurst's eyes had followed Lindsey as she moved away from them with an expression that, Dominic suspected, mirrored his own.

Was there something going on between them? he'd wondered suddenly. It had been Hurst who'd first introduced them, oddly enough at another party, having insisted on dragging himself and Carla across the room to meet her. It now occurred to Dominic that this might have been an excuse to get close to Lindsey himself. Perhaps – an unpleasant thought – Hurst was what Carla referred to as one of Lindsey's 'other irons in the fire'.

As the evening progressed, and he talked and smiled with a succession of people, none of whom he knew, his thoughts continued their less than comfortable analysis, forcing him to admit that he'd never before felt the need to hold a woman at a distance, as he had with Lindsey. He'd been attracted to her since that first meeting, so why hadn't he followed it up in the normal manner? Miranda was no excuse; it was at the tail-end of their relationship, and he'd not then known of her pregnancy. Was it because, subconsciously, he'd sensed right from the beginning that this woman might, if he weren't careful, become important to him – a situation he was anxious to avoid?

Avril was also in the garden that evening. Though rain was forecast for later, there was no sign of it, and since it might never materialize, she set about watering the plants, wondering, as she did so, what her daughters were doing. It seemed a long time since she'd seen them. Was it too late to invite them for lunch tomorrow?

The house had seemed very quiet since Sarah left. Avril had offered her the opportunity of coming back for a day or two during the holidays, should she want to see Clive, but had so far heard nothing. Perhaps she and her father were away on holiday. And before she could stop them, her thoughts turned to Guy Lacey and the evening they'd spent together. It was a long time till September, when he might possibly be coerced by Sarah into bringing back her music centre.

Well, no use building any fantasies there; he'd given her no foundation for them. Resignedly, she replaced the watering can and went indoors to phone her daughters.

At about nine o'clock a trestle table was set up on the patio, and an impressive selection of food carried out. Lindsey felt a hand under her elbow, and found Jonathan at her side.

'I've bagged us a table against the wall,' he told her. 'If you'd like to go and claim it, I'll bring the food.'

'You don't know what I'd like,' Lindsey objected.

'I've a pretty good idea, but I'll bring a wide selection.'

She hesitated, but then, over his shoulder, she saw Dominic watching them.

'OK,' she said, giving Jonathan a smile. 'Thanks.'

There were four chairs at the table, and as Lindsey waited for him, she wondered, with mixed emotions, if Dominic would join them. But it was Margaret Sinclair who came over.

'Well done you, nabbing a table!' she smiled. 'Mind if we join you?'

'Please do,' Lindsey said.

Douglas, she saw, was just behind Jonathan in the food queue. He was a GP at a group practice in town, and Margaret was a theatre nurse at the Royal County.

'Adele seems great, doesn't she?' Margaret observed, watching their hostess as she served her guests.

'Is that a social or medical opinion?' Lindsey queried.

'Both, I'd say, though, like you, I can only go by what I see. Philip's had a difficult time, hasn't he, but he's coped magnificently.'

Lindsey nodded noncommittally. Margaret had no way of knowing the extent to which Adele's breakdown had affected her own family.

The men returned with laden plates, and Lindsey introduced Jonathan as a colleague from work. He raised an amused eyebrow at her, and went on to explain his long friendship with Philip. It turned out that Douglas had also been born in Stokely, and a discussion followed on the attributes of the town, past and present.

Meanwhile the savoury dishes were followed by a delicious selection of desserts, and Lindsey wondered uncharitably who had prepared them. She was pretty certain it wasn't Adele.

They had just finished eating when there was a loud clap of thunder, followed almost immediately by a torrential downpour of rain. Laughing and exclaiming, they all made a dash for the house, shaking the heavy drops off their clothes.

In the mêlée Lindsey had become separated from Jonathan and the Sinclairs, and as people continued to push their way into the room, found herself beside Dominic. She glanced quickly about her, but they were hemmed in a corner and there was no means of retreat. To her embarrassment, she realized he'd seen her search for escape.

'You seem much in demand this evening,' he said evenly.

'This is my home ground, as you know.'

'Yes; I thought you'd be here.'

'You had the advantage of me, then. How do you know the Yarboroughs?'

'I met Philip at the golf club, and we've had some business dealings.'

Lindsey realized she still didn't know what Dominic did,

but she'd no intention of asking. There was a pause, then he said, 'I saw your sister the other day.'

'Oh?' She wasn't going to admit prior knowledge.

'Having lunch at the Bacchus,' he continued, 'with Mrs Willow.'

That, he saw, had caught her attention. 'Yes,' she said, with what seemed to him studied casualness, 'she's researching the history of their firm for an article. She was up in Yorkshire last week, meeting their relatives, the Earl and Countess of Roxford and their daughter.'

Her eyes moved slowly and expressionlessly over his face. 'Friends of yours, I believe.'

So that was it. Dominic felt a spurt of annoyance, the more so since he hadn't known of the family connection.

'Indeed,' he confirmed, and, stung by her coolness to exaggerate his acquaintance with the earl, added, 'I had lunch with Rupert the other day.'

So they *were* still in touch. Lindsey felt like bursting into tears. Instead, she gave him a dazzling smile.

'If you'll excuse me, I think Jonathan has my glass,' she said, and finally managed to evade him.

She and Jonathan left together shortly afterwards. Dominic watched them go, wondering if they were bound for her conveniently close flat. He also thought, sourly, of Carol Hurst, a thoroughly nice and uncomplicated woman, and tried to think harshly of Lindsey. Instead, he succeeded only in envying her companion.

'Have you seen Louise?' Max asked the next morning, hanging Gus's lead on its hook.

'No, why?'

'I noticed their front door was ajar, and thought she might have popped round.'

'Actually, I'm surprised she's not been in touch. I'll give her a ring tomorrow.' She glanced at him. 'It's time we were leaving. Are you ready?'

'Just about. Is Lindsey going?'

'I don't know; she was out when Mum rang, so she left a message. She'd have been at the Yarboroughs', of course.'

'Rather her than me,' Max replied. 'What about Gus?'

'I think we can risk it; Mum's much more amenable these days.'

'How did the party go?' Rona asked her sister later, as they sat over drinks. Avril had taken Max to look at the black spot on her roses – a pointless exercise, in Rona's opinion. Gardening was not her husband's forté.

'Actually, it was an *embarrass de richesse*,' Lindsey replied ruefully. 'Both Jonathan and Dominic were there.'

'Whoops!'

'Whoops indeed.'

'Who came out the winner?'

'Jonathan, of course. I told you I'd written Dominic off.'

'Is he aware of that?'

'If he wasn't, he should be by now.' She paused. 'He said he'd met you and Felicity, so I told him you'd been up to see the Roxfords.'

'Oh Linz, you didn't!'

'I wanted to see what he'd say.'

'And what did he?'

Lindsey kicked at the grass at her feet. 'That he'd had lunch with "Rupert" the other day. So it seems Lady M is still present tense.'

Rona glanced at her face, decided against a direct comment, and asked instead, 'And Jonathan?'

'Escorted me home.'

'As far as the door?' Rona enquired, with innocently raised brow.

'What do you think? It was too good a chance to miss.'

And one in the eye for Dominic, Rona suspected. Feeling it was wiser not to pursue the subject, she asked, 'How was Adele?'

'Exactly the same, even down to the long sleeves.'

Rona pulled a face. 'Better not tell Max that. Seriously, though, she looked OK?'

'Fine – the perfect hostess. I doubt if she had any hand in the food, though; much too professional.'

'Probably Waitrose!' Rona said with a laugh.

It was a pleasant, salady lunch, less formal than Avril's Sunday repasts, and they all relaxed, glad of a respite from their various preoccupations. The previous night's thunder had cleared the air, and it felt fresher than it had for weeks. Lindsey told her mother about the singles holiday she'd booked.

'What a coincidence!' Avril exclaimed. 'I was considering that myself, but I wasn't brave enough.'

'Then why not book the same one?' Lindsey suggested, and her mother's face lit up.

'You wouldn't mind?'

'Not as long as you promise not to cramp my style!'

Avril laughed. 'And the same goes for me!'

They left at six o'clock.

'That was good of Lindsey, to suggest your mother join her on holiday,' Max said.

'Yes. It obviously meant a lot to Mum.' Rona felt a glow of pleasure. It wasn't often that Max found anything to admire in her sister.

They garaged the car and walked slowly home, Gus trotting contentedly beside them. Next week, Rona was thinking, she'd probably finish her article on the Willows. Then she'd have to think of another project.

Beside her, Max came to a sudden halt. 'That's odd,' he said.

Rona glanced at him. 'What is?'

He nodded up the path of the Franks' house. 'The door's still open.'

After a moment, Rona said uncertainly, 'They can't have noticed.'

'But they must have; it's been over six hours.'

They hesitated, looking at each other.

'Ought we to check everything's all right?' Rona asked reluctantly.

'It wouldn't do any harm. Stay there while I let Gus in.'

Rona waited while he opened their own front door and nudged the dog inside. Then, as he rejoined her, they went in silence up the path of number seventeen.

Thirteen

'Ring the bell,' Rona said.

Max did so, and they could hear it echoing through the house. They waited a minute or two, but no one came.

'Perhaps someone broke in while they were out,' Rona suggested.

'Possibly.' Max pushed open the door, stepped inside, and called, 'Hello? Anybody home?'

There was no reply. He turned and looked at her. 'Now what do we do? Phone the police?'

'They could be in the garden.'

'So how do we check?'

'Access is from the kitchen, like at home.'

Max hesitated. 'I don't like just walking into someone's house.'

'Well, if it was the other way round, I'd be glad if someone checked on *our* open door.'

'OK. You lead the way, then.'

They called once more, and when there was still no response, Rona started down the basement stairs. At the entrance to the kitchen, she stopped abruptly and Max cannoned into her.

'What is it?'

'Someone's in here,' Rona said in a whisper. 'Mr Franks.'

'He *must* have heard us.' Max raised his voice, directing it at the figure seated at the table. Rona saw, to her bewilderment, that he was wearing pyjamas.

'Mr Franks? It's Max Allerdyce, from next door. Did you know your front door was open?'

There was no response.

'Perhaps he's ill,' Rona said sharply, and they both moved forward.

Max said, 'Are you all right, sir?' But as he laid a tentative hand on the man's shoulder, he slumped forward across the table, almost spilling a mug half-full of coffee.

Rona instinctively leapt back, her heart in her mouth. After a moment's startled surprise, Max placed his fingers against Franks' neck, then his wrist. He looked back at her, his face suddenly white.

'There's no pulse, Rona. He's – dead!'

Shock slammed into her. 'He can't be!' she stammered.

'There's not much doubt; he feels quite cold, poor chap. Most probably a heart attack.'

'Then where are the others?' She looked about her wildly.

Together, they stared at the lifeless figure sprawled across the table, wondering what best to do. Max said, 'It seems a bit presumptive, my phoning for an ambulance. Should we wait till they get back? It's not as though anything can be done for him.'

Rona tried to marshal her thoughts. 'Let's have a quick look round; there may be some clue as to where they've gone.'

Glad to put some space between themselves and the late Mr Franks, they returned to the ground floor and glanced into the two rooms. Both were empty, though there were glasses on the sitting room table, containing the sticky remnants of alcohol.

They paused at the bottom of the stairs, wondering whether or not they were justified in looking further. Then Rona gave an exclamation.

'What's that?' she asked sharply. On the bottom step were several drops of what looked suspiciously like blood. Her voice rose. 'Max, I don't like this.'

'Nor do I, but we'll have to investigate. Someone may be hurt up there. You wait here.'

'Not on your life! I'm coming with you.'

She reached for his hand and, fearful now of what they might find, they went upstairs, carefully avoiding further splodges on the way.

Max cleared his throat. 'Presumably the parents have the front room, and Louise the equivalent of your study?'

'I should think so.'

He knocked on the door of the master bedroom, but by this time neither of them expected a reply. He pushed the door open, then stiffened. Rona, peering over his shoulder, saw Mrs Franks seated at the dressing table. She was wearing a pale pink dressing gown, and her back was towards them. But her head drooped, and the mirror reflected a white face and closed eyes.

'Not *both* of them!' Rona whispered.

Almost perfunctorily, Max went over and checked for a pulse. He shook his head, then scanned the floor around him. 'The blood hasn't come from here,' he said, 'and I didn't see any in the kitchen.'

'Louise!'

Before he could stop her, Rona had turned and flung open the door of the smaller bedroom. Though, thankfully, it contained no body, this was clearly the source of the blood. A metallic smell was emanating from a large stain on the floor, and beside it, crumpled and smeared with more blood, lay a discarded nightdress.

She held on to the door for support. 'Oh God, Max,' she whispered. 'What has he done to her?'

'Not to mention her parents,' Max answered grimly. 'One heart attack I could accept; two seems too much of a coincidence, especially in view of this.'

She stared at him, horrified. 'You think they were *murdered*?'

'It looks more than likely, wouldn't you say?'

'But – there was no sign of injury, was there, on either of them?'

'Not at first glance, but that's hardly the point. And now I really am going to phone the police.'

He took out his mobile, but Rona said faintly, 'Could we go home and phone from there? I've had enough of this place!'

'Of course. Sorry, darling.'

He took her arm and led her back downstairs and out of this suddenly sinister house. Gus was awaiting them in the hall, tail wagging. Neither of them noticed him. They went into the sitting room and Rona half-fell into one of the chairs.

'You said, "What has he done to her?"' Max commented. 'Who were you referring to?'

Rona looked dazed. 'I think I meant her father; she'd been afraid of him, and the stress of whatever happened could have brought on his heart attack.' She looked up, her eyes widening. 'But if the Franks were *murdered*, then surely it must have been the prowler?'

Max lifted his shoulders helplessly. 'They'll want a description of Louise,' he said. 'What does she look like?'

Stumblingly, Rona told him.

'Right. I'll make the call, then I'll get us a stiff drink. God knows we need it.'

He went into the hall and she heard him speaking on the phone. She was finding it hard to process what she'd just seen, the sheer enormity of it. What could possibly have triggered such carnage? And, overlaying all the horror, came the urgent, all-important question: what had happened to Louise?

Max came back into the room, carrying a tray with two glasses. 'OK, they'll be over here as soon as. In the meantime, get this down you. It should help.'

She nodded, continuing her line of thought. 'They were in their night clothes and the beds were unmade, in both rooms. They'd been slept in, but not made this morning; which seems to imply that whatever it was happened during the night.'

She shuddered. 'Suppose they heard a noise downstairs; they could have gone down to investigate. Whoever it was heard them coming, hid somewhere, and they thought it was a false alarm. Mr Franks made some coffee, and then, from wherever he'd been hiding . . .'

'Have another drink,' Max said gently.

Shying away from the picture she'd painted, Rona backtracked. 'I've not heard from Louise since Tuesday, when she phoned about the stalker. The last thing I said to her was that I'd be in touch. And I haven't been, Max. If I'd gone round, I might have been able to prevent this.'

'And how exactly do you work that out? Listen, darling, there's no way this is anything to do with you.'

'If Archie Duncan hadn't been so dismissive—'

'And you can't blame him, either. With what we had, none of us could have foreseen this. It's a ghastly mess, but you can stop worrying about it; it's up to the police now to sort it out.'

Within minutes, it seemed, there was the sound of cars drawing up outside, and their doorbell sounded. Max went to answer it, to find two uniformed officers on the step.

'Mr Allerdyce?'

'Yes.'

'Sergeant Jacobs and Constable Manning, Marsborough Police.' They held up their warrant cards. 'You rang in to report an incident, sir?'

'That's right; next door.' Max nodded towards number seventeen. 'I left the door on the latch for you.'

'Thank you, sir. I'll have to ask you to make a brief statement, I'm afraid.'

'Oh. Yes, of course. Come in.'

The policemen removed their hats and followed Max into the sitting room, where Max introduced them to Rona.

'They want a statement,' he explained, waving Jacobs to a sofa while the constable seated himself on an upright chair and took out his notebook.

'We have to begin with your full names, address, and dates of birth.'

They supplied them.

'Occupations?'

'I'm an artist, and I also teach art. My wife's a writer.'

Jacobs glanced at Rona. 'You were with your husband when he found the deceased, ma'am?'

'I was, yes.'

'Then we'll treat this as a joint statement.' He turned to Max. 'You stated on the phone, sir, that the deceased are a Mr and Mrs Franks?'

'That's right, yes.'

'First names?'

Max glanced at Rona, who supplied, 'Keith and Barbara.' The constable wrote it down.

'And you say their daughter is missing; was she also resident in the house?'

'Yes,' Rona confirmed. 'And we're very worried about her.'

'What age would she be, ma'am?'

'Mid-thirties, I'd say; but she's very vulnerable, because she has amnesia.'

Under his prompting, Rona recounted what she knew about Louise, which seemed depressingly little.

Jacobs then turned to Max. 'You wouldn't happen to have an address for their next of kin, sir?'

'No, I'm sorry; we hardly knew them.'

'We'll need formal identification,' Jacobs went on speculatively. 'Would you be prepared to step in?'

Max shook his head quickly. 'As I said, we hardly knew them. Surely there's someone more qualified—?'

'We'll come back to that, sir. So exactly how did you come to find them?'

Max detailed the day's happenings, with periodic interruptions for clarification: the time he'd first seen the open door, where they'd been in the interim before noticing it again.

When the account had been brought up to date, Manning passed his notebook to Jacobs, who glanced at it before handing it on to Max. 'I'd like you both to read this carefully, and if you agree it's a true record of what you've told us, please sign it.'

They did so.

'Thank you. This will be typed out, and if you call in at the station on Monday, you can both sign that as well. In the meantime, we'll run you down there now; there's a car outside.'

Max frowned. 'Is that necessary? You have our statement.'

'CID need to interview you,' Jacobs explained. 'And if you've no objection, we'll have a look round while you're gone.'

'Here, you mean?' Max's voice rose indignantly. 'What on earth for?'

'Just routine, sir.' The man held his eye, and Max, remembering police series on TV, envisaged a search warrant should he refuse.

'Feel free,' he said with a touch of bitterness. 'It didn't occur to me that being a responsible citizen would result in being treated as a suspect. Short-sighted of me, no doubt.'

His sarcasm was wasted; Jacobs merely opened the front door, and nodded to some men waiting at the gate. 'They'll lock up when they've finished,' he said.

Max, grim-faced, did not reply.

The next hour or so had an unreal quality. Rona, having been through similar procedures in the past, was less fazed than Max, and threw him an encouraging smile as they were led to separate interview rooms.

She took her place at a table, and minutes later two plain-clothes officers came into the room, introducing themselves as DS Curtis and DC Fowler. The sergeant was a red-faced man in his forties, with curly brown hair and a local accent.

The constable, shifting about to get comfortable, was older and considerably heavier, and, from the beads of perspiration on his face, suffering the effects of the warm evening.

'Now,' Curtis began, 'in your own words, exactly what happened this evening?'

So Rona told him about Max having noticed the open door earlier in the day, and their concern to find it still ajar on their return hours later.

'You left your house at what time, Mrs Allerdyce?'

'Twelve, twelve fifteen.'

'To go where?'

'To my mother's, for lunch. She lives in Belmont.' At his request, she gave Avril's name and full address.

'And you returned when?'

'About six thirty.'

'Right. So what action did you take?'

Bracing herself, Rona described their calling the Franks' names, receiving no reply, and going downstairs to check the garden. There she stopped, closing her eyes as, in her mind's eye, she saw Keith slump lifelessly across the table.

'Would you like a glass of water, ma'am?'

'Thank you, I think I should.'

Curtis nodded to Fowler, and the interview was suspended until he returned with it. Rona took a grateful sip, and continued with her account. When, having described the blood in Louise's room, she came to a halt, Curtis asked, 'Do you remember if you or your husband touched anything in the house?'

'Well, the front door, of course, and the bedroom doors, which were both shut.'

'We'll need your fingerprints for elimination purposes.'

'And my husband checked for a pulse in each case,' Rona added, remembering.

'He didn't move the bodies?' The question came sharply.

'Not intentionally; but when we first saw Mr Franks, Max touched him on the shoulder, which is when he fell forward.'

Curtis tapped his pen on the table. 'You'd have known them quite well, since you were neighbours?'

'Actually, no. The house is rented, and they've only been there a few weeks.'

'So they arrived when?'

'About a month ago. I don't know the exact date, but the

letting agents could tell you. They came from Canada, and
were looking to buy somewhere in the area.'

'Do you know where in Canada, madam?'

'Toronto, I think.'

'Even so, you must have seen quite a lot of them, living
so close?'

'They were very reserved. I knew their daughter better.' But
not that well, she reflected sadly.

'Ah yes, the daughter. What can you tell us about her?'

A little reluctantly, Rona repeated what she'd already told
Jacobs, of Louise's accident and subsequent loss of memory,
her uncertainty about her identity, and Rona's own research
up in Harrogate, while the detectives listened attentively.

She went on to tell them of the mysterious stranger who'd
stared in at her, and who Louise had claimed followed her
round the town last Tuesday, finishing her account with the
receipt of the note and phone call.

'My husband did have a word with DS Duncan,' she ended,
half-accusingly, 'but he didn't think there was anything to
worry about.'

Curtis frowned. 'Do you still have the note, Mrs
Allerdyce?'

'Yes, I kept it. I'm not sure why.'

'Would you hand it to the officer who drives you home?
We might get something from it, though no doubt his mobile
will be Pay As You Go and untraceable.' He thought for a
minute. 'He didn't give his name?'

'No. He said it wouldn't mean anything, and he'd prefer
us to meet face to face.'

'Can you describe him?'

'Thirties, medium height, brown hair. He was wearing a
pink shirt when I saw him.'

'And he claimed, both on the phone and in the note, to
know something about the Franks?'

She shook her head. 'Not on the phone; he'd no time to claim
anything. I hung up straight away.'

'How about his voice? Any kind of accent? Canadian, for
instance?'

'No, nothing unusual.'

There were more questions, but to Rona it seemed they
were going round in circles.

'What's happening about Louise?' she interrupted at one stage. 'She's very vulnerable; she won't be able to stand up for herself.'

'Your husband gave her description when he phoned in. It's been circulated, and a search is under way.' Curtis paused. 'When was the last time you saw or heard any of the Franks?'

Rona bit her lip. 'Tuesday. I was expecting Louise to come round to discuss the stalker, but she didn't.'

'Did you try to contact her?'

'No; I had to drive a friend to Farnbridge hospital, and it put everything else out of my head. I feel guilty now.'

You're the only thing keeping me sane, Louise had said. How could she have let her down so badly?

Curtis pursed his lips. 'It's important to establish when they were last seen alive. We're conducting a house-to-house, but if you remember seeing even a brief glimpse of them, it would be helpful to know where and when.'

He stood up. 'That's all for the moment, Mrs Allerdyce. Your fingerprints will be taken, then as soon as your husband's interview's over, you'll be driven home. And it goes without saying that if this man contacts you again, you report it immediately.'

'Of course.' Rona hesitated. 'If there's any news of Louise, could you let us know?'

But the sergeant wasn't to be drawn on that. He made some vague reply, and, motioning to the constable, left the room. A woman officer came to take Rona for her fingerprinting, then conducted her back to the foyer.

'Can I get you a cup of coffee while you're waiting?' she offered.

'That would be welcome,' Rona said. She wondered how Max was faring, and hoped he was keeping his temper.

His interview, as she learned later, had followed similar lines, and he emerged from it as she was finishing her coffee. Once he too had been fingerprinted, they were driven home. A van and two police cars were still there, and a contraption like a tent had been set up, screening the front door of number seventeen. As they pulled in to the kerb, a couple of men shrouded in white hooded boiler suits emerged from it, and came down the path carrying what looked like black bin-liners, which they proceeded to load into the back of a van. Rona turned hastily away, closing her mind to what they might contain.

Their keys had been returned at the police station, and she ran up to the study for the note, handing it to one of the men who'd driven them home. He took it, she noticed, in a gloved hand, and dropped it into a transparent envelope, though her own prints would have been all over it. Then, with a nod of thanks, he went back down the path to the car.

As soon as they were alone, Max lost no time in checking the whole house to see if the police had left evidence of their presence, and, seeing none, was slightly mollified.

'God knows what they thought they'd find,' he said.

Rona shrugged. 'For all they know, we could have killed them ourselves.'

It was still only eight thirty. She had seldom known a longer evening. She thought back to lunch at her mother's, and Lindsey's account of the Yarborough party. How normal life had seemed then, yet the Franks must already have been dead. Oh, *why* hadn't she contacted Louise, as she'd promised?

'This will be public news tomorrow,' Max remarked. 'It might be as well to warn Lindsey and your parents.'

'I suppose so. The subject never came up with Mum, but we were discussing it at Catherine's.'

'Better get it over.' He brought the cordless phone from the hall, and dropped it in her lap.

Her parents each expressed shock and concern, but it was Lindsey who pinpointed a fact that, in all the upset, Rona hadn't appreciated.

'If it *was* this man,' she said, 'he'll know you can identify him, won't he?'

Rona felt suddenly cold. 'He might even think you could; he mistook you for me, remember.'

'God, you're right.'

'But he won't realize there are two of us,' Rona hurried on, 'and even if he does, he can't possibly know your name, or where you live. You don't need to worry, Linz.'

'But you do,' Lindsey said starkly. 'For God's sake be careful, Ro.'

Rona broke the connection and looked at Max, who'd been listening.

'She's got a point, hasn't she?'

Max shrugged. 'If he thinks you can identify him, he's going to make damn sure you don't have the opportunity. My guess is he'll have put as much distance as possible between you.'

'With Louise?'

Max was silent.

'You think he's already disposed of her?' Her voice rocked.

Max said gently, 'All I think is that he won't want any – encumbrances – that will slow him down.'

'Then why take her with him? Why didn't he kill her on the spot, like her parents?'

'Perhaps because she could be useful to him. In which case, he won't have harmed her.'

'And the blood?'

'There might have been an initial struggle. Perhaps she saw what he'd done to her parents, or—'

'We're just hypothesising, aren't we?' Rona broke in impatiently. 'We haven't a clue what happened, and I bet the police haven't, either.'

'At least they've the means to find out, so let's leave it to them, shall we?'

By the next morning, the fine weather had broken, and a steady rain set in. This had not, however, deterred the first of what Max feared would be a growing number of sensation-seekers, come to gawp at the scene of the murder and, by default, those nearest to it. Feeling it imperative to get away, both from them and the continuing activity next door, he phoned the Ridgeways and suggested they spend the day together.

'I admit I've a special reason for asking,' he said, 'but we'll explain when we see you.'

'Fine, but it's not much fun trudging round the countryside in this weather,' Gavin replied. 'Come over here. We can chill out for a while, then go for a pub lunch. Bring the hound.'

'It must have been traumatic, discovering the bodies,' Magda commented, when Max had given them a synopsis of events. 'Especially coming so soon after that girl.'

Rona, having no wish to revert to her previous assignment, cut in quickly. 'Ironically, it was her parents Louise seemed afraid of. I wonder if she knows what's happened to them.'

Magda replenished their coffee. 'Do you think she really is their daughter?'

'I don't know. It's weird, that there's no record of her.'

'She must have a passport, if they've just arrived from Canada,' Gavin put in. 'Surely that would prove something?'

'That's another thing,' Rona told him. 'Her parents put it in the bank with their valuables. If you ask me, it was to stop her finding it.'

'Come to think of it,' Magda mused, 'it's a moot point which of you this stranger's interested in. He followed you home before he tailed Louise.'

It was an uncomfortable thought.

'On the other hand, he could simply be a weirdo, stalking any woman who takes his fancy,' Gavin offered. 'You do hear of such people.'

After a disturbed night, there was something therapeutic about relaxing in the Ridgeways' familiar room, listening to the rain pattering against the windows and thrashing out with them the intricacies of the last few days. They continued to toss various theories around until, at twelve thirty, they drove out to the Watermill, an attractive little pub just out of town. On this wet Sunday, it was filled with a noisy, chattering throng, and they had to wait for some time before a table became vacant and they were able to squeeze round it.

'At least they serve lunch on Sundays,' Max commented. 'A lot of pubs don't.'

In need of comfort food, Rona ordered beer-battered cod and chips, and the others abandoned their more modest selections and joined her. Gradually, her feelings of guilt and anxiety began to recede. The police were on to it, she told herself. They'd find Louise and bring her back. But back to what, exactly? And once more her mind started its treadmill, and again she had no answers.

After lunch, they returned to the Ridgeways' and spent a lazy afternoon chatting and watching a DVD Gavin had taken out. Consequently it was after seven by the time they reached home. There were still tapes across the Franks' gateway, but the sightseers had gone, at least for the moment, and only one police van remained. A message was flashing on the answer-phone, and Rona pressed the switch to hear her father-in-law's anxious voice.

'Did these people found murdered live near you? The road we saw on the news looked familiar. Please give me a call when you receive this message.'

'I'll speak to him,' Max said, conscious of a familiar sense of guilt. His father, a fiercely independent eighty-year-old, lived in Northumberland, and despite all Max's good inten-tions, an interval had again lapsed since he'd been up to see him. Unfairly, it was his sister Cynthia, living close by, who had to shoulder most of the responsibility, especially the previous winter, when the old man had been ill.

'Don't tell him how closely we're involved,' Rona warned. 'He'd only worry.'

'He'll find out anyway, once the press get on to it. It'll be in all the papers tomorrow, and reports that "neighbours" found the body will be a dead giveaway. He'll want us to go up and stay with him till it all blows over, like he did last time.'

'It mightn't be a bad idea,' Rona said.

Rona's phone call the previous evening had thoroughly unset-tled Avril. She'd spent a restless night, and been brooding over the matter all day, watching or listening to every news bulletin. Rona had been involved in several traumatic events since she'd devoted her time to journalism, but the fact that murder had been committed actually *next* door to her, and presumably while she was at home, was a step too far.

Nor did the dreary weather help. Avril heartily disliked Sundays at the best of times; it was a day for families, and there was no point in cooking a roast for one. The rest of the week she'd managed to fill satisfactorily, and since Sarah had come to lodge with her, she hadn't been alone at night – a situation she'd been anxious to avoid. But Sarah wasn't here at the moment, and unless she made a conscious effort, at weekends Avril spoke to no one from lunchtime on Saturday till Monday morning.

She'd tried phoning first Lindsey and then Rona, just for a chat, really, but neither of them had been home. It was now eight o'clock, and already darkness, accelerated by the rain, was beginning to fall. Unable to bear the thought of the empty evening stretching ahead of her, she lifted the phone and on impulse tapped in Tom's number.

He answered almost at once. 'Tom Parish.'

'Tom, it's – me.'

'Avril?'

'Yes; I've been worrying about Rona.'

'I know; not a happy state of affairs.'

Avril paused. 'Is Catherine with you?'

'No, she's been over to see the family.'

'I suppose . . .' She took her courage in both hands. 'You couldn't come round for a bit, could you? I feel in need of company.'

There was a slight pause at his end, too. Then, 'Yes, of course I can, if you'd like me to.'

Kind, considerate Tom. Why had she ever let him go? 'I'd be very grateful,' she said in a small voice.

It seemed perilously like old times, to see him sitting across the hearth from her, a glass in his hand.

'I don't know anything about those people next door,' Avril began, reminding herself that, however it might seem, it was *not* old times. 'Do you?'

'Well, actually we had lunch at Catherine's last Sunday, and Rona was talking about them.'

'They were here for lunch yesterday,' Avril cut in, childishly wanting to keep her end up, 'but the subject never arose. It was when they got home that they – found them. So – what were they saying?'

'It was all a bit involved. Apparently the daughter Louise, a woman in her thirties, I gathered, is suffering from amnesia after a car crash. She'd begun to have doubts about her identity and whether her parents were in fact her parents at all.'

Avril frowned. 'Why would she think that?'

'Oh, they couldn't produce any photos or papers, saying they'd been destroyed in a house fire in Canada, where they've come from. But they used to live in Harrogate, so when Rona went up there last week, she looked at the electoral rolls but could find no trace of Louise. The parents were listed, but their daughter's name was given as something entirely different.'

'Trust Rona to get involved in some mystery,' Avril said,

with a touch of her old irritation. Then, anxiety overruling it, 'But that won't put her in danger, will it?'

'No reason why it should; it'll probably turn out the murders were the result of a burglary gone wrong.'

'But the daughter has disappeared, she said.'

'Yes; that is worrying.'

'Perhaps she really *is* someone else, and some relative came to claim her.'

'If so, he had a brutal way of going about it.'

'Perhaps the so-called parents wouldn't let her go, and things got out of hand.'

Tom laughed. 'There's no doubt where Rona gets her imagination!'

Avril smiled. 'Seriously, though, you really don't think she's in danger?'

'No, I don't,' Tom said stoutly, as much to convince himself as her. 'And now we've established that, tell me what you've been doing with yourself.'

He stayed an hour longer, and they discussed more general matters, current affairs and news of mutual friends. Then he finished his drink and got to his feet.

'I'd better be going. Try not to worry, Avril. Max is staying overnight while all this is going on, so she won't be alone.'

'I can't think why he doesn't stay every night, like any normal husband.'

Tom smiled; this was an old complaint. At the door, he bent to kiss her cheek. 'Sleep well, now your mind's at rest.'

'I will. And thank you so much for coming, Tom. I really appreciate it.'

'Any time,' he said. But as she closed the door behind him, she knew, sadly, that he didn't mean it literally. She'd forfeited her right to that.

Fourteen

Monday morning, and Max left for Farthings. The vans had returned next door, and there was a group of newsmen with cameras camped on the opposite pavement. From behind a curtain, Rona watched them converge on Max, and though his pace didn't slacken, they trailed him as far as the corner, trying to draw out his monosyllabic replies.

Once in the car, he phoned her. 'You saw what happened?'

'Yes.'

'There was a press conference yesterday. I don't know if our names were given, but the mere fact that we're neighbours makes us newsworthy. Incidentally, the question of Louise's identity wasn't raised, so the police mightn't have released that nugget. I told them it was pointless to approach you, as you didn't know any more than I did, but if they do, keep as detached as you can and don't volunteer anything.'

Rona said anxiously, 'I don't want my photo in the paper. It would remind the stalker that I saw him.'

'That's hardly logical, now is it?' Max said impatiently. 'He already knows your name and where you live. If he'd wanted to silence you, he'd have made a move already. Look, I've arrived at Farthings now, so I'll sign off. Meet me at the police station at twelve, then we can have lunch together. In the meantime, try to keep a low profile.'

As soon as the line was clear, the phone rang again. Rona hesitated, but if she left it, it would mean going down to check the answerphone.

She lifted it cautiously. 'Hello?'

'Up to your old tricks, I see,' said a breezy voice.

'Tess!' Rona wasn't sure whether to be relieved or annoyed. Tess Chadwick of the *Stokely Gazette* was a friend, but they'd clashed before over her coverage of Rona's various exploits.

'I'm outside the house. If you look, you'll see me.'

'I'll take your word for it,' Rona said. She'd no intention of presenting herself at the front windows.

'So how about letting an old pal in and spilling the beans?'

'Max told you as much as I can.'

'Which was pretty well zilch. Come on, Rona; you can do better, I know.'

'Really, Tess, I don't want to be involved.'

'That's what you always say, but if you will make a habit of stumbling over dead bodies, you have to take the consequences. Anyway, if you talk to me, I can hold the rest of them at bay with a bit of judicious bargaining.'

Rona sighed. Tess always got her way.

'All right, but be ready to come in quickly; I don't want a host of flashlights going off in my face.'

'Will do.'

Rona went downstairs and, positioning herself behind the front door, opened it cautiously and Tess slipped inside. The barrage of cameras flashed, but would have been captured nothing more rewarding than Tess's rear view and the wooden door.

She gave Rona a quick peck on the cheek, and followed her into the sitting room. The height of the room above street level meant that unless they actually approached the window, they weren't visible from outside.

Tess perched, bird-like, on the edge of a chair and took out her recorder. As always, she was dressed completely in black, which today comprised a long-sleeved T-shirt, short skirt and ankle boots. Her chestnut hair was as unruly as ever, making her look considerably younger than her forty-odd years.

'So – tell me about the folk next door. How well did you know them?'

'Hardly at all,' Rona said.

Tess raised a sceptical eyebrow.

'Honestly. I barely exchanged more than a dozen words with the parents, though I knew Louise slightly better.'

'The missing daughter. What's she like?'

Rona hesitated. 'A bit strange, really. But that's hardly surprising, considering what she's been through.'

Tess leaned forward. 'Such as?'

Belatedly, Rona remembered that the police had withheld the full story. But they'd put no constraints on her; it had been Max who'd advised her to volunteer nothing.

She glanced at Tess's eager face, still hesitant. How would Louise react to her story appearing in print? She'd not asked for privacy, either; furthermore, the publicity might assist in finding her, could even lead to definitive proof of her identity.

'Go on,' Tess wheedled. 'Tell Auntie Tess.'

Rona reached a compromise: she'd tell Tess as much as she knew about Louise's background – what harm could it do now? – but she wouldn't mention the prowler. Resignedly, she began.

'They lived *next door*?'

Avril nodded miserably. They were sorting out books before the library opened.

'It was Rona and Max who found them,' she added. 'They went in because the front door had been open all day.'

'My God!'

Three pairs of horrified but curious eyes were fastened on her, drinking in every word.

'Were they horribly bashed about?' Rita Jones asked, with ill-disguised relish.

Avril shook her head. 'They didn't look dead at all, Rona said. The only blood they found was on the stairs and in the daughter's room.'

'And she's missing?' That was Liz Pennington.

'It seems so.'

'He's probably done away with her, too,' Rita said ghoulishly.

Avril gave a little shudder, and Mary Price put a protective arm round her shoulders. 'What a shock for you, knowing Rona was nearby when it happened.'

'Why didn't anyone see him?' Liz asked. 'I mean, he must have dragged her out of the house and into a car or something.'

'But it was the middle of the night, surely?'

'I thought Avril said—'

'Max *noticed* the door at lunchtime; it could have been open for hours.'

'Come along, ladies!' the chief librarian called. 'Time to open up.'

Reluctantly they moved apart and took their places, ready to serve the public. For once in their uneventful lives, real life seemed more colourful than the fiction on their shelves.

'So how was the party?' Carla enquired.

Dominic continued to leaf through his documents. 'All right, I suppose. It was held outdoors, but fortunately we'd finished eating by the time the rain started.'

She waited, and when he said no more, prompted, 'And Miss Parish?'

'Was there, as expected.'

'Alone?'

He looked up irritably. 'What is this? The Spanish Inquisition?'

'Just that you've been remarkably grumpy this morning, which usually means things aren't going your way.'

'Quite the amateur psychologist, aren't you?'

'See what I mean?'

Reluctantly, he smiled. 'All right; if you must know, she had an escort, and left with him.'

'Oh dear!'

'I doubt if it's anything heavy, though. I know him, and he has a very nice wife.'

'Unfortunately, that means not a thing.'

'Job's comforter now?'

'I did warn you—'

'I know, I know.'

She looked at him shrewdly. 'It seems to me that you mind more than you thought you would.'

He flung himself back in his chair. 'God, Carla, give me a break!'

'You do, don't you?'

'I don't know what the hell I feel.'

'Well, if you want my advice – and even if you don't, you're going to get it – I think you should take steps to rectify the position, before things go beyond repair.'

'And how,' he asked drily, 'do you propose I should do that?'

'Make a bit of an effort. Apologize for being so bloody

offhand. And now –' she rose to her feet – 'I'm leaving the room, before you throw something!'

Despite Tess's assurances, acceding to her request for an interview had not lessened the attentions of the press. The doorbell rang repeatedly, and Rona tried to ignore it. The phone kept ringing, and she let the machine take it, vowing to delete the messages without playing them.

How, she wondered in despair, was she supposed to work with all this going on, and while she was so worried about Louise? She considered going to Oak Avenue, but in the absence of both Felicity and Julian, it would be imposing on the family at what, for them too, was an anxious time. All in all, she was glad she'd an appointment at the police station; it would at least offer a means of escape.

Yet for all their importunities, the press didn't disturb her as much as the comings and goings next door. From time to time during the morning, she was drawn to the bedroom window where, screened by the curtain, she could see the figures in white going up and down the path. Had they, she wondered, found anything that could conceivably help find Louise?

At eleven forty-five, she'd no option but to brave the press. Though normally she'd have walked to the police station, today the car would afford at least some protection. But first she had to get to the garage. Clipping on Gus's lead, she took a deep breath and opened the front door.

Max was waiting for her in the foyer.

'Were you molested by the press?' he asked, kissing her cheek.

'Moderately, but I took a leaf out of your book, and kept walking. Tess Chadwick gained entry, though.'

'Oh, God!'

'She promised to keep the rest at bay, but failed to deliver.'

'You gave her the story?'

'A slightly edited version. Who knows, it might even help.'

The typewritten joint statement was produced, and again they both read and signed it. Then a man they hadn't seen before approached them.

'Mr and Mrs Allerdyce, good morning. I'm DI Webster, and I'm hoping you can help us. We've come up against a couple of problems; firstly, we've been unable to trace any next of kin for the victims – other, of course, than Miss Franks. Would you have any idea who we should contact?'

Rona hesitated. She'd already told them about the mysterious Karen; it was up to them whether or not they followed it up. 'I'm afraid not,' she said.

'Well, it was worth a try. Fortunately, their bank manager has agreed to identify them, if we continue to draw a blank. And our other problem is that there don't seem to be any photographs of Miss Franks, or, for that matter, any credit cards, driving licence, or NHS records in her name.'

'She told me her passport's in the bank,' Rona said, surprised they'd not asked the manager.

DI Webster looked at her oddly. 'Unfortunately, it seems not.' He hesitated, as though he would enlarge on that, but decided against it. 'So, since you seem to be the only person who's seen her, we're hoping you'll agree to do a photofit. It would be an enormous help.'

Rona nodded. 'Of course I will.'

He led them to one of the small rooms off the foyer, and they seated themselves in front of a computer screen. Rona watched, fascinated, as under her direction, an oval roughly the shape of Louise's face was furnished with a thick dark fringe, blue eyes, and a generous mouth.

'Anything like her?' queried Webster, when the picture was complete. 'Remember, it's not a portrait we're after, more the shape of different features, hairline and so on.'

'There's quite a resemblance, yes.'

'Anything you can add verbally, to flesh it out, as it were?'

'Only that her eyebrows are thick and dark, and her eyes very vivid blue.'

'Good, good; that's the kind of thing we need. Anything else?'

'Not that I can think of.'

'Well, thank you, Mrs Allerdyce; that's been most helpful.'

'Just – find her,' Rona said in a low voice. 'Please.'

Jonathan Hurst stopped in surprise as he recognized the seated figure in Chase Mortimer's reception area.

'Dominic – hello! Were you looking for me?'

Dominic rose slowly to his feet. 'Good morning, Jonathan. No, I wasn't, actually.'

Jonathan waited but he didn't elaborate, and before there
was a chance to probe further, the door to Lindsey's office
opened and she came out, stopping short on seeing the two
men.

Jonathan looked sharply from her to Dominic. Then he said
in a low voice, 'If that's your game, you'll have to take your
place in the queue.' And with a curt nod, he went out on to
the street.

Lindsey, annoyed at not being warned of his arrival, frowned
reprovingly at the receptionist, but Dominic said quickly, '*Mea
culpa*; I asked her not to disturb you.'

In other words, Lindsey thought, he wanted to take me by
surprise. She came slowly towards him, eyebrows raised questioningly. 'Can I help you, then?' she asked coolly.

'I hope so, but not professionally.'

She waited, and he said evenly, 'There are one or two things
I need to say to you, and they can be better said over a good
lunch.'

Lindsey glanced back at the receptionist, but she was on the
phone and unlikely to overhear them. 'It didn't occur to you I
might already have a lunch date? You should have phoned first.'

'It *did* occur to me, but I reckoned that if I phoned, you'd
turn me down flat.'

For a moment they regarded one another, trying to gauge
each other's thoughts. Then Lindsey said, 'I might have done,
at that.'

'*Have* you a lunch date?'

'As it happens, no.'

'Then will you please allow me to take you to the
Clarendon?'

Lindsey hesitated. Part of her was crying out to go with
him, part of her held back. After much heart-searching, she'd
convinced herself there was no future in his on/off approach,
and to avoid further heartache, had decided to end the relationship – if it warranted the name. She guessed he was here
now only because she'd been with Jonathan on Friday.

Steeling herself, she said, 'I really don't think there's much
point in this, Dominic. Let's just leave it, shall we?'

She half-turned away, but he caught at her arm.

'That's what I deserve, I know, but let me explain. Please,
Lindsey: last chance saloon?'

Her eyes held his for a long moment. Then she sighed. 'Very well then; last chance saloon.'

'Thank you.'

He took her arm, and neither of them spoke as he led her out of the building and across the road to the hotel. Chris Fairfax, the owner-manager, was in the entrance hall, and she nodded to him as she followed the maitre d' into the restaurant. Though as familiar to her as her own home, today the surroundings had an unreal quality – stemming, she knew, from the change in Dominic's attitude. For the first time since they'd met, she appeared somehow to have the upper hand.

Only about a dozen tables were occupied; most people lunched in the grill room, where the service was quicker. They were shown to a window table looking on to Guild Street, and provided with large, glossy menus.

'We'd like to order drinks first,' Dominic told the waiter. 'Gin and tonic, Lindsey?'

'Please.' She wondered if he'd remembered, or simply made a good guess. Her heart was beating high in her chest. Why did he have to stir everything up again, when she'd finally found the courage to call a halt?

Their drinks were set before them, and suddenly everything went quiet, as though the room were holding its breath. They seemed isolated at their table, surrounded by empty spaces, and though crowds jostled and laughed on the other side of the glass, double-glazing ensured that no sound reached them.

Lindsey looked up, half-fearfully, to find Dominic's eyes on her.

'You're overdue an explanation of my behaviour,' he began. 'It's been cavalier in the extreme, and I apologize unreservedly.'

She didn't speak, simply sat looking at him. This was not what she'd expected.

He cleared his throat and his eyes dropped to his glass. 'To start at the beginning, some months ago I became involved in a very unwise relationship. From comments you made, I think you're aware of this. It was foolish and irresponsible, and extricating myself proved difficult, and, worse, caused hurt, which had never been my intention.'

He lifted his glass, drank from it, and replaced it on the table, staring thoughtfully down at it. 'The long and the short of it was that I determined to steer well clear of commitments for a long time to come.' He paused. 'And then I met you.' Another pause. 'And alarm bells rang.'

Lindsey reached an unsteady hand for her own glass and sipped at the ice-cold liquid. Blood was thundering in her ears and her mouth was dry. Across the room, someone gave a shout of laughter.

'I knew,' Dominic went on after a moment, 'that the only safe course was to steer well clear of you. But I couldn't. Hence my pathetic attempts at compromise.'

Lindsey moistened her lips. 'And now?'

'Now, on the brink of losing you altogether, I've no option but to throw caution to the winds.'

Intent on each other, neither had noticed the waiter's approach until a voice above them enquired, 'Are you ready to order, sir?'

'No, dammit!' Dominic snapped. Then, looking up, 'I'm sorry. Give us five more minutes.'

'Very good, sir.' He glided away.

'Talk about bad timing!' Dominic muttered.

Lindsey laughed, and the tension was broken. He reached for her hand.

'I'm not really too late, am I?'

'For what?'

'To become a more stable part of your life. To start again, really get to know each other, and – see what transpires. Or have I blown it completely?'

She shook her head, hardly daring to believe what he was saying. But there was one question that still had to be resolved.

'What about Carla?' she asked.

'Carla,' he answered quietly, 'is, as you know, my friend as well as my assistant. And yes, on occasions she's been more than that. But what's between us is affection, nothing stronger. She once described herself as my comfort blanket.'

A corner of his mouth lifted. 'In fact, she's been lecturing me on your behalf. It was because she kept telling me how badly I've been treating you, that I finally saw it for myself. So there you have it, Lindsey. I've put my cards on the table, which is a novel experience for me. Now it's up to you. What do you say?'

A surge of happiness welled up inside her.

'I think,' she said, 'that you should order a bottle of champagne.'

After lunch with Max, Rona took Gus for a lengthy walk in the park. She was in no hurry to go home, and needed time to herself in which to process the train of events that had overtaken them. As she approached the bench where she'd sat with Louise, she glanced over, half-hoping to see her there, but it was occupied by two young mothers, chatting as their children played nearby. Well, the photofit would be in the evening papers and on the news; please God it might help in tracing her.

Her mobile bleeped in her bag, indicating the receipt of a text. She flipped it open to read: *Can't speak to you now – I'm in the office. Just to say I had lunch with Dominic and everything is WONDERFUL! More later. Lindsey.*

Rona smiled; good news was more than welcome at the moment, and Lindsey was overdue for a lasting and worthwhile relationship. With luck, this could be it.

When she finally reached home, the press were still camped in the Avenue, though to Rona's relief, they appeared to have given up on her. Averting her eyes from the shrouded door, she turned into her own gateway.

However, as she reached the study the doorbell rang, and she swore softly. It seemed she'd congratulated herself too soon. Gus barked a warning, and after a minute the bell rang again.

Rona went into the bedroom and took up her position behind the curtain. Then, recognizing the figure walking back down the path, she ran downstairs and, ignoring the camera crews, flung the door open.

'Felicity! Sorry! Do come in!'

Felicity Willow, a large bouquet of flowers in one arm, turned and retraced her steps.

'Whatever's going on?' she asked. 'All these vans – I had to park at the end of the road – and as I walked back, a continuous stream of cars passed, driving slowly, while the occupants stared up at the houses.'

Rona smiled ruefully and gestured her into the sitting room. 'Been living on Mars for the last few days?'

'Not quite, but I've been more or less incommunicado since Thursday.'

'Of course you have. Sorry. How's Julian?'

'Much better, thanks. He should be home at the end of the week.' She held out the flowers. 'This is with my thanks for all you did.'

'Oh Felicity, they're lovely, but there was no need.'

'So – are you going to tell me what's been happening?'

'Unfortunately, we've had a tragedy. Oh –' at Felicity's gasp – 'not personally. The elderly couple who were renting next door have been killed.'

'God, how awful!' Felicity paused. 'Killed how?'

'Murdered, actually. And to make matters worse, it was Max and I who found them.'

Once again she went through the story.

'And the daughter's still missing?'

'Yes, and to complicate matters, she's suffering from amnesia.'

'Did you know her?'

'Slightly. They were – a very private family. Look, can I get you some tea? Coffee?'

'No, thanks, I've just had some. The reason I called – apart from bringing the flowers – was that I felt you deserved an explanation. About how Julian came to be in Farnbridge.'

'It's really none of my business.'

'It was good of you to be so discreet about it; not everyone would have been.' Felicity looked down at her hands. 'You were right in thinking Tara wanted him to partner her at the dinner. And he *had* spent the day in London, as he said, but instead of staying the night there, he caught the train to Farnbridge, and Tara met him at the station.'

Rona said carefully, 'I thought there'd be a simple explanation.'

'Not all that simple. I wasn't born yesterday, Rona, and nor were you. They *have* been seeing each other; Julian was sympathetic over the break-up, and – his sympathy went too far. He bitterly regrets it now. I wanted you to know the facts, so that you wouldn't be left wondering.'

'Thank you, but really—'

'The accident's being investigated, of course, so things will be a bit strained for a while, but once that's all over, we'll put the whole thing behind us.'

'And – Tara?'

'Has been discharged, and is being looked after by her mother.' Felicity gave her a bright smile. 'So, enough of all that. How's the article coming along?'

'It's almost finished. I need to check a couple of things, so if it's not inconvenient, I'll pop back later in the week.'

'And stay for lunch?' Felicity asked with a smile.

'Strictly sandwiches. You have enough on your plate.'

'You could be right; Graham and Erika are staying on for a while. But we will still be friends, won't we, Rona? When the article's finished and everything?'

'Of course we will. Another lunch at the Bacchus, perhaps?'

'I'll look forward to it.' She rose to her feet. 'I must be getting back; Minty needs collecting from a birthday party, and Robin's due to play cricket. I'll see you later in the week, then? We can at least have a cup of coffee.'

'That would be good.' Rona saw her to the door.

'And I do hope they find your friend safe and sound,' Felicity added.

'So do I,' Rona said. 'Oh, so do I.'

'Avril? It's Guy.'

Avril's heart gave a little jerk. 'Guy! How nice to hear from you.'

'How are things? Nice and peaceful, now my daughter's out of the way?'

'I wouldn't exactly say that.'

Something in her voice must have alerted him, because he said quickly, 'There's nothing wrong, is there?'

'Well, I suppose you've heard of the double murder that's in all the papers?'

'Yes? But it's nowhere near you, surely?'

'They lived next door to Rona. And it was she and her husband who found them.'

'Not again!' Guy exclaimed. When Sarah had first arrived, Avril had felt bound to tell him of Rona's involvement in the Curzon case.

'My own feelings exactly.'

'I'm so sorry, Avril. I'd have rung sooner, if I'd had any idea.'

'That's kind of you, but there's nothing anyone can do. How's Sarah?'

'Well, that's partly the reason for this call. She's gone off to France with Clive at a moment's notice. Which means she won't be coming to the theatre with me on Friday, as planned.'

Avril waited, hope stirring inside her.

Guy gave a little laugh. 'You'll think I make a habit of making use of you when my daughter lets me down, but I was wondering if you'd care to come with me? It's the modern-dress production of *The Merchant of Venice*. It's had rave reviews, and I remembered we discussed Shakespeare in modern dress at the pub that evening.'

'It's – good of you to think of me,' she said. 'When did you say this is?'

'This coming Friday, the seventeenth. Are you free?'

'I'm almost sure I am. That would be lovely, Guy.'

'Excellent. Now all that remains is to fix the mode of transport. I'm not too keen on driving down; would you mind going by train?'

'Of course not. And meet you at the theatre?'

'Good Lord, no! I'll drive over to collect you, and leave the car at Marsborough station.'

'That's fine going down, but it will be nearly midnight before we get back, and you'd still have the drive to Stokely.'

'Don't worry about that; I'm quite a night bird.'

'Wouldn't it be more sensible if you stayed overnight? You could have Sarah's room.'

She stopped short, heat washing over her. 'That is,' she stammered, 'I didn't mean—'

God, she was making it worse!

Guy said quickly, 'That's a very kind thought, but I wouldn't want to put you out.'

Though she desperately wanted to back-pedal, she couldn't in all conscience leave the invitation hanging. 'It would be no trouble,' she said, 'but of course, if you'd rather—'

'Avril.' His voice was gentle. 'Please don't be embarrassed. I know exactly what you meant, and as I said, it's a very kind thought. Provided you're sure it wouldn't make too much work for you, I'd be delighted to stay.'

She drew a long, tremulous breath. 'That's fine, then. I'll see you on Friday.'

'I'll check the train times, but to be on the safe side, I'd better collect you at five. If we're too early, we can always have a drink before the show. And in the meantime, I'm sure you needn't worry about Rona; she seems a very capable young woman.'

Avril put the phone down with a rush of conflicting emotions. Only a couple of days ago, she'd been regretting the loss of a kind and considerate man like Tom. Possibly – just possibly – she'd found herself another.

Fifteen

Lindsey's call had been ecstatic. Seeing Max's long-suffering expression, Rona had taken the phone to the privacy of the hall, and sat on the stairs while her sister repeated, almost verbatim, what had passed between her and Dominic.

'I told you playing hard to get would work,' Rona put in, when Lindsey paused for breath. 'And wasn't it I who said it was too soon to give up on him completely?'

'Oh, aren't you the wise old owl! But seriously, Ro, he is gorgeous, isn't he?'

'I admit I liked him,' Rona replied. 'More than I expected to, having heard a fair bit about him. But what are you doing, phoning me? Why aren't you with him, making mad, passionate love?'

'Because, unfortunately, he's had to go to London for a couple of days, which is why he came to the office at lunchtime, instead of waiting till this evening. Ro, he wants me to go on holiday with him. He mentioned South Africa.'

'Hang on: I thought you were going to Italy with Mum?'

There was a pause. Then Lindsey wailed, 'Oh, God, I'd forgotten about her! I was just thinking I could cancel my singles booking.'

'Well, you can't let her down; you saw how pleased she was. Anyway, it's only for ten days. You have four weeks' holiday, don't you?'

'Yes, but I've already had a week, and it was September Dominic mentioned.'

'Then you'll have to tell him. He won't think the worse of you for sticking to your arrangement.'

'I suppose not,' Lindsey said disconsolately.

'And if he does, it'll tell you quite a bit about him,' Rona added sharply.

'All right, all right. I'll suggest we go in October.' She paused. 'Jonathan was pretty unpleasant this afternoon.'

'Are you surprised?'

'Said I was looking very pleased with myself, like the cat that got the cream.'

'Perhaps,' Rona said, 'it will encourage him to return his attentions to his wife.'

They watched the news in silence. The photofit of Louise received wide coverage, and Rona wondered uneasily if her abductor had seen it.

'It looks quite like her, doesn't it?' she commented.

'I wouldn't know.'

Rona frowned. 'How do you mean?'

'I can't say if it's like her, because I've never seen her.'

She turned to him incredulously. 'But you *must* have, Max! They've been there nearly a month!'

'Nevertheless, I haven't – apart from a cigarette glowing in the dark, which could have been anyone. And what's more, from what that detective said, I'm in the majority.'

'Yes, but living next door . . .'

'Strange, I agree, but true. Come to think of it, the police and I have only your word for it she even exists.'

Rona stared at him, and gave a little shudder. 'That's weird.'

He put a hand on her knee. 'All of which puts you in a unique position, my love. To help them with their enquiries, and so on.'

'As long as the phrase isn't used euphemistically,' Rona said.

This was the last week of Max's classes, which, unusually, had stretched into August to compensate for the four weeks they'd been away.

'Once they've finished and you've handed in your article,' he said at breakfast the next morning, 'I think we should go up to Tynecastle and spend some time with the old man. It'll be lovely up there at this time of year.'

'Better check with Cynthia that we can stay with her. We can't impose ourselves on Roland and Mrs Pemberton.'

'Well, we'll give him the option. God knows, the house is large enough; he rattles around in it.'

'Is he working on anything at the moment?'

Roland Allerdyce was a gifted artist and member of the Royal Academy, and it was from him that Max had inherited his talent.

'He mentioned some commission or other, but it's hard to find him when he *hasn't* something on the go. It wouldn't interfere with our visit.'

'Another thing,' Rona reminded him. 'You'd better finish that painting of Michael's car before you show your face up there again.'

Cynthia's elder son had bought a red MG earlier in the year, and extracted a promise from his uncle to paint it – an obligation Max had not yet fulfilled.

Max pushed back his chair, bent to kiss her, and made for the stairs. 'Don't talk to any strange men,' he said, only half-jokingly, 'and I'll be back round ten.'

Rona cleared away the breakfast things. There'd been no further developments on the news, but Max's comment the previous evening, about having only her word that Louise existed, had lodged in her mind. The police had been unable to find any record of her; would they come to the same conclusion, and stop looking for her?

Shaking her head in frustration, she resolved to put all these worries out of her head, and concentrate on finishing the article.

Max had put the post on the hall table, and on her way to the study, Rona stopped to flick through the half-dozen envelopes. One was typewritten and addressed to her. She slit it open and drew out the single sheet of paper. Then, as she glanced through it, she sat down abruptly on the stairs to read it more slowly.

There was no address at the top of the page, merely the date, yesterday's, before the letter began.

> *Dear Miss Parish,*
>
> *I appreciate that I must be the last person you want to hear from, but I trust you'll at least read this letter through before throwing it in the bin.*
>
> *It is now more imperative than ever that I speak to you, but before going further, let me swear categorically that I had nothing whatever to do with the deaths of Keith and Barbara Franks, and have cast-iron alibis for*

the supposed time of their deaths. Nor have I any idea what has become of their daughter. I'm aware that you have given my description to the police, which is fair enough after my less than wise approaches to you.

Since they are anxious to question me, I intend to go to them voluntarily within the next couple of days, but before I do, I ask you most urgently to meet me. Obviously you would want a public place, where any fears you may have, however unfounded, would be minimized. I suggest therefore that we meet in the lounge of the Clarendon Hotel at 4 p.m. tomorrow, Tuesday. I can't, of course, prevent you simply informing the police of my where-abouts, but I would implore you to give me this last chance of a private word with you. I can guarantee you'll be very interested in what I have to say.

There is no need to reply. I shall be at the Clarendon at the appointed time, and if you don't come, I'll make no further attempt to contact you, but go straight to the police station.

HS.

Rona leant back against the stair, her heart pounding. She read the letter through again, and the detective's voice echoed in her head: *It goes without saying that if this man contacts you again, you report it immediately.*

She glanced at the phone on its glass-topped table. So what was she waiting for? And yet . . .

Suppose she did inform the police: they would be waiting for HS, whoever he was, at the Clarendon, and take him away for questioning. And she was quite sure they wouldn't let *her* know what he had to tell them. Whereas if she met him herself, somewhere safe like the hotel lounge – where, at four o'clock, afternoon tea would be in full swing – well, what harm could come to her? And he said he'd then voluntarily go to the police. Could she believe that?

Clearly, it was no use informing the police where he'd be, but asking for time to talk to him first. They'd laugh in her face. But Max . . .

She pushed herself up off the stair, went to the phone, and pressed his button.

'I want you to listen,' she began, 'and not interrupt until

I've finished. I've had a letter from the stalker – "HS" he signs himself this time – and he wants to meet me this afternoon at the Clarendon.' She raised her voice above his immediate protest. 'Max, I want to go. I've been puzzling over this whole business too long, and if I simply tell the police now, I'll never know what he has to say. He promises to go to them straight after seeing me—'

'You don't *believe* him?' Max interrupted. 'Rona, this—'

'I almost think I do. But the point is, I want *you* to be there, just across the room, and if anything goes wrong – though I can't see how it can, in those surroundings – then you can charge to my rescue. What do you say?'

'I say you're mad.'

'No, just curious. Heavens, all this desperation to see me; he must have something important to say.'

'Then let him say it to the police.'

'He will, but afterwards.'

'No, I'm not going along with this. If you don't ring the police straight away, I shall.'

'I shouldn't advise it,' Rona said levelly. 'I'm telling you this on trust.'

'That's nonsense. Suppose something happens to you, and I'm quietly sitting back, letting it?'

'Now you're being ridiculous.'

'Humour me. How long would it take for him to whip out a knife? I'd only be halfway across the room before he used it.'

'In front of all the tea-drinkers? And I thought I was the one with imagination! Honestly, honey, I won't be in any danger. I promise.'

There was a long silence. She said tentatively, 'Max?'

'What?'

'You will come, won't you?'

'Well, if you're determined to go into the lions' den, I'm sure as hell not letting you go alone.'

'Bless you. I knew you'd help.'

'With one proviso, and hopefully to prevent us both being clapped in irons. Once he's told you everything, glance over at me and touch your hair. That'll be the signal for me to phone the police on my mobile. Just in case it slips his mind to go to them afterwards.'

'All right,' Rona said after a moment. 'But don't give any sign that we're together, will you? It might inhibit him.'

'I thought that was the idea,' said Max grimly.

After speaking to Max, Rona couldn't settle. She went upstairs and sorted through the papers on her desk. Then she took out the notes she'd made following her visit to Harrogate, rereading the comments of the Franks' ex-neighbour. *Why* was there no mention of Louise, either in the records or in anyone's memory? And who was Karen? Where was she, and what had happened to her? Perhaps, she thought with a twist of excitement, this afternoon would provide the answers.

Somehow, the time passed, and at a quarter to four, she left the house to walk to the Clarendon. There were fewer cars parked outside today, the press had finally left, and the crowd of onlookers, realizing there was nothing to see, was dwindling. After the hiatus of the last few days, Lightbourne Avenue was settling back into its normal ambience.

As she passed the *Chiltern Life* building, Rona remembered that she'd not spoken to Barnie for a while. Still, she'd soon be able to hand him the finished article. At least this time, the murders had nothing to do with what she was writing, thank God.

The Clarendon looked as it always did and always had. Hard to believe she was about to meet a potential murderer there.

She drew a deep breath, walked through the swing doors and turned into the lounge, hesitating in the doorway as she wondered for the first time if she and the man she'd come to meet would recognize each other. Then, across the room, someone stood up, a man of medium height in a pink shirt – no doubt to aid identification. He half-smiled and, on legs that were suddenly shaky, she walked over to him, catching sight of Max as she did so. It will be all right, she told herself. It has to be.

'Miss Parish.' He made to hold out his hand, then thought better of it. 'It's very good of you to come.'

He pulled out a chair and she automatically sat down.

'Can I get you something to eat? Cakes, sandwiches?'

'I'm not hungry, thank you.'

'A cup of tea, then?'

It might help the dryness in her mouth. 'All right. Thank you.'

He signalled to the waitress and ordered a pot for two. As he did so, Rona studied him, wondering if she could have improved on the description she'd given to the police. She didn't think so; there was nothing outstanding or memorable about his appearance. He had mid-brown hair, conventionally cut, a square chin and grey eyes. There was not much more to say.

He turned back to her, catching her in her scrutiny.

In an attempt to take the initiative, she said, 'Perhaps, for a start, you'll now tell me who you are?'

'Of course. Sorry for all the cloak and dagger, but I knew my name would freak out the Franks. I'm Harry Swann.'

The last part at least was familiar. Rona frowned. 'Are you Karen's husband?'

He looked surprised, as though she should have known. 'No, that was my brother, David.'

'Well, you can at least tell me who Karen was? Or is?'

He stared at her blankly. The waitress came and set down a pot of tea, cups and saucers, milk and sugar, while Rona waited impatiently.

As she moved away, he said uncertainly, 'I thought you . . . It seems I'd better fill in the background. When I was young, my family lived in Harrogate. My brother met Karen at the tennis club when they were both sixteen, and they started going out together. Though they went to different universities, they kept in touch, and eventually got engaged.'

He looked up. 'I should say at this point that Karen has never liked me; she was jealous that David and I were close, and was always trying to stir up trouble between us.'

Since he'd made no move to pour the tea, Rona stirred the pot and then did so, pushing the milk and sugar towards him to take if he wished.

'What about Louise?' she asked. 'How does she fit into all this?'

Again he looked puzzled, then his face cleared. 'I thought the name was familiar; you were asking about her in Harrogate, weren't you? Afraid I can't help, though; I don't know anyone called Louise.'

'But surely – I mean, she must have been Karen's sister or something?'

He frowned. 'I never heard of any sister. But the Franks lived on the other side of town, and as Karen disliked me so much, I never went to her home. I didn't even meet her parents. Until last week.'

Rona caught her breath. 'You saw the Franks last week?'

'I'm coming to that. But to go back to David and Karen, the opportunity came up of a job in Toronto, and they decided to bring the wedding forward and move out there.'

He paused, and took a sip of his tea. Rona noticed he'd added neither milk nor sugar, but was unsure if this was intentional.

'I said David and I were close, and that's true. But we both had tempers, and we'd always fought as children. Even when we grew up, there were heated arguments, but they never lasted long. Until Karen. She built on it, making snide comments, criticizing me to Dave, and so on. It came to a head just before the wedding; we had an almighty row, and the upshot was he didn't want me as best man.

'I was bitterly hurt, as you'd imagine, but convinced he'd come round. However, thanks to Karen, he stuck to it. So I refused to go to the wedding, they went off to Canada, and I – never saw him again.'

Another quick drink of tea. Questions were teeming in Rona's head, but she daren't interrupt the narrative.

'After a year or so,' Swann continued, 'I had a letter from Dave, suggesting we bury the hatchet and I go over and spend a holiday with them.' He gave a twisted smile. 'She couldn't have known he'd written. But I was still nursing the slight over the best man business, and I never replied.

'Then I met my wife, and naturally David and Karen were invited to the wedding. But by then she was pregnant and couldn't fly, and she caused a fuss when Dave suggested coming over by himself. I can just imagine it: *He refused to come to our wedding; why should you go to his?* No matter that it was all her fault.

'But Susie, my wife, knew all the bad feeling was making me miserable. So, after a few months of her nagging, I swallowed my pride and wrote to him, saying I was sorry for my part in the row, and would like to see him.'

Swann came to a halt and sat staring down at the table.

'And did you?' Rona prompted.

He looked up, and she was shocked by the expression in his eyes. 'No. The next thing we heard was that he was dead.'

'Oh, no!'

Again the odd look. He said abruptly, 'What exactly is your connection with the Franks?'

'Connection? I haven't one, other than they rented the house next to ours.'

He stared at her. 'So you've only known them – how long?'

'About four weeks. But it was Louise I knew.'

'This Louise again. Who is she, exactly?'

It was Rona's turn to stare. 'Their daughter. The woman you were following round town.'

His eyes bored into hers. 'Are you being straight with me?' he demanded.

'Of course I am. Why?'

'You mean you really don't know?'

'Know what?'

'The woman you keep calling Louise is Karen Swann, my brother's widow.'

'No!' Rona said involuntarily. 'She can't be!'

'What I don't understand is, if you don't know the Franks, why were you making enquiries about them?'

Rona barely heard him. Her mind was spinning, refusing to accept what she'd just heard, and, blocking it, she fastened instead on his earlier reference to Harrogate. 'That's how you tracked me down isn't it? From Harrogate? I'd been wondering.'

'It's how I heard of you, yes. We live down here now, but a friend rang to tell me you'd been to their old house, and since you'd left a card, he gave me your address. But you've not answered my question: what were you trying to find out?'

'About Louise,' Rona said drily. She took a sip of tea, hoping it would steady her. 'She told me she had amnesia, and could remember nothing of her past life.'

'How very convenient,' Swann said harshly.

'She'd been in a car crash in Canada, and everything that had happened before was a complete blank. She even began to wonder if the Franks were really her parents. There were no photos of her, or anything to do with the past, but they said it had all been burned in a house fire. I had to go to Harrogate on business, and she asked me to find out what I could while I was there.'

'And what did you find out?'

'That the Franks had lived where they'd said they did, had a daughter who'd married and emigrated to Canada, as they'd told her she had, but that the daughter's name was Karen and her husband was David Swann, whereas Louise had married Kevin Stacey.'

'And what did they say had happened to this Kevin Stacey?'

'They divorced and he went to work in the Far East.'

'Did he, now. I think it's time you had a look at these.' He bent down and retrieved a briefcase from under the table. Rona watched as he took out a cardboard folder, opened it, and withdrew a sheaf of yellowing news cuttings. He selected the top one and handed it across the table to her.

It was headlined HOUSEWIFE ACCUSED OF DOUBLE MURDER – and beneath it, unbelievably, was a photograph that, though the hairstyle was different, was undeniably Louise.

Rona felt the bile rush into her throat. Instinctively she put a hand to her mouth, and out of the corner of her eye, saw Max start to his feet. Distractedly she shook her head at him – they couldn't be interrupted now – and after hesitating a moment, he subsided.

She dragged her eyes back to Swann's. 'Who . . .?' Her voice came out in a croak.

'Dave and the baby.'

'God, no!'

'Would you like to see the rest of the clippings?'

'Not – now. Just tell me what happened.'

'The only known facts are that the cleaner found them, early one morning. Karen was sitting on the nursery floor, covered in blood and nursing the dead baby, with Dave's body beside her.'

'But what did she say? She must have said *something*?'

'Oh, believe me, she said plenty. That Dave had been having an affair – which turned out to be true – that he had a violent temper – also true – and that when the baby wouldn't stop crying, he'd picked him up and shaken him violently. *Un*true. She maintained that she'd flown at him to try to make him stop, and when he wouldn't, she'd seized the nursery lamp and cracked it over his head.'

'How unbelievably awful,' Rona whispered.

'What is even more unbelievably awful,' Swann said in a

low, bitter voice, 'is that she got away with it. Because of what was referred to as "provocation" – i.e. the affair – and the fact that she'd been suffering from severe post-natal depression, she was given a suspended sentence. For killing my brother and his son.'

'I thought you said—'

'*She* said. There's no way Dave would have harmed that baby. Oh no; the boot was on the other foot. *He* found *her* shaking him, and tried to stop her. And when she realized Timmy was dead and Dave had seen her do it, she bashed him over the head. The God-awful thing, though, is it was her story that held, and everyone believed it. Everyone, that is, except those who knew Dave.'

He lifted his cup again, saw it was empty, and put it down. Rona refilled it.

'It almost killed my mother,' Swann continued in a low voice. 'It became her aim in life to clear Dave's name, but there seemed no way of doing it. She's terminally ill now, and when I heard, indirectly through you, that the Franks were back in this country, I felt I owed it to her to get Karen to retract the accusation. It couldn't make any difference to her now, and it would give such comfort to Ma.

'And, of course, I also had a personal reason for contacting her. I've been torturing myself, wondering if he ever got my letter. I can't bear to think he died believing I wanted nothing more to do with him. However much she dislikes me, Karen owes me that.'

He drained his teacup.

'So I decided to look you up and ask you where I could find them. I called at your house and rang the bell, but there was no reply. So I started to walk back to my car, stopped to light a cigarette, and that's where we almost bumped into each other. I half-wondered if it could be you, so I waited to see where you were going, and when you turned into your gateway, I went back. I was going to ring again, but before I could, the kitchen light suddenly went on. Instinctively, I turned to look down, came eye to eye with you, and, realizing how it must appear, decided to leave it for the moment.

'So I wrote the note, and when you didn't call me, phoned, but still you wouldn't meet me. There seemed nothing for it but to try the house again; but to my amazement, just as I was approaching, who should come out of the next gateway but Karen herself, as large as life. At least, I was ninety per cent sure it was her, though she did look slightly different. I didn't want to speak till I was certain, and what really threw me was that she gave no sign whatsoever of recognizing me. I mean, OK, she might have cut me dead, but that's a different thing entirely. There was no flicker of recognition, which seemed – bizarre, somehow. Enough to make me hesitate, anyway.

'So I followed her at a distance, and when she turned into the café, I went in after her, glad of the chance for a better look. The last time I'd seen her, she'd looked as she does in that photo – short, spiky hair, and so on. But apart from the fact that she blanked me, I was pretty sure it was her, and it seemed to make sense, her living next door to you.'

'She didn't recognize you because of the amnesia,' Rona said. 'That bit at least must be true.'

'Perhaps. Oh, and while I think of it, there's another thing: have you by any chance got a doppelganger?'

'Otherwise known as a twin; yes, I have.'

'So that explains it. When I left the café, I saw you coming from the other direction, but before I could reach you, you turned into that furniture shop. So I went on up the road – and then, lo and behold, there you were again, right in front of me! It gave me quite a start, I can tell you.'

'And your reaction alarmed my sister. But you said you met the Franks?'

'Yes. I'd an appointment in Marsborough on Friday afternoon – I actually live in Chilswood – and after it, I decided to beard the lions in their den. If I could make Karen admit Dave hadn't killed the baby, Ma could die in peace. And I could also ask about my letter. But when they opened the door and I said who I was, they went into a blind panic, and wouldn't let me in the house. They almost slammed the door in my face.

'So once more I had to retreat. I was wondering what to do next when I heard of the murders, and it really put the wind up me, I can tell you. I knew that since you'd seen me hanging around, you'd report me and I'd be a prime suspect. But even overriding that, it seemed my last chance of proving Dave's innocence had gone. My only hope was that Karen might have said something to you.'

He looked at her without hope. 'In view of the amnesia, I presume she didn't?'

Rona shook her head.

He sighed, picked up the cutting and put it back inside the folder. Then he looked at her again, and his face changed.

'I wonder if you're ready yet to think what I'm thinking?'

Rona said uncertainly, 'And that is?'

'That it was Karen herself who murdered her parents. After all, she'd killed before.'

Sixteen

The room seemed to tilt around her. Could this nightmare get any worse?

Rona tried to swallow past the obstruction in her throat. 'My husband's across the room,' she said hoarsely. 'May I call him over?'

Swann looked startled, and his eyes quickly scanned the room. 'Yes,' he stammered. 'Yes, of course.'

But Max had already seen her reaction, and was on his way over. 'Darling, what is it? What's happened?'

She gestured weakly at Swann. 'You tell him,' she said.

Briefly, Swann did so, removing once more the yellowed clippings from the Canadian newspapers. Max glanced at them briefly, swore under his breath, and reached for Rona's hand.

'There's no doubt?' he asked then.

'Not about who she is. Who killed her parents is a moot point.'

Max flung him an accusing look. 'Whatever your motives, you put the fear of God into my wife.'

'I know, and I've already apologized. It was quite unintentional.'

'You have a job, presumably, and you say you live in Chilswood. How have you found time to keep coming here and following people?'

'Max!' Rona protested weakly.

Swann made a placatory gesture. 'It's a fair enough question. The first time I saw your wife was a Sunday evening, and I'd come over specifically to speak to her. But I have a business meeting in Marsborough every Tuesday; when I was here last week, I saw Karen and your wife's sister, and later put the note through your door. Then something cropped up at work, and I had to come back on Friday; so when I'd finished, I took the chance to call on the Franks. And today, as you know, it's Tuesday again.

'Incidentally,' he glanced at Rona as he took another clipping from the pile, 'you said they told Karen they lost everything in a fire. That happens to be true. The brother of the woman Dave had been seeing was so incensed at the lightness of the sentence that he torched their house. They were lucky to get out alive. There's a report of it here.'

He pushed it across, but neither Rona nor Max made any attempt to read it.

Max said dully, 'So what will you do now?'

'As I said, go straight to the police station. Armed with these cuttings, together with my cast-iron alibi, I doubt if they'll detain me.'

'Max and I could still be suspects,' Rona pointed out.

Swann shook his head. 'Not for long. The first thing the police will do is contact their opposite numbers in Toronto. The case might not have reached the papers here, but it was headline news for weeks in Canada. The name Karen Swann was plastered all over them. No wonder they wanted to change it.'

'That would be why they hid her passport.' Rona remembered the detective's hesitation when she'd mentioned it; the one the bank held would be in Karen's name, not Louise's.

'But it still doesn't mean she killed them,' she added. 'And if she can't remember what she did, isn't it possible she's a different person now? A different personality, at least? I really can't see Louise harming anyone; she's too timid.'

Swann shook his head. 'In all conscience, who else could it be? Not a burglar; it said in the papers nothing was taken. And the Franks weren't the kind of people to make enemies.'

'Why didn't they tell her the truth, though?' Rona pursued. 'Her memory will come back in time, and it'll be even more of a shock.'

Swann shrugged. 'I suppose they were trying to protect her, reckoning it was all for the best if she couldn't remember. God, she's got it made, hasn't she? Unlike Dave and little Timmy, she's alive and well, away from all the hoo-ha and with a new life ahead of her. And the icing on the cake is that she doesn't even remember what's she done.'

There was no more to be said. Rona and Max stood up,

and Swann with them. This time he did hold out his hand, and both of them took it.

'Good luck,' Rona said.

'Thanks. You too.'

They left him at the table and walked out of the hotel into the blinding sunlight, by unspoken consent turning into Dean's Crescent North.

Only as they reached the little sitting room at Farthings did Rona say, 'Do you really think she did it, Max?'

'Killed her parents? God knows, but it seems quite likely.'

'But *why*?'

'Perhaps Swann's visit somehow upset the apple cart.'

'So if she's not being held somewhere, as we thought, where is she?'

'Again, God knows. Done a runner, no doubt. Don't worry, darling; I doubt if we'll see her again, other than on the news if they find her.'

'I just can't *believe* . . .'

'I know,' he said gently. He glanced at the clock on the mantelpiece. 'The sun probably hasn't reached the yard-arm, but I'm opening the bar. For medicinal reasons, if nothing else; you've had one shock after another, and by default, so have I.'

He glanced at her downcast face. 'Would you like to stay here for the evening, and we can go home together?'

She straightened, shaking her head. 'No, Gus will be waiting. I'll be all right. I'll just have a drink with you, and be on my way.'

Max handed her a glass. 'Then let's drink to the resumption of normal services.'

'I'll join you in that,' she said.

After the next press conference, the news hit the papers. MISSING DAUGHTER TRIED FOR MURDER IN CANADA, screamed the headlines, and this time, alongside Rona's photofit, was a reproduction of the picture from the Canadian press. The net was tightening; surely it could only be a matter of time before Karen/Louise was found.

Lindsey phoned, and both parents, in varying degrees of anxiety.

'But you were *friendly* with her!' Lindsey kept saying. 'She could have slit your throat!'

'Well, she didn't, did she?' Rona snapped, her own discomfort shortening her temper. 'Just forget it, will you, Linz? I'm trying to.'

'God knows how you keep getting into these situations,' Lindsey snapped back, irritable in her turn. 'Journalists on glossy mags don't usually require danger money!'

'Being a journalist has nothing to do with it – at least, not this time. I just happened to be living next door to a murderer; lots of people find themselves in that position. You see them on the news, saying, "But he was always such a quiet boy," and so on, as though he should have had "murderer" stamped on his forehead. Well, now I know how they feel. I was taken in, too.'

Lindsey's voice softened. 'Sorry, sis; I didn't mean to jump down your throat. I'm worried about you, that's all, and so is Dominic.'

Rona couldn't help smiling. 'Now, that makes me feel a whole lot better!'

'There's no need to be sarky, he really is.' She paused. 'At least we don't have to worry about the stalker any more.'

'That's something, I suppose,' Rona said tiredly.

After a quick phone call to check she'd not be in the way, Rona spent the next two days at Oak Avenue. One would have been sufficient, but the last week had left her shaky, and she needed to have other people around.

Julian, having continued to make steady progress, was due back at the weekend, and in the meantime his parents were still in residence. Rona and Felicity had their planned coffee together, and later Graham came up to the archive room for a chat, glancing with interest through the typescript she handed him.

'It'll be good to have it all collated,' he commented. 'We knew there was a wealth of information buried in there, but it was a daunting task to find anything. Now that you've indexed it, specific information will be readily accessible.'

He laid the typescript back on the table. 'I hear from Felicity that all this business in the papers relates to your neighbours.'

'Unfortunately, yes.'

'A bad business all round. Personally, I doubt if they'll ever track down the daughter; she could be anywhere by now –

she'd a good few hours' start before her parents were discovered. If she's any sense, she'll have fled abroad.'

'She hadn't got her passport,' Rona said, and explained it was held at the bank.

'Ah! Then that will have limited her choices.'

'I still can't believe she did it, any of it,' Rona said sadly. 'I always thought she was the vulnerable one.'

'Appearances can be deceptive,' rejoined Graham Willow owlishly.

Friday. The week had seemed interminable. Max had spoken to his father, and provided the police had no objection, they hoped to fly up to Northumberland on Monday. It would be good to see Roland again, not to mention Cynthia, Paul, and the boys; even better, to get away from Marsborough for a while.

The day was overcast and humid, and Rona saw from the study window that the plants in their containers were beginning to droop. Abandoning her computer, she ran downstairs and went into the garden. Gus followed her, amiably wagging his tail.

'We'll go for a walk later,' she promised him, filling the watering can at the outside tap. As she moved methodically among the tubs and urns, returning every now and then to refill the can, her actions seemed suddenly charged with significance: and she remembered the day the Franks had moved in, when, while watering, she'd looked up at the house and seen a curtain move.

Automatically, she glanced up again – and froze. Seated on the window sill of Louise's bedroom was the ginger cat. Rona dropped the watering can, staring up at it, and as she watched, it stretched a paw up the pane.

How had it got in? she wondered distractedly; there'd been no cat flap in the old-fashioned back door. Perhaps it had slipped in unnoticed as the forensic team was leaving; Louise had said it made a practice of that. But that was a couple of days ago now, and since then the house had been empty. It must be hungry, or, more importantly, thirsty. She tried to remember if there'd been a water bowl in the kitchen, but even if there had, the water wouldn't have lasted this long.

She went back inside, looked up the RSPCA in the phone
book, and rang their number. After several rings, a machine
clicked on. *This office is open Monday to Friday, between the
hours of nine and eleven a.m., and four to six p.m. Please
leave a message and we'll get back to you as soon as we can.
In case of emergency, phone . . .*

Rona looked at her watch. It was ten past eleven. She hesitated: was this an emergency, or could the cat last until four?
It hadn't looked particularly distressed. She considered
phoning the police, but dismissed it. She'd no wish to bring
herself back to their notice. God, what should she do? How
about the fire service? They were known to rescue cats out
of trees, but breaking into a house was another matter.

The keys would have been handed back to the letting agents.
Was it, she wondered, remotely possible that the Franks had
left one for emergencies under a stone somewhere? It wasn't
recommended practice, but a lot of people did it, and such a
key could have been overlooked.

Gus looked up at her, sensing her indecision.

'Stay here,' she told him, 'I shan't be long.'

She took a tin of dog food from the cupboard, not knowing
whether or not it would appeal, but guessing if the cat was
hungry enough, it would eat anything. It was only as she ran
up the basement stairs that she considered Gus's reaction,
should she return with the cat. But perhaps, if she fed and
watered it before letting it out, it could fend for itself. It had
been a stray before the Franks adopted it.

She slipped the front door key into her pocket and let herself
out of the house, pulling the door shut behind her. The street
was deserted – which, for the last week or so, was a state
she'd been longing to have restored. Now, she'd have given
a lot to see a passer-by, some sign of life.

She shook herself; she was being neurotic. She turned into
the next gateway and walked up the path, trying not to think
of the last time she'd been there. Without much hope, she tried
the door handle, and was not surprised when it resisted her
pressure. Helplessly, she looked about her. The tired-looking
plant was still in its stone pot at the bottom of the steps. Rona
tried to lift it, but it proved too heavy; nor, when she felt around
in the soil, did her fingers encounter anything unexpected.

Think! she commanded herself. If you wanted to hide a key,

where would you put it? She turned to the narrow flowerbed running down the left-hand side of the path. The contract gardeners had continued their visits during the Franks' occupancy; since the garden could only be accessed through the house, might a key have been left for them? Rona walked slowly along the length of the bed, pausing now and again to peer under shrubs and lift aside leaves. And then, half-hidden in the undergrowth, she saw a little stone figure of a hedgehog. With a surge of hope she lifted it, and sighed in relief. Nestling underneath it was a shining key.

She picked it up, dusted off the soil, and replaced the figure. Then, before her resolve could falter, she went up the steps, put the key in the lock, and opened the door.

It was the silence she noticed first, heavy and oppressive. She stood listening, unsure for what. Again, she shook herself. She'd feed the cat and leave as soon as possible. What name had Louise given it? Something to do with its colour . . . Amber! That was it!

'Amber!' she called, wishing she'd brought some biscuits to rattle and catch its attention. 'Dinner, Amber!' Did it know the word? At any rate, there was no response. Perhaps it had been shut in the room?

Cautiously, unwillingly, Rona went up the stairs. Patches of carpet – presumably where the splashes of blood were – had been cut away, showing the bare boards underneath, and the banisters were covered in a light, greyish dust: fingerprint powder, she thought, and was careful not to touch it.

'Amber!' she called again, her voice echoing in the listening house. 'Where are you? I've got some dinner for you!'

Louise's door was, in fact, ajar. Rona pushed it open, noticing that, here again, the patch of carpet bearing the stain had been cut away, and that all the surfaces were coated in powder. There was no sign of the cat.

It could be anywhere, she thought in frustration. She went to the window and looked down at her own garden from this unfamiliar angle. The watering can was on the flagstones where she'd left it, and Gus lay stretched out beside it. On impulse, she tapped on the glass, and when he looked up, ears cocked, she waved to him. Had he seen her? Whether or not, the sooner she got back to him, the better. Her garden seemed suddenly a most desirable place to be.

It was as she was turning from the window that there was
a sound behind her – a soft click – and she spun round to see
Louise leaning against the closed door, smiling at her. But
this was a different Louise – a Louise with cropped hair, the
trademark fringe combed back from her forehead, and an odd,
feverish glint in her eyes.

Rona's heart seemed to stop as she frantically reassessed
her position. 'Louise!' she stuttered.

'Karen, actually.'

God, her memory had come back! How exactly would that
affect things?

'You found the spare key; well done,' Karen continued. 'I'm
so glad you've come, Rona; I was hoping to see you.'

Rona moistened her lips. 'I've been worried about you.
Where have you been?'

'At the commercial hotel, in Windsor Way. It's amazing
how unobservant people are. But once the news about Canada
broke, it seemed wiser to leave, and this house was the one
place no one would think of looking for me. So, as soon as
the police moved out, I moved back in.'

Rona tried to think of a safe response. 'I was looking for
Amber,' she said, holding up the tin of dog food. 'I saw her
at the window.'

Karen nodded. 'She slipped in past me when I came back;
nearly gave me a heart attack, brushing against me in the dark.
She must have been hunting, because although she was hungry,
she wasn't starving. Now, she's annoyed with me because I
won't let her out. But if anyone saw her asking to come in . . .'

As she'd been speaking, Karen had casually turned the key
in the lock and slipped it into her pocket. She moved into the
room and sat on the dressing stool.

Rona watched her with alarm. What was she planning?

Trying to keep her voice light, she asked, 'When did your
memory come back?'

'Last Friday, when Harry called. They didn't let him in, but
I was on the stairs, and I heard him. He sounded just like
David, and when he asked for Karen, everything snapped into
place. Or almost everything. Odd bits keep coming back.'

She looked up at Rona, still standing at the window.

'You've read the papers, and since it was through you that
Harry traced us, no doubt you've spoken to him. God knows

what he said – he never liked me. So now, I'd like you to hear my side.'

'Of course.' What else could she say? Oh God, Max wouldn't be home for hours yet. Even then, how would he know where she was? It wouldn't occur to him that she'd voluntarily come back to this house.

'You'd be more comfortable if you sat down.' Karen nodded towards the stripped bed, with its old, stained mattress, but Rona was reluctant to leave the window. Illogically, as long as she was visible from her own garden, she felt reasonably safe. She half turned to glance down again, but Karen moved swiftly. Rona shied away, but all she did was draw the curtains.

'That's better,' she said calmly. 'Now, sit down.'

There was no option but to obey, and in the green light coming through the curtains, Rona seated herself on the edge of the bed while Karen launched into her narrative.

'I'd loved David since I was sixteen,' she began. 'There was never anyone else. When we were both at uni, he phoned every evening and came up whenever he could, and as soon as we graduated, we got engaged. We weren't planning to marry for a year or two, but not long after, David was offered this great job – in Toronto, of all places. It was too good to turn down, so we brought the wedding forward and went out together.'

She was quiet for a moment, staring back into a past Rona couldn't see. 'And we were so happy,' she said softly, 'so much in love. I found myself a job – we'd both read sciences – and for several years everything was wonderful. During that time, Father retired. They'd been out to see us a couple of times, and fallen for Canada. There was nothing to keep them in the UK – I was their only child – so they decided to retire out there, and because they had family in the country and were financially sound, they were accepted.'

She was silent for a longer space. 'Then I discovered I was pregnant, and soon after, we heard from David's parents that Harry was getting married, and we were invited to the wedding. But Harry'd always been jealous of David, and there'd been a terrific row before our own wedding, resulting in his not coming. I knew David was unhappy about it; he admitted writing to Harry, trying to patch things up, but hadn't had a

reply. He thought if they could meet face to face, all would
be well, and when I told him I wasn't able to fly, he suggested
going alone. I wasn't having that, though. I wouldn't have put
it past Harry to try to turn him against me.'

'Harry told me he *did* eventually write,' Rona ventured.

'Yes, yes, he did. You'd have thought David had won the
lottery when he got that letter. He was full of plans for Harry
and Susie to come over, but that was just before—'

She bit her lip.

'What happened, Karen?'

'Timmy was what happened. It was a difficult birth – long-
drawn-out and very painful, and there were complications, which
didn't help. And when I finally went home, I was suffering
from post-natal depression, and couldn't even begin to cope. I
loved my baby – of course I did – but he wouldn't stop crying.
Night after night, day after day, till I thought I'd go mad. Mother
tried to help, but she couldn't do much. I wasn't getting any
sleep, and nor was David. We were living on our nerves.'

Tears filled her eyes. 'Just talking about Timmy upsets me.
Now everything's come back, I'm grieving for him all over
again.'

Rona, thinking of Harry Swann and his dying mother, steeled
herself. 'So why did you kill him?' she asked softly.

Karen put her hands to her head, her face tortured and tears
streaming down her face. *'Because he wouldn't stop crying!'*

Rona stared at her. Unbelievably, Karen had taken the bait,
and in doing so, proved Harry right; it *hadn't* been David who
killed the baby. But she was continuing:

'He cried all day and all night, unless I was actually nursing
him. If I tried to put him in his cot, he'd start screaming,
going so red in the face that I was frightened, and had to pick
him up again. And that was the state I was in, when I bumped
into Sally Benson at the pharmacy.'

She looked at Rona. 'Sally's one's of those people who
likes to tell you unpleasant things, because she "thinks you
ought to know". And, to cut a long story short, what she
thought I should know was that David had been having an
affair with a girl in his office for the last few months. All the
time, in fact, that I'd been carrying his child.'

Impatiently, she brushed her tears away. 'That was when it
all blew up. I taxed David with it the minute he got home,

and I could tell by his face it was true. Oh, he tried to bluster, say there'd been nothing in it, but I didn't believe him. It had been going on for nine months, for God's sake.

'When we went to bed that night, I insisted he sleep in the guest room. But no sooner had I dropped off than Timmy started again, and I just – disintegrated. I think now that I was blaming him for David going astray – if I'd not been pregnant, it wouldn't have happened. That kind of thing. But all I knew at the time was that I *had* to quieten him, so I could get some sleep.

'I scooped him up, and started shaking him, over and over. I never even noticed he'd gone limp. Then David came rushing in, yelling, "Karen! What are you doing?" and snatched the baby from me. I watched him lay Timmy on the changing trolley and begin trying to revive him, but I could see he was dead. That's when I started screaming. David shouted at me to phone for an ambulance, but I knew he'd tell them what I'd done. By that stage, I was almost out of my mind; the shock of Timmy's death, David's betrayal, the prospect of prison, all swept over me in a suffocating wave. I picked up the nearest thing and hit him with it. He went down like a stone.'

She paused, added calmly, 'I told everyone he'd killed the baby, and that was why I hit him. It was a way to get back at him, for the affair.'

Rona's own eyes were wet. It seemed, despite the criticism, that the Canadian judgement had been a merciful one.

'If you saw the papers,' Karen said dully, 'you'll know what happened next. I received a suspended sentence subject to medical treatment, and was allowed "home". But there was no way I could go back to that house, even temporarily. So we sold it, contents and all apart from a few personal possessions, and I moved in with my parents.

'It didn't end there, of course. There was graffiti on the wall, anonymous letters, phone calls in the night. And to cap it all, one night someone set fire to the house. That was the final straw. A couple of days later I took the car, which had somehow escaped damage, drove until I was almost out of petrol, then put my foot down and aimed for a brick wall. God knows why I wasn't killed, but they managed to drag me back to life. Or half-life, without any memory.'

'And your parents?'

'Moved into temporary accommodation near the hospital, and made arrangements to fly back here as soon as I was well enough. That was when they decided to call me Louise – my grandmother's name – and bury the notorious Karen Swann for ever. They also suggested I grow my hair, but they said it was to hide the scars, not to change my appearance.'

'They did their best for you, then.'

Karen stopped crying as suddenly as she'd started, and her face changed, became hard and cold.

'They wanted to keep me dependent on them,' she said.

'Surely not? I mean, they were elderly; why would they want that? They'd be trying to save you the pain of remembering, having to go through what you're reliving now.'

'They lied to me,' Karen said implacably. 'They invented a complete life for me, with a fictitious husband and a divorce, to stop me finding out the truth.'

'But with the best of intentions. They—'

'No. How could they expect me to recover, if they fed me all those lies? They preferred me with half a brain, believing what they wanted me to believe.'

After a moment, Rona said, 'So when Harry had gone, and your memory came back . . .?'

'I made them tell me everything, and as they went through it, it confirmed what I remembered. Not all of it at once, but the main facts were clear enough. We thrashed over it endlessly all evening. I was desperately upset about Timmy, and David, too. In spite of everything, I still love him. But most of all, I blamed them for keeping it from me.'

She stood up suddenly, making Rona jump. 'All this talking has made me thirsty – and hungry, come to that. It's lunchtime. I'll go and make us something.'

Rona stood up eagerly. 'I'll help you.'

'No. You stay here.'

'But Lou— Karen, I—'

'You might try to leave,' Karen said, 'and I don't want that.'

'I – don't understand.'

'You're my friend, and I need a friend. You're coming with me, to make a new life together.'

Rona stared at her, aghast. 'Going where? Karen, be sensible! You haven't got your passport, and neither have I. It's at home somewhere.'

'We needn't go abroad. There's the north of Scotland; we could drive up there. Don't argue with me, Rona,' she added quickly. 'You *are* my friend, aren't you?'

'Yes, of course.'

'Then don't let me down. Like David did, and my parents.'

Their eyes met, the unspoken sentence hanging in the air between them: *And look what happened to them.*

'Now, I'm going down to make some sandwiches – I brought a supply of food back with me. But I warn you – don't try to jump me when I bring them; I'll have a knife.'

She went to the window, lifted the curtain, and scanned the gardens below. Then, apparently satisfied, she took the key out of her pocket and left the room, turning it in the lock on the other side. Rona ran to the window, but as Karen had checked, there was no one to be seen. Even Gus had gone indoors. No matter how much she knocked on the glass, no one would hear her.

The threat of the knife had escalated the danger level. Would Karen use it, when Rona refused to leave with her? Harry's voice sounded in her head. *After all, she's killed before.* And in this very house. Oh God, why had she ever come here? That bloody, bloody cat!

An idea came suddenly, and, immediately acting on it, she picked up the tin of dog food, pulled back the curtain, and hurled it through the window, shattering the glass. Karen would have reached the hall by now; with luck, she wouldn't have heard the crash, and nor, since the back door was solid, would she see the glass on the terrace unless she actually peered through the panel. Heart pounding, Rona pulled the curtain across again, concealing the broken glass. Possibly, just possibly, someone might notice it.

Max stretched and looked at his watch. He'd done as much work on the canvas as he could for now, and he needed a break. Since it was almost lunchtime, he decided to phone Rona and suggest she met him at the Bacchus. It would do her good to get away from the house. Thank God they'd the prospect of the Tynecastle visit next week. With luck, by the time they returned, this mad woman would have been found and they could get on with their lives.

There was no answer on the landline, which surprised him;

Rona hadn't said she was going out. He tried her mobile, but it went to voicemail, surprising him still further. Where the hell was she? He decided to ring again in ten minutes.

But ten minutes later, he met with the same results. Irritated by now, he tried Lindsey's office, only to be told that Miss Parish was lunching with a client. No go there, then.

Max frowned, considering his options. Under normal circumstances, he'd have shrugged and let it go. But these weren't normal circumstances, and, slightly uneasy, he elected to go home and check for himself.

'Rona!' he called, as he let himself into the house. 'Are you there?'

There was no reply, but Gus came bounding up the basement stairs to greet him.

'Where is she, boy?' he asked, bending to pat him. Unusually, the dog evaded his hand and ran back down the stairs. Max shrugged and went up to the study. The computer screensaver was on, which was odd; when Rona finished work, even for the lunch break, she invariably switched it off.

Increasingly anxious, he called again, glancing into the en suite to check she'd not been taken ill, but like the rest of the house, it was empty. And she was still not answering her mobile.

He went back downstairs, to find Gus waiting for him in the hall. Again, as soon as he saw Max, the dog turned and ran down to the kitchen. Perplexed, Max followed, stopping short on the threshold. The patio door was open.

Thoroughly alarmed now, he ran outside. But the garden, surrounded by high walls and paved throughout, offered nowhere to hide, and while it was patently obvious no one was there, the watering can stood abandoned by one of the tubs. Rona always, but always, replaced it by the tap when she'd finished using it. Gus, who had followed him, barked encouragingly, thereby adding to his unease, since he normally barked only when the doorbell rang.

Max returned to the kitchen, and, with a sense of shock, saw what had escaped him on his dash outside: Rona's mobile was on the table. Which explained why she'd not answered – but not why she'd left the house without it.

He paused to take stock, mentally listing the anomalies which were now building up. 1) Rona had gone out without her mobile – something she never did. 2) She'd left the back door open. 3) The computer hadn't been switched off. 4) The watering can was out of place. 5) Gus was behaving strangely. Any one of these things would have been uncharacteristic, to say the least. Taken together, they were seriously disturbing. God, what was going on?

There had been no cry from downstairs, no pounding of angry footsteps, and Rona steadied her breath. As she'd hoped, the broken window had gone undetected. For the rest, her only chance was to remain calm – as, she admitted ruefully, she'd told herself in similar situations before. So when Karen returned, balancing the tray and eyeing her cautiously, she was again seated on the bed, and made no move as it was placed on the dressing table.

It bore a plate of sandwiches and two glasses of the lemonade that, Rona remembered with a pang, had been a speciality of Barbara Franks. Karen must have found it in the fridge. A bread knife was also ominously in evidence, but the door hadn't been relocked, perhaps because it was difficult to juggle with the tray. Or perhaps she considered the knife sufficient deterrent.

Rona nodded at the bare patch on the floor, and forced herself to say conversationally, 'Whose blood was on the carpet?'

'Mine,' Karen replied. 'Father lashed out, hitting me in the face, and making my nose bleed. It went on for some time.'

Lashed out? While he was being murdered? Rona feared the sandwiches would stick in her throat, but when Karen passed her the plate, she'd no choice but to take one. Had something been put in them? she wondered fleetingly, but it seemed unlikely; Karen was tucking in herself, and there were no separate piles, which might have raised suspicions.

She said, 'At what point did your father lash out?'

Karen sighed. 'You want the 'i's dotted and the 't's crossed, don't you? I suppose that's what comes of being a journalist. Well, as I said, we argued the matter back and forth, but they refused to see my point. Eventually we went to bed, but I couldn't sleep. I lay there, on that bed, weeping for David and Timmy and letting the rage boil up inside me.'

Through the broken window, Rona suddenly heard Gus

bark, and her heart jerked. She looked fearfully at Karen, hoping she wouldn't register the increase in volume, but she was lost in her story. Why was Gus barking? Was Max there? Oh God, let Max be there! Let him find her!

Karen was saying, 'I must have been half-dozing when I heard my parents' door open, and Father go downstairs. It was five o'clock, and already getting light. I wondered if Mother was awake, and if so, whether she'd be more amenable to apologizing if Father wasn't there. So I tapped on her door and pushed it open. She was sitting at the dressing table. She didn't turn, but our eyes met in the mirror, and her very first words lit the touch-paper. Would you believe she asked if *I'd* come to apologize, for the things I'd said the night before.

'I said something like, didn't she realize she'd taken away my life by denying me my memories, and she said she was amazed that I wanted them.

'I screamed at her to admit she wanted to control me, that it wasn't for my sake, but theirs, that they'd kept me in the dark.'

'And at that she lost her temper, something I couldn't remember happening before. She yelled that if I was determined to know, then she'd tell me, and of course they didn't want my memory to come back! I might let something slip, then they'd be back in the same position they were in, in Canada.'

Karen paused and took a deep breath. 'Then she said, "Don't you think we've had enough of being labelled the parents of a murderess?"

'I saw her eyes widen in the mirror as she realized what she'd said. She hadn't meant to, but it was so clearly how they'd been thinking, that I just lost control. I seized the dressing-table mirror and cracked it over her head. It was like history repeating itself, like killing David all over again.

'And, like the last time, I knew Father would come up and see what I'd done. So I had to act first. I crept downstairs, the mirror in my hand, and down again to the kitchen. He was sitting at the table with a mug of coffee — I can still smell it. He half-turned, and, like Mother, said, "Come to apologize?"

'So I lifted the mirror again, but he saw the movement and flung out an arm – either to deflect me, or defend himself. His fist landed on my nose, and the pain of it almost blinded me. I could feel the blood coming, and before he could get to his feet, I lashed out, and this time made contact with his head.'

She paused. 'I've just thought of something curious; there was no blood with either of them, but there'd been a lot with David. But admittedly the lamp had shattered and cut him quite badly, whereas the mirror didn't break. Either that, or both my parents had thick skulls.'

The sheer callousness of that took Rona's breath away, and with it, her last hope of talking Karen round.

'I went back upstairs,' Karen said expressionlessly. 'The blood was soaking into my nightdress and some of it dripped on the stairs. Back in my room, it took me a while to stop the bleeding, but eventually I managed it. I washed quickly to get rid of the blood, then, when I was dressed, I wiped the mirror to remove fingerprints, and replaced it on Mother's dressing table. She hadn't moved; she was just sitting there with her head bowed, as if she was thinking. A pity she hadn't thought more clearly when she was alive.

'And that's about it, really. I took what I needed with me in a carrier bag – the police would check the suitcases – and left the front door open, to make it seem someone had broken in.'

Max ran down the path and looked up and down the street, in a vain hope of seeing Rona coming home. It was deserted; everyone would be at lunch. He turned and went dispiritedly back inside. Should he call the police? They took little notice of missing adults until some time had elapsed; could he convince them that the accumulation of happenings was significant? Oh God, Rona, where *are* you?

Gus was awaiting him in the hall, and yet again, on seeing him, galloped down the basement stairs, barking. Max frowned; was the animal trying to tell him something? He followed him down to the kitchen, and Gus promptly ran outside. Again, Max followed, and to his astonishment, the dog started jumping up at the dividing wall, barking excitedly.

'Seen a cat, old boy?' he asked. Then his eyes went beyond the wall to the next-door house, and he was suddenly on high alert. Surely those curtains hadn't been drawn this morning? Nor, most definitely, had the window been broken.

He turned and dashed back upstairs, out of the door, and up the next path, where he saw, to his amazement, that there was a key in the door.

His impulse was to crash in, shouting Rona's name, but he restrained himself. Instead, he went stealthily up the stairs and paused outside the room where the patch of blood had been. Voices were coming from it – and one of them was Rona's.

His hand closed silently round the door knob, and very gently he turned it. Then, when it had gone the full extent, he pushed the door violently back on its hinges, and launched himself into the room, not knowing what he would find.

Everything happened at once. Rona was seated on the bed, but between her and the door was someone who could only be the mysterious Louise. Her face, turned towards him, was frozen in surprise, and at the same moment Rona lunged forward, giving her a violent push which knocked her to the floor and at the same time catching up an evil-looking knife from a tray.

'Quick, Max! Outside!'

He allowed himself to be pushed from the room, and Rona pulled the door shut behind them, managing to turn the key just as Karen, regaining her feet, hurled herself at the door, rattling the handle and banging repeatedly against the panels.

Max reached for Rona, and they clung together, gasping for breath. Then she pulled away and gave him a shaky smile.

'I think you'd better phone the police,' she said.

So it was over. They remained on guard until the police arrived, and escorted Karen out of the room and down the stairs. Max and Rona followed, and as they reached the hall, an orange streak came racing towards them. Rona bent swiftly, and scooped the ginger cat into her arms.

Karen, totally calm now, looked back over her shoulder. 'Give her to Harry,' she said. 'A belated peace offering.'

And allowed herself to be led down the path to the police car.